GHOST AT DUSK

KEVAN DALE

Ebook ISBN-13: 978-1-7337504-3-1

Paperback ISBN-13: 978-1-7337504-4-8

GET SORCERY OF THE STONY HEART
FOR FREE

To instantly receive the free novella *Sorcery of the Stony Heart* and the exclusive novelette *A Spark of Will* (unavailable anywhere else) sign up for Kevan's free Readers Club at kevandale.com

PART I

1

———

Twenty-two minutes until sunset, maybe twenty-three.

Almost time to hide. I get jumpy even without a clock left in the house, from the light from the windows, creeping up the bare walls. The shadows gobbling up the dusty corners. Some afternoons, I stand in the hallway, watching. As the afternoon drains, I listen to the muffled sounds of life outside. Cars passing by on the street. Kids shouting after each other on bikes. Crows. Wind sighing around the walls and roof. A house sounds different when it's empty. The windows pop in their frames when the sunlight hits them long enough. The boiler coughs on with a rattle, setting the radiators to knocking. Boards and stairs creak as the house breathes with the weather.

Twenty minutes.

This is the first October I've been alone. I miss the sound of people. Footsteps. Plumbing running, shutting off. Whispers and coughs and throat clearing. Talking on the phone. Radio. TV. Enough to cover up the sound of emptiness. It's worse in October. Lower light. Shorter days. And me, by myself.

The world's dumbest ghost.

Trying to find new places to watch a day come to a close. Up in a corner of the ceiling. The attic crawlspace with the ancient insulation and abandoned mousetraps, filled with must and resin from the roof joists.

I didn't think death would be like this. I didn't think about death at all. What junior high school kid does? I guess if you'd forced an answer out of me, I'd have said: Something like sleep. Not emptiness, not that part of sleep. The other part, where you feel safe, lulled to sleep by all the familiar sounds of the house around you—except in death, you'd be hearing the good sounds of the universe around you. God clearing His throat. The spin of the planets. The low hum of the stars and the distant rumble of the universe's gears turning.

Well. Nope. It's nothing like that.

It's this. Watching the days pass by. Keeping an eye out for sunset, when the nightmare games begin. Stuck in this one place, the house I grew up in, apparently forever. And if there is something else to it, then I'm missing it. I've tried everything I can think of.

Eighteen minutes.

So when I hear a car door slam in the driveway, boy does it catch my attention. A minute later, a key works the lock on the front door. Takes a couple of tries—my family used the kitchen door, and it has the newer lock—but the door swings open. A woman steps inside. She's pretty, but old. Probably near forty. Dressed nice, jacket, long skirt, boots. Blond hair. I stand at the bottom of the stairs, unseen. No one's been in the house since my sister locked it up last winter and drove off with my dad.

The woman looks over the entryway with a quick eye, then purses her lips and looks up the stairs. She looks right through me, which is a weird feeling. When I was alive, there were plenty of times I'd wanted to be invisible, like at school. East Junior High. When a teacher like Mr. Fitzgerald was looking for his next unprepared victim in class—usually me. Or when a dickhead like Mike D'Angelo—one of our three class psychopaths—went stomping down the hall in his shit-kicker boots, training his beady eyes on anyone stupid enough to look in his direction. Then, not being seen was sweet relief.

But that's different from someone standing four feet away, looking right through you. Makes me feel like some kind of peeping Tom. Not that I can see her naked or anything. It's that looking at someone who's totally unguarded is weird. Like peeking into someone's head in a way you'd never be able to if you were actually there. She walks right in front of me. I'm close enough to see the mascara on her eyelashes, to see the smoky makeup on her eyelids, the light green pattern of her iris. She frowns, her lipstick a muted red.

I can't tell if she senses I'm there, or not. Some people can.

Back when my family was still here, a few did. My sister, Beth, had a friend in high school named Chrissie. This was seven years after I'd died. Chrissie made me think of a nervous mop. Quiet. Shy. But an amazing artist. She used to draw pictures of her pet rabbit that were better than anything I'd ever seen. Chrissie knew I was here. Every time I stepped close to her, she wrapped her arms in front of her flat chest and frowned. I'd follow them around the house as they did whatever they were doing—something for school, usually—and it was one hundred percent reliable. She also got chills when I blew on the back of her neck. I'd watch her get goosebumps, and tighten her shoulders as a chill rolled up her back.

After a while, Chrissie stopped coming around.

The woman walks right through me. Feels like a wave of warmth and force, uncomfortable. As a ghost, I can't stop her. Can't touch her. Nothing. After a quick shiver of my own, I follow her into the kitchen. She stops and looks around. Goes to the sink, turns on the tap. The water gurgles out and when she shuts it off, the pipe bangs. Her black heels clack on the linoleum as she opens and shuts cabinets, tries light switches, looks out the window into the yard. She goes through the door to the breezeway connecting the house to the garage. When she tries the garage door opener, I step up behind her and blow on the back of her neck.

Nothing. I get a whiff of perfume and a hint of coffee. I inhale. Life. Not that I care too much for either smell—but still, she woke up somewhere this morning, showered, shampooed her hair, filled her coffeepot and drank a cup or two, left her house, moved through an autumn day, alive. So wrapped up in being alive she probably doesn't even realize she is. That's what I drink in. Life. I'd almost forgotten what it's like.

She turns and walks through me again.

"Wait up, lady," I say.

She doesn't hear me, of course. The mice and spiders in the garage don't hear me, either. No one hears a ghost. I can hear myself.

I catch up to her in the backyard. The fence is gray and splintery, the tall grass next to it faded, leaning now that summer's gone. Leaves from the big sugar maple cover the yard and the corners of the roof. Orange, yellow, red. The wind sends a dozen more leaves floating down, twirling like dizzy birds. She walks the yard, stepping carefully, trying not to get her heels stuck in the ground.

I only follow her so far. I know from experience I can make it a yard or so past the fence, but no more. Trust me, I've only tried about twenty thousand times. Here's what happens: I reach a certain point, and something holds me back. It's like being a bug stuck at the bottom of a porcelain sink. Can't get a grip, gravity does its thing, bug goes round and round. The house and yard are the sink.

I'm the bug.

The lady takes something out of her pocket and taps it. Like a deck of cards, only thinner. Like a quarter of a deck. A little picture shows up in her hand. She points it at different corners of the yard. Tap. Picture. Tap, another picture. Coolest thing I've seen in years. Then, she holds it up to her face and talks to it. "Hi, Brittany. Call Phil over at Pine Street. There's a fence that needs to go, and a general cleanup for 162 Chestnut. Also, call Dave Sutton and schedule something for him. It's cold inside, and the paperwork mentioned something about the furnace being questionable. Thanks."

She taps the device too quickly for me to figure out what she's doing, and then it makes a noise like a miniature rocket taking off, and she puts it back in her jacket. She eyes the roof and the gutters, then walks through me yet again. I'm still thinking about the thing that took the pictures—it's like something from *Star Trek*.

After that, she walks through the whole house, trying light switches, running faucets, looking in closets, her boots loud and sure. At my old room, she pauses with her hand on the door-frame. I feel something then, a quick opening into her thoughts. A weird jumble of images, ranging from an office that looks like a house, with a board with pictures on it, to a kid about my age, her daughter, to a Halloween costume in a mirror. A fairy, with a sparkly wand, a poofy skirt, and a glittered gold mask. Hers, when she was younger. She knows the story, the history of the house. She remembers it from when she was a kid.

How do I know?

The other thing about being a ghost is that when people think about you—not you the ghost, but the life that you had—it opens up a glimpse into their life. Usually just for a moment or two, but sometimes longer. And she was thinking about what'd happened to me. And it got to her.

By now, maybe you're thinking about what happened to me.

Here's all you need to know: I died on Halloween night, 1981, at age fourteen.

I don't like to talk about it.

2

BY THE TIME THE LADY LEAVES, I'M IN A STATE. UPSET BECAUSE OF being reminded of Halloween. Worried, because what kind of camera is that? Have I missed a decade or two? Also curious, because it probably means Beth has finally convinced my dad to sell the house. Beneath all that, a tiny flame of hope flares. Will selling the house finally set me free? An idea I've only entertained approximately ten gazillion times.

I snap out of my thoughts.

Oh, shit.

Zero minutes.

The sun is down, leaving just a faint wash of color in the sky. Pipes knock in the walls and the radiators rattle and ping. The old fear crashes over me.

Mr. Groan is near.

I kick myself for getting caught out in the open. Scrambling, I fly down the hallway to the closet I hide in, feeling the dry, brittle wood of the door as I pass through it. I squat in the corner, wrapping my head in my arms, terrified he saw me. The furnace shuts off in the basement with a clang, and the house slips back into quiet. I will myself still, silent. Safe in the one place he can't get me. Why here? I have no idea. No other place in the house can keep Groan out. I'd learned that the hard way, right at the beginning. No other nook, no eave, no crawlspace. Just this one closet in the hallway on the first floor.

And suddenly Groan is in the house. He's so horrid the air itself holds his nastiness, a crawling sensation. I shut my eyes and rock back and forth, hoping he'll just leave. Sometimes he does.

Nope. He's not leaving. A scraping sound, faint at first, grows closer. His fingernails, claws really, drag along the walls of the kitchen, across the glass of the window, metallic on the old spoon rack on the wall. He whispers. I can't make out the words at first, just dark muttering, like he's having a conversation with himself, like he's preoccupied with something. Something that upset him.

That isn't good.

The scratching sound comes out from the kitchen and into the hallway. I start to catch some of his words.

"No, no, no," he whispers. "Someone's been naughty, naughty, letting ladies walk around. Click, clack. I bet you liked that. Wouldn't you like to eat those legs? I know I would, little man. Wouldn't the little man like that?"

I turn away from the door, burying my face in the corner of the closet. The sound of his voice always gets to me, pure malice. I think he likes this best, when I'm so scared I basically fall apart. Like a trapped animal. He taps his claws on the plaster of the wall beneath the stairs.

"Lips and hips. Chests and breasts. Did it make you ache? Did it?"

He stops, not far from the closet, his voice echoing out across the empty house. Bangs explode on the walls, hard enough that I feel them through the floor.

"Did it? Did it? Did it?" he screams with each hit. "I told you never, ever let anyone in here. Didn't I tell you that, you weak, shivering, drooling piece of human scrap? I told you that ten thousand times."

He's never told me that, not even once. I hear him shifting, like he's getting on his hands and knees. Oh, God. He comes right to the closet. I squeeze my eyes shut. The door rattles. He's on the floor, putting his face in the gap below the door.

"Then please listen very closely to me this time, request number ten thousand and one," he says, his voice calm, reasonable. "This is for your own good. I'm only looking out for you here. Please. Work with me on this."

He pauses. I hear his breathing. The stench filling the closet is unbearable, like charred rot stewing in a full toilet.

"If that gorgeous piece of woman-flesh walks in here again, her eyes running all over everything, her painted lips pursing and rubbing, frowning and deciding . . ."

He pauses, and lets out a long, weary sigh.

"I'm going to have to kill you. Rip you into little shreds. Then, I'm going to sew you back together again, and hold you in my lap no matter how bloody you are, and we're going to have a little talk, you and I, about responsibility. And expectations. And I'm going to need you to look me in the eye, and promise me that you'll never, ever make a mistake like that again. I just can't—"

He stops himself, as though struggling to keep his temper in check.

"If we don't have trust, Timothy," he continues, "we don't have anything. Do you understand?"

I can't speak. My mouth is dry, so dry it's glued shut.

"And don't you dare squeak when you talk," he says. "You need to answer me like a man."

I try to say something, but I can't.

"I can wait here all night," he coos. "I don't have anywhere to be. Say, that might be fun. Just the two of us. We could have a sleepover. We could play all night. All night. What do you think? Or maybe you could answer me when I ask you a simple question."

"Yes," I say. My voice is uneven, not loud enough, but it's all I can manage.

"Did you just squeak at me, mouse turd? Didn't I just say—"

"Yes," I repeat, louder. "Yes!"

Silence. The stench gets even worse. "I hope you didn't just raise your voice to me, Timothy."

"I'm sorry," I say quickly. "I didn't."

"Didn't let her in? Because you did."

"Didn't raise my voice. I didn't mean to."

"But you did."

"I'm sorry."

"You don't sound sorry."

"I am. I promise."

"In fact, you sound like you've had the best afternoon of your tiny little life."

I shake my head, just wanting him to go away.

"How do you think that makes me feel?" Groan says. "After all I've done for you, this swinging drink of gorgeous lady water pours herself through here, and you lap it all up, bright-eyed and curious, following her around like a young dog sniffing his first whiff of heat. Do you know how disappointing that is?"

"I apologize, I'm sorry," I say, speaking quickly, not too loudly. "I didn't know. I couldn't help it. It had nothing to do with me. I won't do it again."

"Do what again?"

"Follow her around."

"You're not listening!" he shouts. "Don't let her in, Timothy. Don't let anyone in. This house isn't for them. This is for me, and I let you stay here because I like you. This is mine. Mine. Not theirs. Just ours. You and me. Best friends, forever. Okay? Are we good? Are we straight?"

"We are," I say. "We're good. We're straight."

"And you'll never, ever break your promise to me?"

"I promise. I'll never break it. Ever." Anything to get him to leave.

"Great," Groan says. "Then I'm off."

I hear him get up. Claws scrape the walls, then tap the three long chimes that hang from the doorbell. With a rattle, the front door opens—and then slams shut hard enough to make the pipes clatter for a full five seconds afterward.

3

So, Mr. Groan.

I don't even like talking about him, but you need to know, so here goes: he's the demon that killed me. Strangely, I don't know that much about him. Where he came from. What he wants. How he showed up in the first place. And more practically, I don't know how to get rid of him. What I do know is that he's my personal, eternal, afterlife cross to bear. My jailer and tormentor. And a total asshole.

Now when I say Groan killed me, it isn't what you're probably thinking. I didn't summon a demon. I didn't fool around with a Ouija board. I didn't play my Judas Priest albums backward.

What I did is go trick-or-treating.

Then I ate a bunch of poisoned cookies.

Those stories about kids dying on Halloween because of eating deadly homemade treats?

Hi, that's me.

Halloween, 1981.

And, yes—being fourteen made me a little old to be trick-or-treating. Agreed. My friends and I weren't even planning on doing it. But Mark Babson, part of our little group, was bummed out because his parents were divorcing and his dad was moving to Oregon, so I came up with the idea of trick-or-treating, just for laughs. As a goof.

Terrible idea.

I'm not going to tell you the details, like I said, because they're horrible. So there you have it. Poisoned cookies. And, yes, it was just me—the other guys were fine. Again, I'm not getting into it.

So where does Groan come in? Well, the poisoned cookies weren't handed out by a leering demon who'd taken up baking and murder, if that's what you're thinking. No, they were baked and handed out by a nice old lady—Mrs. Eleanor Rose Gracie of 16 Rock Ridge Road. Twenty-six years a widow, aged seventy-one. Three grown children. Five grandchildren. Retired elementary school music teacher. Beloved.

And, somehow, possessed by Mr. Groan.

My theory is that Mrs. Gracie started losing it. My great-uncle on my mom's side did. One day he was fine, then he started complaining about the Japanese family that kept floating outside his bedroom window. He complained that the paintings of trout fishing around his house were framed with ground beef dusted with powdered sugar. He eventually became convinced that he was on a cruise ship.

With Mrs. Gracie, I think her loose marbles made her vulnerable. Maybe demons look for a certain frequency, or a certain vacancy. I'm pretty sure Mrs. Gracie wasn't holding black masses between mahjong sessions and trips to the library, in any case.

Dozens of kids ended up in the hospital. A few, like me, died. It made the national news. People in town were stunned, naturally. Heartbroken, horrified—but it was a tragedy, not a crime. And they were right. Kind of. Mrs. Gracie had accidentally put mouse poison into her cookies because the package was mixed in with her other baking stuff. By then, it was clear she was out of it. From what I heard later, she barely understood what'd happened, and everyone, including the police, felt terrible about having to put her through the process of criminal charges—not that they got very far, because she died a week after Halloween when her heart gave out on her.

For a long time, I wondered if maybe Groan did her in. At this point, I doubt it. If he could've kept her alive, he would've loved the attention. He would have found any and every way to make the situation worse. He would've given a master-class performance as the sweet old lady who blurts vile things. He'd have fucked around with everyone who dealt with Mrs. Gracie, each in a different way, keeping everyone off-kilter. He would have loved that. So now I think that Mrs. Gracie either lucked out, or willed her heart to stop. Or maybe the sadness just killed her.

Finally, I sit back, straining my ears. Nothing. A lot of nothing. I decide to take a chance, and I peer out into the hallway, leaning through the door. Empty. I pass through the door. Moving through a wall or a door is uncomfortable. Wood is splinters, brick is grit, wires feel like needles, and the whole thing feels like a field of pressure. Sometimes like a powerful, narrow waterfall. Other times like magnets repulsing each other. Whatever rules dictate physics for ghosts, I don't get them.

I wander the house (ghosts don't sleep) thinking about it being sold, thinking about Groan's warning. Up the stairs, down the hall, turn around, pop in one room, then the next. Down the stairs, living room, hallway, dining room, kitchen. Cellar, just a quick spin past the furnace, which struggles to keep the house at sixty degrees. Up the stairs, do it all again.

I stay away from the windows at night. Groan's favorite trick is to leap up suddenly, just outside a window. Or sometimes drop, hanging upside down like a messed-up spider. Hiding silently for hours just so he can spring up into a window I'm passing isn't out of the question. So I stay away from the windows. He doesn't show up again, though I'm wary all the way until dawn. Sometimes he disappears for weeks at a time. Sometimes only hours. Sometimes he's here, sometimes not. If there's some pattern to it, I've never figured it out.

And here I've been thinking lately that I haven't seen much of him.

So much for that.

4

———————

HERE'S A THING I CAN DO AS A GHOST: WATCH THE LIVES OF PEOPLE I've known. Family, friends. Sometimes—rarely—other people. They needed to be thinking about me for me to see them. It's weird. One minute I'll be wandering the empty hallways, and then I'm suddenly pulled into a daydream. Like actually *pulled*. I feel lifted, spun, and yanked—and then, bam, I've got a fly-on-the-wall view of what's happening with the person thinking about me.

In the beginning, once I'd gotten over the whole shock of being dead, it was sort of cool. Looking into the secret lives of your friends and classmates—what's not amazing about that? Even Martin Warner, who was probably the most popular eighth-grade guy at East Junior High, bawled his eyes out in his bedroom after I died. He held on to an old stuffed animal, a tattered bulldog or something. No one would have believed that —I barely did, and I saw it.

Other kids from school thought about me, too. Tons of girls, which completely surprised me. Maybe it's just a girl thing to grab on to strong emotions like that, or maybe I was just the biggest idiot to ever walk the hallways of East, but I've spent years kicking myself for not saying so much as "hi" to most of them. That bit of sadness they had for me was wrapped up in a thick blanket of *he seemed really nice* or, even worse, *he was cute.* These were some of the prettiest girls in my grade. Kristen Bailey. Jennifer Appleton. Tina Ducette. It took dying to realize I might have had a chance with them. That haunted me.

Get it?

But nothing good lasts, and pretty soon, it was hard to find any of them thinking of me. My friends kept thinking of me, though. They'd get together in the woods, walking around during a long summer dusk, kicking stones, hanging from thick branches, throwing pine cones at each other, working their way through the grief. They'd have a sleepover at Craig's house, or Hugh's—and I could see them, hear them. A couple of times, it was almost like I was there with them: D&D set up on the table, a blue lightbulb in the corner, posters of AC/DC and Rush on the walls. Soda, chips and pretzels, a bag of marshmallows. A stack of records. On the edges of the table, little cones of sandalwood incense burning. Ghosts can smell, remember. Stupid jokes, dumb imitations, farts. And the laughter that tied us all together breaking over them like waves, way into the night.

Heaven.

But time worked its magic. Healed all wounds. Shut them off from me. Oh, I still get the occasional glimpse, even now, thirty-seven years later. Sometimes on my birthday. Almost always on Halloween. Over the past few years, I've seen a little more. I'm guessing it's because most of them have kids now, some of whom are getting close to how old I was when it happened. Although Hugh has thought about me more this year than in decades, and he doesn't have kids. Maybe it's that they're all sliding into their fifties—which, by the way, sounds totally unbelievable to me. Let alone what they look like. Craig is bald. Hugh has a stomach the size of a tipped-over wheelbarrow. Even freakier, most of them look so much like their own dads that I don't know how I never saw that when we were young.

I try to see Beth. I figure, if she's getting Dad to sell the house, she's probably thinking of me somewhere. I go upstairs and glance out the windows of my parents' old bedroom, which faces east. The sun shines through the trees, lighting up the orange leaves of the woods down behind the house.

Beth is the easiest person for me to see. Originally, it'd been my mom, until she'd died fifteen years ago. Maybe it was just that Mom was pretty much always thinking about me, so she pulled me into her thoughts all the time. My dad was another story. He doesn't think about things that he doesn't want to. A wall that he puts up through hard work. Nothing coming down, nothing getting through. That changed a little when he started losing his grip on things, growing forgetful as he got older. Then, he'd sometimes open up, but in a way that was weird. Once, probably just two years ago, he was standing by the kitchen sink eating a disgusting sandwich (sardines, onion, mayo) while listening to the classical music station on the radio. The phone rings, and my dad turned and looked right at me and said, "I bet that's your sister." Chalk that up to one more thing that I never understood about my dad.

So I reach out for Beth. I unfocus. Everything melts away, and then images appear. Sometimes it's clear, other times, it's like a warped, fish-eye view.

It's nice to know when people are thinking about you (and horrible to realize how often they're not, which turns out to be most of the time for most people that you'll ever meet, sorry). It also has its horrible side. Let me give you an example that still makes me want to puke. My friend Craig went to Bard College, down in New York State. When he was a junior, Beth, who was a freshman at Salem State here in Massachusetts, went out to visit him in Annandale-on-Hudson. They'd apparently started talking on the phone after running into each other when Craig'd been back during the summer.

Now Craig and I used to practically torture Beth. We did things like make nooses and hang her dolls. We'd make her laugh until she wet her pants. We knew just how to set her off, and didn't hold back. Her screaming at the top of her lungs, throwing shoes at us—well, it was a pastime. But things changed (except for me, because I'm dead, har har). They got older. They were in college. They were suddenly in each other's pants.

Okay, so you're probably thinking *How would you know all that, Mr. Ghost who goes where people are thinking about you?* Was I reaching out to them, looking for that kind of thing? Dear God, no. I only caught wind of it because I'd passed through Craig's mind as he'd been masturbating about Beth one night in his dorm room. And next thing I knew, they were thinking about each other, calling, writing letters. Every time I tuned in to them —which became easier than it had been, I guess because I'd become some sort of undercurrent to their romance—they were building up this great love that spanned time and space.

I told you it was revolting. It gets worse.

They finally get together, with Beth driving down to Bard to spend the weekend. Early October. Romance in the air. They'd made out before, I discovered as Beth wrote in her journal. I had mixed feelings about the whole thing. Craig had this easy charm with girls, something I'd never had—but I also knew the real Craig, and his charm with girls was a trick, a phony mask. He did this stupid laugh, and plastered a weird grin on his face. He spoke differently. He made his voice softer, laughed, and said *no way* all the time. And you know what? It worked. Girls bought it. Ate it up.

To me, that's bullshit, because what they were buying wasn't what Craig was really selling. He wasn't really that guy. I've thought about that a lot over the years, to be honest—and maybe that's just the way the world works, and I was the one who didn't get it. Me? Well, I'll just put it this way: I have a vivid memory of arguing that any girl who didn't play D&D had no chance with me, proud to hold fast to principles.

Guess which one of us had dates?

So there I was, my feelings well and truly mixed, knowing that Craig and Beth were kindling a romance. He was talking in that soft voice, saying *no way* to her. She was lapping it up and filling her diary with questions like *I wonder if this was meant to be all along?* Whatever. There wasn't much I could do but ignore it—which is exactly what I was trying to do when Craig suddenly thought about me, hard. Pulled me right in . . .

. . . as he was screwing Beth. Like, in the bed with her. Like, inside her.

Even thinking about it now, I get the shivers. Horrible. Thinking back on it, I'm pretty sure that's why their romance didn't survive that weekend at Bard. As he was pumping away on my sister, he started thinking about me. And believe me, as hard as he was trying not to think of me, I was trying not to see what was going on. He couldn't get me out of his mind (which is creepy on some whole other level, I know).

So that was that, the farthest and final stop of the Craig and Beth train.

I can't say I was sad to see that end.

Beth is in her forties now, living down in Florida, near my dad. She's been living down there since the mid-1990s. She's an architect, and also teaches at a small college. Her husband, Ron, is an entertainment lawyer. He's okay. Round face, going bald, but funny. Oh, and I'm an uncle! Two nieces and a nephew. I'm also convinced Beth had three because of me. That way, if one of them dies, it won't leave an only child in the process.

I reach out, and there she is. Warm air. Palm trees. A road

behind her, and in front of her a soccer field. I get a glimpse of my nephew, Dylan. Beth looks normal, I guess. Her hair is a lighter color than I've seen it. I have to say she looks pretty good. Healthy, in good shape. She's held up better than most of our other friends and family. Started running in junior high. That's when she'd think about me most often—I've probably run a thousand miles with her, which is kind of sweet, and just a little bit boring. The running helped her deal with her dead brother. Later, the running helped her deal with Mom being sick (cancer) and dying. Then, the running helped her deal with Dad's gradual mental decline, and everything leading up to her moving him out of the house and bringing him down to a retirement place near where she lives in Fort Lauderdale.

That was my handiwork. I'll get to that.

Now, you can't get too far into people's thoughts when you're watching them as a ghost. But with Beth, I have a better time figuring things out. As I watch her pretending to watch Dylan's soccer game, she has a weird blend of emotions and thoughts: part worry, part frustration, part sadness, part money stress, part stubbornness, and part guilt. I dig a little deeper, and get images of her arguing with my dad, who looks old and shrunken and confused and not at all happy that she's selling the house.

Yep, selling the house.

Ghost included, apparently.

5

———

NEXT MORNING, THE REAL-ESTATE AGENT PULLS INTO THE DRIVEWAY. I watch her from the dining room window. It's where my friends and I used to play D&D, surrounded by books, character sheets, DM screen, dice, pencils, and junk food. We'd start early in the day, and sometimes play late into the evening. I still like the room, since it reminds me of those days. I've also hated it for that very reason. There was an entire year where I didn't set one ghostly foot into it. A brown van with white lettering (*Diamond Oil & Heating*) pulls in behind the Realtor's car. She gets out. The driver of the van gets out, and they talk for a minute, then head to the house. I crack up when I see the furnace guy take a long look at her butt as they approach the door.

Look, I know Groan made me promise not to let the Realtor —or anyone—into the house. The truth is—which he knows as well as I do—that I can't actually do anything to stop them. I can't hold the other side of the doorknob. I can't block the key from the lock. I can't float in front of their faces yelling, *Leave, the powers of Hell command you!* No, nothing.

So when the Realtor opens the door, I stand to the side. She pushes her sunglasses up on top of her head. She's wearing a different color lipstick this time, a kind of brown that matches her fingernails. The furnace guy follows, carrying a metal toolbox. She smells like flowers, just a dab. He smells like oil and cigarettes.

"Original works in there?" He has a cigarette tucked behind his ear, thinning hair, and goofy eyes. He glances at the Realtor's chest as he asks the question.

She doesn't catch it. "Pardon?"

"Original boiler."

"I think so, yes."

He puts the toolbox down. He sniffs away a smile, and walks over to the thermostat. He flips the worn lever up to around eighty degrees and listens. Nothing. "He'd have been here himself, but his kid got into a little fender bender on her way to class this morning."

"I hope she's okay," the Realtor says.

"Ah, she's fine." The furnace comes on in the cellar, starting up its racket. He claps his hands, rubbing them together. "My son gets into an accident, he knows better than to call me. He'll take the accident over his old man's temper."

The Realtor just smiles. I'm guessing she wishes Dave was there.

I look at the furnace guy more closely. Why does he look familiar?

"I'm just messing around," he says. "Love my kid."

"How old is he?"

"Twenty. Thickheaded, stubborn, young, dumb, and you know the rest." He gives another little clap and grabs his toolbox. "Basement?"

"Right over there." She points to the door next to the kitchen.

"Keep telling him to do something useful," he says. "Learn a trade. Join the army. Something. But, nope—he wants to make funny movies for his YouTube, waiting for the dough to come rolling in. Nuts, I say."

I step in front of him. *Holy shit.* I look at his face, then down at his work shirt. An embroidered tag reads: Papadakis. I look at his face again. *Oh my God.* I went to junior high with him. Joe Papadakis. It's him. Same eyes, same hunch, same grin.

Same clap.

He used to clap all the time, like putting a period at the end of his sentences. A weird habit. We used to call him Joe *Clap-a-dakis.* Or sometimes *Papa-clappis.* He looks old—but it's him, no question about it. He opens the door to the cellar.

"I'll go take a peek," he says with a wink to the Realtor. I follow him down the stairs, watching him duck his head at the bottom. He gives the cellar a quick look-over and heads to the boiler. The whole space is empty, lit by four casement windows. At the west end, a partial wall separates the boiler from the rest of the cellar. Joe finds the light switch. The fluorescent lights flit on and buzz.

Joe puts down his toolbox, and claps. "What've we got?" He opens his toolbox and takes out a flashlight, then starts looking over the lines and pipes, shining the light behind the furnace. He looks at a faded label on the furnace itself. "You're older than I am."

He flips open a small, thick cast-iron door that says Heat King in raised letters. A blue flame roars on the inside. Joe squints at it. He tucks the flashlight into a side pocket of his work pants.

"Joe Papadakis!" I yell. I know he probably won't hear me, but I'm curious.

He claps his hands, softly. Puts his hands on his waist. He finds a switch on the furnace and presses it. The fire shuts off with a snap.

"Mr. Clap-a-dakis!" I scream, right in his ear. He runs a hand over the back of his neck. He glances around. He gets down on his knees, looking in the chamber where the fire burned.

"Dirty, dirty," he says. "Just the way I like 'em."

There's a metal box off to the side, and Joe gets a screwdriver and opens it. He looks at the inside with the flashlight, pushing around the old wires with a nicotine-stained finger. I lean over his shoulder and holler "Papa-clappis!" Both his hands are full this time, but he taps the screwdriver against the flashlight. He gets up and turns the switch back on. After a click, the fire starts up again. He shuts the door with the tip of the screwdriver. It squeals. He watches a dusty temperature gauge for a minute. Knocks the glass with his knuckle. Watches some more.

Don't let anyone in.

I decide I need to do something, so I can at least tell Groan I tried. I can move things, if they're small—but only just a little. Like a screwdriver—I can't move that, unless it's balanced on the edge of something. Then I could maybe tip it over. A scrap of paper, yes. A pencil, not quite. I can't actually make them float or anything, just shift. Once, I turned a light switch off, so that's an idea.

As Joe walks around the furnace, following the pipes and wires with the beam of his flashlight, I try to turn off the lights. My hand keeps going right through the switch. I feel a little pressure, some friction from the metal switch box and the wires inside, but I can't catch anything. I go over to the furnace and try the switch I'd seen him turn off. It's even worse than the light switch. No chance. I put my hand inside his toolbox and shake it back and forth. Nothing. I kick it, but my foot just flies right through it, nothing but a little tickle where the wrenches, sockets, and other tools pass through my foot.

"Joe!" I yell.

He puts the flashlight back into his pocket and claps. I seem to be able to make him do that—but making a furnace repairman clap on command probably won't satisfy Groan. Joe steps around the furnace and squats by what I guess is the oil line.

One thing I've done a few times—I got the idea from Groan, as a matter of fact—is make a smell manifest in the air. It's hard to explain exactly how it's done. It takes concentration, thinking about the object that makes the smell. So I try it. I hold still. When I feel that I'm partially *not* there anymore, I start to think about a big, fresh, wet dog turd. A steamer, like our old dog Bomber used to drop, the size of a kitten. I'd stepped into one of those barefoot once, when I was little. I still remember the warm, moist squish as the poo curled up between my toes, the way disturbing it like that had released a stink so strong I could taste it.

There we go. I have it. I feel it.

I relax and concentrate, remembering hopping across the yard, my mom rinsing my foot down with the garden hose. The chunks clinging between my toes, ripe and nasty.

Joe looks up, and sniffs. "What the fuck?" he whispers. No clap this time. He sniffs again, then cranes his neck and sniffs at his armpit.

I keep the stench coming.

Joe stands with a grunt and puts his hand on the crack of his own butt, checking his pants. I lose my concentration—why is he checking his own pants? Does he think that he accidently crapped himself? *Joe Crapadakis.* I hear it clearly. I bust up laughing, and he claps his hands, which makes me laugh even harder. The smell starts to dissipate.

Joe sniffs his fingers and shakes his head. "Something died inside me, holy shit." He looks in the general direction of the stairs, pulls the cigarette from behind his ear, fishes a lighter out of his pocket, and lights it. He inhales and blows the smoke out of his nostrils, then waves the smoke around. He steps over to the casement window and tries to crack it open, but it's stuck. He takes another drag, knocks the glowing tip off against the side of his toolbox, and puts the partially smoked butt into his shirt pocket. He waves the smoke around.

"How's it looking?" the Realtor calls from the top of the stairs.

Joe straightens his shirt and looks at the smoke still curling up by the lights.

"It's a temperamental one, all right," he calls back. The sound of boots coming down the cellar stairs fills the space. The Realtor wrinkles her nose at the smoke-and-poop smell, and Joe's neck flushes a little at his collar. He points at the furnace, and pretends not to notice any faint smell of poo or cigarette smoke. "These Heat Kings are great furnaces, maybe the best ever made. Run like champs for fifty years."

"How old is this one?"

"Sixty years, easy."

The Realtor nods.

"It's an old man," Joe goes on. "It'll still get places, but it'll take longer getting there, and it's gonna hem and haw and groan along the way."

The word *groan* doesn't make me feel good.

"But is it working?" she asks.

"Much as it's going to. Lines are good. Blower looks okay. You want to get another couple of years out of it, I can replace the burner, it's seen better days. But it won't be any more efficient, and right now, at best, you're getting fifty, maybe fifty-five percent efficiency. New furnaces are better. They have gas on this street?"

She nods.

I picture that giant turd again. *Oh, they have gas on this street.* It only takes a second. The Realtor notices it first and her gaze flicks immediately to Joe.

Joe catches on a second later. "You smell that? That ain't me." Spoken with all the chivalry of a Knight of the Round Table. The Realtor puts the backs of her fingers to her nose.

"And I'm sure it ain't you," Joe adds, with a clap. "Noticed it earlier. Like sewage."

The Realtor starts looking around. Joe goes with her, shining the light around the corners of the cellar. Once, he shines the light on her butt when she's walking in front of him, and smiles.

"Town sewer?" he says.

"Septic," she answers.

I can't hold on to the image well enough to keep the smell coming, especially after Joe's line about it not being her. No, I lose it. By the time they make it back to the furnace, the Realtor says, "I'll have someone take a look into it," by which she means, as far as I can tell, *you farted.*

Well, that's only the start of it, because by noon, there's a For Sale sign in front of the house, put up by a guy in a pickup truck with Stonewall Realtors on the side. The sign is white and blue, with a nice picture of the Realtor. Her name: Deborah Landi.

As I stare at it, listening to the radiators tick as they cool back down to the *nobody here* setting, the big question—really, the biggest question—bounces around in my head: Will I finally be able to move on when 162 Chestnut Street is owned by some other family, or am I doomed to haunt it forever?

It's the question that's haunted me since I made the awful decision to chase my aging and frightened father from the only home he'd known for half a century.

PART II

6

____

I DIDN'T DRIVE MY DAD OUT FOR FUN, I DID IT BECAUSE I HAD TO.

My dad, by that point, was still fine. Oh, I noticed a few things here and there, but nothing too odd. He lost track of things. Put the wet laundry into the dryer, but forgot to turn it on. Wandered into the kitchen to look through the drawers next to the stove, and then straightened up, shaking his head. Told the same story to the same person, more than once. Things like that.

He didn't really do a lot, not since he'd retired. He'd talk with Beth on the phone—she called him just about every night around 7:00 p.m. He'd chat with the mailman, he'd run errands, he'd call his younger brother, who lived in Pennsylvania, and the two of them would talk over each other, barely listening to what the other was saying. He kept the yard up, said hello to the neighbors, kept the sidewalk clear of snow in the winter, paid his bills, went to the bank, did his grocery shopping and went to the pharmacy for his blood pressure medicine. Put gas in the car. Swept the breezeway. Put out seed for the two bird feeders outside the kitchen window.

That was about it.

He'd stopped most everything else by then. No getting

together with friends. No Sox games at Fenway. No anything. He'd started closing off when I died—but I think he kept up as much as he did for Beth's sake. By the time she finished college and moved south, he and Mom had gotten into a groove that rarely took them anywhere beyond work, home, and errands. Mom drank, Dad watched TV, and I watched them both grow apart. It pretty much went that way for years, until Mom got sick.

She never drank much when I was alive. Nope. She'd just needed to see her son die in front of her to light that fuse. So she drank to cope. Coping eventually turned into Vodka City. Oh, she was able to work and everything. Keep up appearances. She never got behind the wheel of a car with a drop of booze in her. She didn't drink during the day. But, like clockwork, she cleared the table after she and my dad had dinner, then got out the vodka and vermouth and went to the den to read. By nine o'clock, she was blotto. She'd put her book down, glassy-eyed and unsteady on her feet, tell my dad she was going to bed (she thought she wasn't slurring, but she always was), and pass out upstairs. When she drank, she liked to smoke. And drinking and smoking are the cancer superhighway.

Ergo, therefore, the proof of the theorem is solid: I killed my mom.

I know, I know. I can hear you saying: *But, Tim, it wasn't your fault. If you're going to go down that road, you'd have to admit it was really Mr. Groan who killed her.* Or maybe *People make their own choices, Tim.*

Maybe all that's true.

But it'd been *my* stupid idea to go trick-or-treating, and it'd been *my* stupid idea to make Craig crack up by shoving eight poisoned cookies into my mouth at the same time. I almost choked to death in the process, wouldn't that have been ironic?

My idea.

Mine.

So, yeah—maybe it wasn't my fault, if you put it down on paper, looking at all the facts.

But the heart isn't the head, and never will be.

Okay. So Mom got cancer. Mom died. And, no—I never saw her again. Her ghost, I mean. I watched her die, right there, along with my dad and Beth. She'd been home from the hospital for about three days. She'd also had some kind of stroke, so she wasn't quite with it. Here's how it went, at the end: she'd been unconscious for a day, and doing this gasping breathing. Big inhales. Horrible. Beth could barely handle it, and my dad focused on the clock, waiting for the next time he could put medicine in her IV. When that kind of thing is happening, you cling to something concrete, something to do.

Beth and my dad could deal with medicine, they could clean the kitchen, they could give updates to relatives on the phone, they could deal with the people coming by to offer support, or to say goodbye. It's like they were hosting an event, which I guess they were, and they could pay attention to their hosting duties as a way of forgetting that the most significant person in their lives was in her last days and hours, just in the other room. I'm not criticizing them. It's how they got through a desperately painful and sad transition.

Me? I couldn't do shit.

So I made it my thing to look for Mom's ghost. Her soul. Spirit. Whatever it is, it didn't have too much time left in her failing body. That was my mission. I was going to greet her—and hope to hell she knew something I didn't about where to go at that point.

Because that's what moms are good at, right?

Well, apparently not my mom, because she was gone in a heartbeat. It'd come down to heartbeats, as I guess these things do. Those gasping breaths stopped, followed by these shallow, faint breaths. Those got farther and farther apart. I could see her winding down, like an old clock with only the tiniest bit of tension left in the spring. Her color changed. Her face got pale, like an alabaster statue I'd seen at the Museum of Fine Arts. Her feet got dark, bruised. A stillness came over her, and the rest of us, as we stood around the bed, watching in a kind of fascinated agony. Then, it was just down to heartbeats. One after another, growing faint. I could see her pulse on the side of her neck, a tiny dimpling of flesh. Beat. Beat. Beat. Pause. Beat. Pause. Tiny beat. Pause. Pause. Pause.

Done.

I was worked up, and ready. *Hi, Mom*, I was going to say. Give her a hug, tell her everything's going to be fine, we're together, it doesn't really end, oh, and—by the way—do you know where we're supposed to go?

But, no. Nothing happened. There was no flash of light. I didn't see her ghostly double sit up from her corpse and look around. I didn't see streams of glory rushing up through the living room ceiling, carrying her spirit to the heavens. Nothing.

What had I missed? That's what I kept thinking. How could I be a ghost, and watch my own mother die, and *not* see her spirit. What kind of idiot was I?

So there I was, stunned. My dad and sister were embracing, sobbing. I went all through the house, looking, calling for Mom. Nothing. I kept going back to the body—which looked entirely like something carved, still and empty—wondering if there was some sort of timer, something like a caterpillar needing to chew its way out of its chrysalis, some delay in the spirit tugging itself free of the body.

But there was nothing. And there never was anything.

Seriously, how does the fucking universe work?

. . .

Mom died in 1999. After a couple of years, my dad adjusted. I guess I did, too. That's what you do. It's never the same, but you find a way to get on. Probably close to what it's like if you lose a limb: it's gone, it's not coming back, it sucks, better get used to it, you learn to open the door with your left hand, and that's how you open doors for the rest of your days, because there are still plenty of doors, and you still need to get through them. The next eighteen years were pretty normal, other than me being a ghost who could float through any doors anyhow. Dad had his routine, he stuck to it. Beth got married, and he went to Florida for the wedding. I got a few good glimpses of that, from both Beth and him. So that was nice. Beth had Emma, then she had Alexandra, three years later. Dylan, two years after that. My dad got used to traveling down there to see them. They came up a few times for Christmas.

But slowly, Dad started slipping. Once I really saw what was going on, I tried to think of ways to let Beth know. After all, I saw him pretty much all the time, so it was easier for me to get the picture. I didn't have a lot of luck with that. And he was such a creature of habit by then that he could get through any conversation with Beth on the phone with no problem. He could say hi to his grandkids and ask them silly questions. It all sounded fine— and then he'd finish the call and put the phone in the refrigerator.

That was problem number one, and it was a big one, and I had no good ideas.

Problem number two was, you guessed it, Groan.

I was used to Groan's craziness by then. He'd been harassing me for pretty much thirty years at that point. Don't get me wrong, he still found ways to scare the shit out of me, but I got used to it. That's one part of the universe that I *do* understand. You get used to things, no matter how crazy they are, or painful, or ridiculous.

Sigh.

In any event, Groan had pretty much always ignored anyone else in the house. It was all *Hello, Timothy* and then torture, torture, torture. When Beth was a teenager, he started mentioning her. He'd accuse me of watching her get undressed (as if I could do that without puking), of jerking off while watching her shower (I stayed clear, if you must know), of enjoying sitting next to her as she took a big dump (please). Sometimes he'd sit on my chest, crushing me, and launch into an insane soliloquy about how lovely she was, usually ending it with some revolting meditation on her butthole or nipples or something.

And of course, once my mom got sick, he'd regale me with exactly how he'd given her the cancer, which I knew was bullshit. Evil technique of a demon? Sorry, I'd seen her smoke ten thousand packs of More cigarettes, I know how people get cancer.

But Groan never touched my family. He never made anything happen around the house. Not a single bump in the night. He'd threaten to tear their heads off, pin them down and you-know-what them in the butt, nail them to the walls with kitchen knives through their hands and feet.

All talk.

Of course, it took me a good five years to figure that out, and his threats used to drive me to tears. I'd beg and plead with him not to touch my family, or hurt them. He'd give in, like he was doing me some huge favor.

Dickhead, like I said.

So all through the years Beth was there, nothing. When my mom was still alive, nothing. After the fact, yes, but at the time, it was nothing. When my dad was alone at first, Groan came up with a lot of threats, as usual. He said he'd push Dad down the cellar stairs. He'd trip him while he was getting out of the shower. He'd shove his hands into the blades of the lawnmower. Garbage disposal. Car exhaust. Scissors. Anything. Everything. I didn't give it any more thought than I'd given all the other stuff he'd said over the years.

Me, he could mess with. Them, he couldn't.

Until, suddenly he could.

Groan started trailing my dad. More than once, he came by, but he didn't talk to me, didn't wait outside of the closet for me, none of his usual crap. I found him sitting in a chair in my dad's bedroom, watching him sleep. Pale skin, dark circles around his freaky eyes. Long chin. Long ears. Long fingers. Teeth like broken tombstones. Hair like tufts of a dead lion's mane. Filthy clothes, old-fashioned. He didn't even realize I was there as he just stared sinisterly at the dark shape of my sleeping father.

That's when I decided something was up—and since that something involved Groan, I knew it was bad. I think what ended up saving my dad was that my ability to tell that Groan was nearby had become so finely tuned over the decades that he wasn't able to keep it secret from me, which was what he was trying to do. He watched the house more often. He sometimes passed through, very quickly. He once spent an hour moving in circles in the basement, without stopping by to say *Hello, Timothy.* I crept out of the closet one night to find Groan hovering near the ceiling of the dining room, which was just beneath my dad's room. He moved his long fingers in strange patterns, spinning slowly.

I saw something different in my dad, too. He was more agitated, confused. His hair was messed up. He'd go a few days without showering. One morning, instead of his own bathrobe, he put on one of my mom's, and didn't notice until he went to hang it up later. But that wasn't as bad as the other stuff he started doing, like spending extra time in the basement, just going from corner to corner as if he was looking for something. The same corners that Groan had spent time in. My dad lingered in the dining room a lot more than he had before. Sometimes staring up at the ceiling.

Groan got a little cocky, which was what tipped me off. Out of caution, I'd started spending the nights outside my dad's bedroom. Just sitting in the hallway, watching the moonlight shift and rise as the hours passed, seeing the sky to the east eventually pale as dawn approached. No sign of Groan. Nothing. But around 3:00 a.m. one night I heard my dad mumbling. I thought he was talking in his sleep. Then, I realized it sounded like a conversation—half of one, anyway. I poked my head through the door and saw him sitting up in bed, hair messed up, eyes closed.

Groan sat at the foot of the bed. His skin had a corpse tinge to it, and his uneven, pointy teeth were yellow. Two stubby horns sprang from the side of his head, curled like a ram's. He turned to me, said "Boo," and disappeared. My dad slumped over, and then half woke, looked around, pulled his blankets up, and went back to sleep.

Groan could have just disappeared before I got a good look at him. But, no. He had to say *Boo*. After making sure that my dad was all right, and that Groan was really gone, I realized exactly what he was up to. It all came clear to me.

He wanted to possess my dad.

Groan had an opening into my dad, because my dad was slipping into some kind of senility. Slowly, but it was happening—and somehow I knew, I just knew without a doubt, that it was what had happened with Eleanor Gracie. That was Groan's way in.

So I knew two things.

One: Groan couldn't manage it yet, because my dad hadn't gone far enough down the road to crazy old man yet.

Two: I had to get my dad out of the house for good.

Whatever it took.

7

My dad wasn't going to leave on his own. Too stubborn. Which meant I had to make the guy who brought me into the world—who raised me from a baby, who put up with me going from a sweet kid to a stubborn teen who thought he knew everything, who suffered through my death, who suffered through my mom's death—to fear being alone in the house he'd lived in for fifty years.

It was the right thing to do.

It was.

My strategy was to get him off center. What I needed to do was get him frazzled, and the way to do that was to mess with his routine. So I'd wake him with the smell of smoke. I'd manifest the smell, and after half a minute, he'd snap awake and fly out of bed, staggering around the house, sniffing, looking at the smoke detectors, checking the furnace. He called the fire department the first two times. They came and of course found nothing but a worried old man in his bathrobe.

No, sir. No sign of anything, but we'll be here in five minutes if there's a problem.

That left my dad scratching his head. The firemen, too—which was part of my plan. Because by the time Beth started asking around (and she would) I wanted to make sure there were people in town who might also be wondering if my dad was losing his stuff.

So smells? Check.

I woke him other ways. I could rattle the shower curtain, and that would usually bring him out of a sound sleep. I couldn't quite get a door to slam anywhere in the house, but there was one shelf in the hallway closet that was warped enough that I could get it to rock back and forth, which created a decent enough *squeak-thud* to wake him up, too.

Being a ghost should be easier than it is.

You think of the classic ghost: moaning, eerie whispers, rattling chains, floating glasses and pens. None of that worked for me. One of the best things I figured out was that, while I couldn't manifest a moan or scream or whisper, I could create the effect of a yell having *just happened.* I'd hover over my sleeping dad at random hours of the night and yell his name as loud as I could. He'd wake up, not as if he'd heard it clearly, but with that weird sense of someone having called your name. Between all that, my dad's sleep was wrecked.

Congratulations to me, I'm a terrible son.

Whatever was going wrong with his thinking got worse when he didn't sleep well. He'd forget more, pause longer when he opened the refrigerator, struggle with finding his keys. Of course, I worried that now he was going to crash his car and kill himself, or someone else. He was going to forget how to get home and catch pneumonia as he wandered around in thirty-degree weather. He'd choke on a hot dog, his exhaustion getting the better of him. He'd forget his medicine.

Wrecking his sleep?

Terrible idea. I stopped.

The key had to be Beth. She was the one who needed to see problems. So I thought about the phone calls. Like I said, those were pretty much every night, right around seven o'clock. No more than five, sometimes ten minutes.

That was my window.

Naturally, I went straight for filling the kitchen with the smell of turds when he talked to her. He stopped talking for a minute, and looked around, carrying the phone to the sink, looking at the garbage underneath it, looking at the disposal.

"No, I'm here," he said. He looked in the refrigerator for something rotten, checked around it for anything he'd forgotten to put away. Beth didn't have a clue. My dad was good at covering up.

Fine. I needed bigger guns.

I tried a couple other things over the next days, always when he was on the phone with Beth. I rolled a pen off the counter as he looked at it. I got the spice rack to rattle. I pried loose a picture of Mom held on to the refrigerator by a magnetic calendar. It spun to the linoleum, landing facedown. He kept talking to Beth as he bent down and got it, looking at it for a moment before cradling the phone with his shoulder and hanging it back on the fridge. I tried to rip it down again, but I couldn't get it to budge.

All the small-bore stuff wasn't working. Worse, I caught Groan shadowing my dad around the house just after sunset. Everything Dad touched, Groan touched, mumbling: his chair, the clicker for the television, his glasses, the light switch, a glass on the counter, the button on the fridge for filtered water, the doorknob and dead bolt that Dad checked every night, the banister, bathroom door, toothbrush, toilet handle, alarm clock. Groan didn't even notice me following him, watching. The whole while, I fully expected him to turn and attack me—or at the very least, do that once my dad was asleep. But no, he just left. Vanished.

I switched tactics after that, turning to the one thing I'd never gotten the hang of: appearing. You'd think that was basic, intro-level stuff. Ghosts are called apparitions, right? They should appear. *Like they just saw a ghost.* Why the hell would people say that if no one had ever actually seen a ghost?

But no matter how hard I tried over the years, nothing. Waving arms, yelling, trying to throw myself into people or furniture. Standing between my parents and the television. Nope. I tried to put myself exactly where I thought a person was looking. All that did was freak *me* out, because it sure felt like they were looking at me. Sunlight, moonlight, starlight—none of those worked. Full moon. No moon. Equinox. Solstice. The anniversary of my death. My birthday. None of those held any special power. By the time I'd been dead for a few years, I'd given up trying to appear, and hadn't tried it anytime since.

So I tried it the next night for my dad. It didn't work. I strained, willing myself to appear, groaning and grunting, but my dad looked through me as though I were any other random air. The next night, I tried the opposite: total relaxation, basically tricking myself into it. *Don't try, don't try, laid-back, calm—BAM, here I am!* That didn't work, either.

I discovered the secret to it by accident.

The next night, seven o'clock rolled around, and my dad had loaded his plate into the dishwasher. *Jeopardy* played on the little television he kept in the kitchen to watch while he ate supper alone. It was December, and the smell of the air outside was saying we were in for the first snowfall of the season. Earlier that afternoon, he'd gone out to the garage to make sure the snowblower was ready to go. In doing so, he'd glanced up at the joists that ran along the top of the garage, where some old junk was stored. His gaze landed on a big wooden toboggan we'd used as kids. The memory jiggled a splinter of grief still wedged painfully in his heart. I felt the stab of it. He'd let out a sigh that had a little shake to it, then moved the recycling bins to the other side of the garage to make room to get the snowblower out.

That's what gave me an opening. A touch of fresh grief made

the connection stronger. So when he talked to Beth that night, leaning against the counter by the sink, staring into the middle of the kitchen, I thought about the toboggan. Those winter afternoons carrying that thing up and down the small hill behind Craig's house. Cold winter air. Wet wool mittens. The vinyl pad of the toboggan. Lip balm. Down jackets. Steaming laughter. It came to me so clearly I didn't think about it—I just pushed it out, and filled the kitchen with the scent of sledding. It surprised me how well I was able to do it.

My dad stopped talking midsentence.

"Dad?" I heard Beth say, tinny and small from the phone.

"Yes, okay," he said, his face pinched. "Well, I told them they'd better come out and take a look at it, probably get one of the tree services to take it down."

I stood right where he was gazing, and relaxed, looking at him. I felt it happen. The air changed around me. It was a weird sensation, like I was being pressed—very lightly—all over.

My dad's eyes widened. His mouth went slack.

It was so weird, because I knew he was looking at me—really looking at me. What now? Wave? Do a little dance? Windmill my arm like Pete Townshend? I didn't do anything. I just stared back at him. It's hard to explain what it felt like, because it was the first connection I'd had with someone in thirty-seven years. I looked at him, he looked at me. I smiled, hoping I wasn't going to start bawling, feeling like pretty much the lamest ghost imaginable.

He dropped the phone, blinking, staring right at me. I was five feet away from him, just underneath the frosted glass ceiling light. His eyes filled with tears. He went pale.

"Timothy?" he said in a weak voice.

"Hello? Dad? Are you okay?" Beth's voice squeaked from the phone on the floor.

I nodded. He straightened, resting one hand on the counter.

What should I do? I was flustered. Should I tell him that I love him? That I'm always there?

"Are you . . . ?" he managed to get out.

"Dad? Dad?" Beth said.

I lifted my right arm and pointed to the kitchen door, like a ghost from a Charles Dickens novel would have done.

"You have to leave," I said. As soon as I said it, I was certain that he hadn't heard my voice, because his gaze looked at my hand, not my face. I used my other hand, waving. *Go. Go.* Like a traffic cop.

"I think my dad fell or something," Beth said, not into the phone. Her voice grew louder. "Dad?"

That snapped him out of it. He took his eyes off me and reached for the phone.

And I lost it, my manifestation. Just like that.

I tried to get back into that feeling, but the harder I tried, the further it slipped. My dad blinked, breathing hard like he'd just run up a flight of stairs.

"I'm fine, I'm fine," he said into the phone. "I just dropped this darned thing."

"*Are you sure?*" Beth said.

"I'm sure."

His voice trembled. Beth heard it, I could tell.

"Tell me what happened, Dad," she said.

"Nothing. I dropped it."

"Well, how long does it take to pick it back up?"

"As long as it took," he said, a hint of irritation in his voice.

"Well, what if you fell for real? Who would know? What if I wasn't on the phone with you when it happened?"

They went back and forth like this for a little while, but I didn't listen.

Okay, that worked.

It'd worked. Somehow, I'd managed it. And it'd gotten to my dad. That much was clear. Beth heard something in his voice, but I saw it on his face.

So I knew what I had to do.

8

———

GROAN CAME BY AGAIN THE NEXT NIGHT. HE WOUND HIS WAY around the house, one room to another to another, going to all of the corners. I followed him, staying almost entirely within the walls, just poking my eyes through. He didn't notice I was there. Normally, he knew exactly where I was. Not this time. He kept quiet—I wouldn't have even known he was there if I hadn't been vigilant. He repeated this strange circuit of the house. Three times. Then, he was gone.

My dad cried out in his sleep.

Whatever Groan was planning, I wasn't going to let it happen. So what I'm going to tell you, I'm not proud of.

I used every scent from childhood. Baby powder. Diapers. Pudding. Warm banana bread. Skateboard wheels (they have a smell). Wallpaper glue. Hamster cage. Christmas tree. Finger paint. New tennis balls in the can. Thanksgiving stuffing. Laundry hamper. Glue and paint for plastic models. The old Head & Shoulders shampoo. Construction paper. Chapter books. Piles of leaves. Modeling clay. Popcorn on the stovetop.

Anything that could bring me—and my dad—back to those years before everything fell apart.

And let me tell you—I was getting the hang of this ghost thing, because I turned into some kind of superhero of smells. Push a marble on a hardwood floor? Barely. Fill a room with the scent of red licorice? Bam, done. What was weirder, though, was that once I'd used a scent, got it really good, it was hard to catch that one again right away.

I got better at appearing, too. Although I couldn't always do it. I still don't know exactly what the trick is to that. Sometimes it's the easiest thing in the world—I think it, and there I am, like stepping through a doorway. Other times, I trip up, and can't quite get it to stick. That's more like trying to adjust a radio station with poor reception by pointing the antenna in different directions. I drift in and out, unclear. And sometimes I can't do it at all. Not a hint. Not a spark, not the slightest bit of transformation. Nothing. Like willing yourself to walk up a wall and out onto the ceiling over your head. Just not possible.

Sometimes Dad would squint, like he wasn't sure of what he was seeing. Other times, his eyes would widen and he'd fumble for his glasses, only to lose where I was. I worried that he'd start thinking he was imagining it. After those first couple of nights— him searching the house, him not sleeping, him sitting in my old room, holding a few of my old painted lead wizards (they still looked pretty awesome)—I realized he wasn't terrified. Sad, yes. Confused, yep. Hoping? Eager? Happy? I think there was some mix of all of that. Worse, he became focused—exactly the opposite of what I'd expected. He wasn't just sleepwalking through his days, so deeply embedded in his routine that he never had to actually stop and think about anything anymore. No. He wanted to find me. And aside from his pathological stubbornness and unending refusal to deal with any emotions, he was a pretty smart guy. So the next day, he went out, and came back with an armload of books from the library. On ghosts and hauntings.

Great.

He also became less forgetful. No more putting the phone away in the fridge. No more grumbling about cereal while looking underneath the sink. That started a strange couple of weeks. Dad spent hours and hours reading these books, books with titles like *The Scientific Search for Ghosts, New England Hauntings, Spirits: Emissaries from a Holographic Universe*, and *Voices from the Undiscovered Country*. I read them over his shoulder as he sat at the dining room table. There wasn't anything in any of those books that mentioned anything I'd experienced since I'd died, other than vague pronouncements like *A ghostly manifestation frequently is connected to the site of a traumatic death*. Well, duh. Everyone knew that. Or *Spirits often don't realize that they're stuck in a transition between one plane of existence and the next, unaware of their state of being, fixated on the life that they've moved on from to the exclusion of all else*. Not exactly, Owen Lighthorse, PhD. Pretty much all I've thought about since my *traumatic death* was the fact that I was a ghost. A stuck ghost. Seriously, who wrote these books?

But they gave my dad some ideas. He dug up an old cassette tape recorder from the 1970s. Craig and I had used it extensively in the documenting of farts when we'd been in sixth grade, budding geniuses that we were. He brought it up to my room. I saw where this was going, after we'd skimmed through *Voices from the Undiscovered Country* (which, incidentally, purported to show that ghosts were full of some kind of secret knowledge and wisdom—plainly nonsense, as I'm sure you've realized by now). I was curious if it would work. He popped in a new tape he'd bought from RadioShack (after mumbling about *how they think people are supposed to open these God damned things*) and looked around. He checked that the machine worked, exactly as a dad would—*Testing, testing. One, two, three. Is this working?* Stopped. Rewound. Listened. He nodded. Rewound it again, and hit record. The little wheels of the cassette spun.

"Timothy." He cleared his throat. "Can you hear me?"

"Yep. I'm right here. Here. I'M RIGHT HERE." I spoke, but no go. Didn't work. I put my face right on the little part of the tape recorder where the mic was, and shouted, but the only sounds in the room were the quiet gear noises of the machine and my dad's breathing. I tried to tap it, bump it, blow on it, smash it. Nothing. I tried to stomp on the floor next to it, to clap my hands, to whistle. Nothing.

"Are you here?"

And, of course, I couldn't appear. Nothing. I couldn't even get a smell happening. All I could think was that if it would somehow *work*, I could get him out faster. Part of me also just wanted to communicate. I was glad I could make the room smell like Play-Doh, but that wasn't communication. Even when I appeared in front of my dad those times, it was barely communication. Just to be able to say a simple thing, and get a simple response—well, that would have been amazing, and seemed about as impossible as coming back from the dead. So I got pissed. I tried to wrench the curtains, slam the closet door, kick a hole in the wall. Foot, fingers, and fist all passed effortlessly through it all.

"The temperature seems to have dropped in the room," my dad said, suddenly narrating a documentary. "Timothy?"

I stopped my tantrum. I tried to manifest a voice, tried to picture the sound like a bubble from one of those little bubble wands: start with nothing but a film of bubble mix, and gently, slowly blow it up. I thought I felt something getting some traction, but lost it. After a minute, my dad stopped the recorder. He rewound it, and listened back. The only interesting part was that after he mentioned the temperature and then said *Timothy?* there were a couple of faint hisses, almost like static—and I was pretty sure they matched what I'd been trying to say, trying to get out, the way I'd felt sound start to catch before I lost it.

So that seemed like a dead end.

But actually, my dad's efforts with the tape recorder took a dangerous turn before I knew it.

9

———

DAD DIDN'T GIVE UP ON THE TAPE RECORDING AS FAST AS I DID. HE repeated the experiment in every room of the house as the after-noon wore on. In the first couple rooms, I tried to come up with something—anything—that would register on the recording. No luck. In fact, it felt even less possible than earlier. Some of these ghost things are like that—your best shot is usually your *first* shot, and the harder you try, the harder it gets. I tried to get myself into the right headspace for it, but it felt like chasing the tide out. I ended up just watching as he tried to catch some sign of his dead son.

Bummed me out.

I also couldn't manage to get any smells to manifest. Not a whiff of anything. I decided it was because my dad was focused, and when he was focused, it shut down the parts of his mind I'd been able to use to do what I'd done earlier. The emotional part of him was locked away. My plans unraveled exactly because I'd nudged him down this path. I didn't even bother trying to do anything that evening when Beth called.

And then Groan made it ten times worse.

•　•　•

Turned out he'd caught on to what we were doing. During the night, I'd only heard my dad snoring in his bedroom upstairs, and I'd seen nothing but quiet hallways lit by the moon. But when Dad got up, instead of padding down the stairs in his slippers and bathrobe to make breakfast, he went to my old bedroom. Curious, I followed him. He walked in, and went over to the tape recorder, which he'd put on the nightstand next to my old bed. He'd plugged it in so the battery wouldn't die. He hit the rewind button, and stood there looking at it as it rewound an entire side of tape. He must have set it up to record just before he'd gone to bed. It took a good three or four minutes to rewind to the beginning. Once it did, he pressed the play button and turned the volume up. There was the normal tape hiss and then the sound of the recorder being moved around. Then, my dad's voice.

"It's just a few minutes before midnight. December third. Soon to be the fourth. I'm placing the device in Timothy's room. On the nightstand."

On the recording, I heard my dad's footsteps receding, followed by the sound of the door closing. Then nothing. A hollow silence. Hiss. It sounded like the house at night. The heat coming on. Pipes filling with water after the upstairs toilet flushed.

My dad sat on the edge of my old bed—my old Star Wars blanket folded into a rectangle, still at the foot of it—and put his hands on his knees as he listened. He looked old. Skinny legs. His back bent, his bathrobe frayed, his hair gone white and poking out at Albert Einstein angles, just shorter. A minute went by, then another, then five. And he listened carefully to all of it. I felt a surge of love for the guy. He and I couldn't have been more different—I was my mom's son. You could tell, just looking at us. We thought the same way, reacted to things the same way, were basically cut from the same cloth. Beth and my dad—they were the other tribe within the family, no doubt about it. Stubborn, convinced they were right in every situation, super smart in some ways and total idiots in others. By the time I'd died, my dad and I were already in the midst of the collision that would certainly have racked us for at least another decade or two. Neither of us really understood the other. Hell, even after three decades of watching the guy when he didn't know he was being watched, I still couldn't figure him out. Oh, I could predict—to the microlevel—everything he'd ever do. Prediction is different from understanding, I think you can agree.

All that said, there was love.

And as I watched him patiently listening to nothing playing back on that tape, I felt that love. Even thirty-seven years after I'd died.

Love.

The sounds started up after about a half hour. By then, I don't think my dad expected to hear anything, so at the first sound, he lifted his gaze up from the floor in front of him to the tape recorder. It was a bump, some kind of thud. I leaned in closer. So did he. At first, I figured that it was nothing more than a house creak. Another sound followed it. Then another. Each one a bump. My dad peered at the little turning counter on the machine to see where the noises started. Squirrel on the roof? Branches knocking? No—it couldn't have been anything like that, because I'd been downstairs the whole night, and it'd been quiet.

"Dad?" the recorder played.

My dad gasped. He'd been holding his breath. What the hell? It sounded like my voice, kind of. More of a whisper.

"I'm here."

What? It's probably obvious to you, but my mind shot off in a bunch of crazy directions: Did I do that? Had I done it when I'd been zoned out? Was I somehow doing it right at that moment? No, no, and no. I even went more bizarre, before I reeled myself in. Is my room haunted by some other ghost? Is there some loop in time that I got myself caught in? Am I the ghost of a ghost, haunting myself?

"My God," my dad muttered.

Then I understood: Groan.

I listened more carefully as the voice spoke again, and heard that it was Groan, doing a fantastic imitation of me. He was a demon of a thousand voices to begin with, but this was impressive—and my poor dad, who hadn't actually heard my voice in decades, wouldn't have been able to tell it wasn't me.

"Can you hear me? Say so if you can hear me."

My dad's hands started to tremble and he sat up, straight as the bedpost behind him.

"I hear you." His voice broke.

"It's not me!" I yelled, but of course he couldn't hear me. I tried to shut off the tape recorder, focusing all my will on pressing the stop button. Nothing, couldn't do it. I tried to pull the plug from the wall. Nope. I tried to jam myself right into the electrical outlet and wires, trying to cut it, but that didn't work.

Dad took in a deep breath, and reached out and shut off the tape recorder. He listened. The house was quiet. He rewound the tape, just a little. Pushed play.

"I'm here" played again. Then "Can you hear me? Say so if you can hear me."

What was Groan doing? The tape played on.

"I miss you." Pause. "I love you."

Oh, that fucker. I looked at my dad. His nose was red and his chest was hitching.

"I love you, too," my dad whispered around the tears. "I love you."

It killed me to see his heartbreak. Tore at me—but it gave me an opening, because my dad was flooding with emotions. I stopped worrying about turning off the tape recorder. I focused. I felt myself manifest.

"You have to help me," my false voice said, wavering from the tiny speaker. "I'm stuck. All alone. Don't leave me, Dad. Don't leave."

Even as I started to appear, I knew I wasn't super solid. My dad looked up at me, looked through me, then did a double-take.

"Timothy?" he said.

"If you leave—I—I don't know what will happen to me, Dad. And I'm afraid."

My dad looked right at me as Groan's words came out. I shook my head. I pointed at the tape recorder. Shook my head some more.

"My God, I hear you," my dad said, his voice like he'd been punched in the chest.

I walked over to the tape recorder and shook my head again, pointing at it.

My dad nodded. "I hear you. I won't leave. I won't."

No, no, no. I tried to think of some way to make him understand. I swung my arms over the machine, like an umpire calling a strike.

"There's more?" he said.

What? I shook my head.

"I won't stop it, no," he said.

Talk about different wavelengths. It amazed me not just that we were father and son, but that we were on the same planet. There was more silence on the tape. I started to fade—again, I couldn't really control this appearing business—so I stepped between my dad and the tape recorder.

"DON'T LISTEN," I shouted, mouthing the words with exaggerated movements. "THAT'S NOT ME. YOU HAVE TO LEAVE."

My dad squinted at me, not understanding, shaking his head.

"I hear you, yes. I won't."

"Mom can't help me," Groan said in my voice. It grew faint. My dad leaned in farther. "You need to. She loves you. She told me to tell you—but she also told me to tell you to help me. To stay."

"I'm not going anywhere."

Again, he's nodding. I'm shaking my head, slipping out of sight in the sunlight.

"I've been so frightened, and lonely. You're all I have."

The voice was barely audible. I was so pissed at Groan. A few more noises warbled through the speaker, the sound of sniffling, as though the ghost me were crying. Pathetically. Like a little kid.

Groan was such a prick.

"Timothy?" my dad whispered. He looked around the room. I was gone. Damn it. He listened to the rest of the tape, another ten minutes of nighttime silence. Once the tape ended and the machine clicked off, he reached over and rewound it back to the 534 mark, where the voice of Groan had begun. *Thunk, click, sppzzzz, click*, as he stopped it, played it, fast-forwarded it, then played it again.

"Dad? I'm here."

The sound of the voice was a quarter of the volume it had been the first time he'd played it. Dad reached over and snapped it off before it could go any further. He got up and went to the hallway, then to Beth's old room, which my mom had turned into a study after Beth had left. He went into a couple of drawers and then returned to my room with a pen and a sheet of printer paper. He scratched out in his nearly illegible handwriting *Dad. I'm here.* And then he let the tape play again, and wrote down everything Groan had said. Even as it played, the voice grew softer, until it was nothing more than the whisper of a mouse in the far corner of a hissing room. He rewound the tape recorder once again, looking over what he'd written out. Played it again. Nothing. A hint of those thuds, but then nothing. The knock of a radiator at one point. The faintest hint of some hissing variations, but nothing more than that.

My dad played it through three more times after that, then

listened to the entire side of tape again. Not stopping. Not eating. Making sure. He looked over the words, rereading the whole false soliloquy. *If you leave—I—I don't know what will happen to me, Dad. And I'm afraid.* His gaze stayed on that line. He put his hands on his bony knees and nodded, sure of what he needed to do. He stood up, taking the paper with him. He turned off the tape recorder, but left it where it was, plugged in. He couldn't see me, hear me. I tried to get a smell to show up—I was going for shit, as in *This is all bullshit, don't believe it, it's bad*, but I couldn't get anything to happen.

Dad walked out of the room. "I won't leave you, Timothy. And you can leave me another message tonight. I'm here for you. Don't worry. Dad's here."

I wanted to cry. I wanted to hit something. I practically wanted to laugh. It was unbelievable. What was I supposed to do?

I wanted—needed—my dad to leave. And now he wanted—needed—to stay.

Because of Groan's lies.

Because Groan wanted him to.

Because Groan wanted *him*.

I had no idea what to do.

10

———

Groan had unintentionally done me a favor over the decades: he taught me how to scare the shit out of someone. So I took a page from his book of assholery and used it on my dad. Better still, Dad wasn't just clinically curious anymore—he was emotionally involved beyond anything I could have done with my ghostly miming.

If you leave—I—I don't know what will happen to me, Dad. And I'm afraid.

Your dead child tells you that, and no emotional wall can hold. I had more access to his raw emotions that ever. And with that as fuel, I could do more than I'd ever thought possible. No more struggling to come up with the smell of a fart. No more straining to shadow up in bright sunlight. No, if I could think it, I could do it.

Confuse him. Inconvenience him. Bug him. I looked for any opportunity. Push his keys off the counter. Break all the pencil tips (he liked pencils). Drag the hanging end of the toilet paper down into the water. Ring the doorbell at midnight. Turn the lights on and off. Unfortunately, I think he welcomed these acts as messages. I guess I can't blame him—but really. What kind of message is a strand of toilet paper hanging in the toilet? *Stay clean?*

So I brought on the scares.

Oh, I did all the classic horror movie stuff. Standing behind him, reflected in the medicine cabinet mirror when he closed it. Leaping up outside the window over the sink when he was rinsing dishes. Staring at him from the corner of his bedroom as he tried to fall asleep. Peering out from under the bed, in my room. Closets. Tops of stairs, bottoms of stairs. Poking my head down into the fireplace.

Boy does that stuff work. My dad would cringe, step back like he was hit. And then he'd try to figure out what it meant. I appeared right behind him one night while he was talking with Beth, and when he turned (he paced a lot when talking to her), he yelped and dropped the phone. He talked his way out of it—claiming a spider had crawled onto his sleeve—but I could hear the doubt in the silence on her end of the phone. Normally, Beth talked an appalling amount, to the point where I've sometimes wondered if she lacked the ability to actually have a silent thought. It was only when she *stopped* talking that you knew something was up.

The problem was that the harder I tried to scare him, the more convinced he became that he was unlocking the mystery of what I was trying to tell him. The tape recorder became a battleground. He tried to capture more of my voice on tape. I tried to hide or move the tapes, the plug, the recorder itself (the most I could manage was to slide it off the nightstand a few times, which sadly didn't break it). Dad set it up to record a few more times, and I dutifully, carefully turned it off after about ten minutes.

I took things further, after a week or so. I pushed the shower curtain while he was showering. I slammed the toilet lid closed while he brushed his teeth. I rattled the knives while he made toast. I came close to taking his fingers off when I flicked on the garbage disposal while he was pushing some leftover Brussel sprouts into it. I actually scared myself with that one—I wanted to scare him, not mutilate him.

So a few nights later I was trying to get a bathrobe to float across a bedroom, when I sensed His Nastiness. As always, I flew back through the floor, to the downstairs hallway, and zipped into the closet. He was in the house. Something went weird in the air. My hackles went up. There was a sense of threat, moving nearby. The closest I can come to explaining it is this: imagine you're in the ocean, at night, maybe even diving, and the biggest, freakiest, blank-eyed, open-mouthed great white shark is out there with you, circling, behind, below, in front, getting closer. That vulnerability and that threat—that's what it's like to have a demon nearby.

He didn't come by the closet, but I still felt him, so after a while I inched my way out of the closet, sensing him on the second floor. I took my time, passing up through the wood and flooring, the carpet and the drywall, until I had a glimpse of my dad's room.

Dad was asleep. Groan stretched out on the bed next to him.

He stared at me. "Timothy, Timothy, Timothy. What am I going to do with you?"

I ducked back down into the floor.

"No, I'll wait," I heard him say.

Shit shit shit.

Every bit of me wanted to fly back to the closet, but I didn't. I rose through the floor again.

"Oh, look who's not quite the coward I thought he was," Groan said. Shadows clung to him. He lifted his hands and steepled his long fingers in front of his face. His nails were long and dirty.

"What do you want?" I said.

"What do *I* want? You're questioning me? Who do you think is in charge here, my little closet mouse?"

"You know what I'm talking about." I tried not to let him get to me. I tried to sound sure of myself.

"*You know what I'm talking about*," he said, mimicking me. "No, Timothy. I don't know what you're mumbling about. What am I, a mind reader? How should I know what's passing between your gross little ears?"

"Leave him alone," I said.

"Leave *who* alone?"

"My dad."

"Is that what this pathetic display is all about? You can't grow up? You can't let go of the edge of his fart-perfumed bathrobe? Wow. I'm surprised."

"I know what you're trying to do." I'd never talked back to Groan like that before. Ever.

He smiled.

"You have *no idea* what I'm trying to do, turd," he said. "If you did, you wouldn't dare stick one single hair of your insubstantial head outside of that little whack-den of yours. You wouldn't flap your haunted lips at me like that. You wouldn't open your eyes. You'd squeeze them shut and keep your weak little mind focused on not shitting yourself."

"He never did anything to you," I said.

"Yes, he did," Groan said. "He did everything to me. He made you, which, tragically for me, turned one evening of hysterical, unforgettable, laugh-out-loud comedy into what feels like a thousand years of soul-crushing drudgery as I have to deal with you. How could you possibly think that's *nothing*?" He cocked his thumb at my sleeping father. "I owe this one some serious payback, don't you think? I sure do. And don't act surprised. I hate it when people act surprised when they're really not. Surprise is like this." He jammed his nails right into my chest, reaching for my heart. It wasn't like passing through stuff, barely there. No, Groan and I were just as substantial to each other as you and the last person you saw, so it stunned me, agonizing. I tore myself free of his hand and flew backward. He was behind me before I could see where he'd gone.

"And like *this*," he whispered in my ear, his breath burning like a torch. His hands wrapped around my throat and he dug his nails into the flesh of my neck. He slid his fingers out with a wet sound and rubbed his hands around in the blood, then started licking my neck with a tongue that felt like a moray eel. He blew on me again, rubbed his hands all around my neck—and the wounds on my neck and chest were gone. "That's surprise."

He sprung up onto the floor and crossed the room, doing a weird, gimpy walk.

"Don't. You. Tell. Me. What. Sur. Prise. Is," he said, staccato.

I wasn't the one who brought it up. I felt around my neck and chest, but they felt whole again, even though the warm stickiness of my blood drenched my sides. Groan stopped walking, his back to me.

"Are you still here, Timothy?" he whispered.

"Look," I said. "Leave him alone. You can do whatever you want to me. You can kill me. You can kill me every night. You can—"

He spun and stomped back to me, his eyes wide.

"I can kill you anytime I want to already!" He bent over, shoving his face right into mine, contorting his back like a cobra to do it. He grabbed the back of my head, then ground his index finger into my eye.

The pain was unbelievable—his nail scraped against the back of my eye orbit. I couldn't even yell, the pain was so intense.

"See? Should I pop the other one? Why shouldn't I? I don't even care anymore—don't you understand that? Of course you don't—you're a dipshit. Dipshit, dipshit, dipshit."

Each time he said *dipshit*, he poked his finger harder into my skull. He sat back on his heels, squatting in front of me, then lifted me by my collar, grabbed my head with both hands, and licked my ruined eyehole until my eye reformed itself. He shoved me backward. I staggered, falling through the bedroom wall and out into the hallway. I got myself up and went back in. Groan was back on the bed, sitting by my father's head.

"I hope you have something else to offer me, kid," he said. "Because I'm so bored with killing you that I'm about ready to kill myself for a change. Hey, here's an idea: maybe you could help me. Would you do that, if I asked? Honestly, I can't handle this much more. Would you?"

He rolled his eyes and held his palm to me. "No. Don't answer. And don't not answer. Neither one works for me, not right now. God, you're tiresome. And do I get any credit for putting up with you? Nope-nope. So let's just shuttie-uppie. I don't need to hear the obvious grinding of your feeble mental gears. Watching you try to work out the right thing to say is like watching a blind kitten chasing after a wind-up mouse. Just sad. S-A-D, sad."

He closed his eyes for a moment, then flicked them open. "But here's the thing. This nonsense of yours stops. Tonight. Now. Get it?"

"I—"

"I just told you not to talk, and not to not talk—so why are you not not talking to me right now?" He stuck out his tongue, slowly, and chomped his teeth on it, gently. He pulled it back in. "Justshutthefuckup, and listen. If I catch wind of you playing any of your reindeer games with Daddy here—the spooky-wooky garbage you seem to think is frightening to him, the utterly predictable *haunting* shit—then you and I will have a problem bigger than all the rest of our problems combined. And I don't handle problems well, do I?"

He held his hands over my dad's sleeping face. He straightened out his fingers. His claws grew an inch longer, accompanied by a ripping sound. Little curls of gray gunk squeezed out from his cuticles. He lowered his hands until the nails nearly touched Dad's neck.

"I'll rip his throat out," he said, his face going blank. "And I'll make it look like *you're* the one doing it. How's that? Decent way to die—killed by your son's ghost? And don't give me a frowny-face, thinking to yourself *my good friend Mr. Groan is just teasing, he can't actually* do *something like that*. Let me explain something to you, dummy. I can do whatever I want to. Just because I haven't, doesn't mean I can't. Or won't."

He was lying. I'd worked out a long, long time back that he couldn't actually touch my family. Not physically, anyhow. But with the dementia—who knew what havoc he could wreak?

"I can tear him apart," Groan continued. He placed a nail on Dad's cheek. "I can hurt him."

He pressed harder. I watched as his nail pushed into the skin.

"I can make him see me, any way I want to." As he said it, he started to change, his flesh and hair wriggling and rearranging. It only took a few moments, and he looked like me. Instead of a nail pressing my dad's cheek, it was a knife in *my* hand. I'd never seen him do anything like that before and it made my stomach drop. "You like? Pretty good—except I haven't quite mastered that dense, mouth-open look that's your trademark. Something like this?"

He let his jaw flop down, half rolled his (my) tongue out, and basically looked like a drooling idiot. It wasn't a good look on me (and it wasn't any look I ever made, to be clear).

"I almost went with this look when I killed your mom," he said, talking with his tongue out. "But, instead, I went with this."

He scrunched his face up into something much more demonic. I had a second or two where I thought I was going insane, because he looked so terrifying—*my face* looked so terrifying.

"You didn't kill her," I said. "Cancer, remember?"

"*Cancer, remember?* Yeah, I remember. Who do you think *gave* her the cancer? And when she was lying there, right at the end?" He made the horrible death-rattle sound that'd filled the house for those last twelve hours. He did a pitch-perfect rendition of it, and it chilled me. "When she was staring up at the ceiling—do you want to know what she saw? She saw *you*. Young Timothy, the teenage cookie monster. Oh, and Timothy, the droopy-drawers toddler. Oh, and Timothy, the lazy-eyed, patch-wearing first grader with the bad haircut and the thick glasses. Oh, and Timothy, the baby who couldn't breathe right at first so they had to stick him in an incubator for a few days."

I wanted him to shut the fuck up, even though he was lying.

"Poor Mommy, dying in the living room, gasping her last few thousand smelly breaths, staring in horror at the vision of her dead son. On her chest. *Strangling her.*" He pressed the knife farther down, and a drop of blood grew on Dad's cheek. "So don't be so fucking sure of what I can and can't do, Timothy—because you'd be surprised at how much pain *you* can cause your poor parents."

Groan suddenly morphed back into himself, a leering corpse hunched over my father. He pulled his fingernail from the flesh of Dad's cheek, and licked the blood off it. He turned to me.

"Such a shitty son you've been," he whispered. "Don't push me."

With that, he shot up through the ceiling as though he'd been yanked by a rocket. He was gone. I hurried over to my dad, who'd started to shift. He muttered something, then felt at his cheek, his hand coming away with blood on it. He sat up, and looked at me. Right at me. Then at my hand. I looked down—and saw a perfect vision of a butcher knife in my hand. The knife disappeared right after I noticed it.

"Timothy?" my dad said, his voice thick with sleep. And fright. He flinched backward, putting his arm up between us.

I backed out of the room, disappearing.

11

———

I could handle Groan finding new ways to torment me. But now he was going after my dad at his most vulnerable.

Fuck that.

He wasn't going to kill him. That was bullshit. No, possession was his goal. And he'd get him at a certain point. Maybe that point was still far off, but my gut told me it wasn't. Once he possessed him, things could get even worse. Just ask Eleanor Gracie.

I wasn't going to let that happen to my dad.

Groan had outmaneuvered me. Fine. All I had to do was do the same to him. The answer was as simple as that, and once I started thinking that way, I came up with the right plan. Groan had made my efforts to scare my dad look like attempts at communication. I had to change direction—dig into Groan's *own* bag of tricks. He knew how to fight dirty. He knew how to go beyond any boundary.

So that's what I did.

I've felt terrible about it ever since. But it worked.

· · ·

First, I tried something I'd never done before: changing my appearance. Now, I've told you just *appearing* in the first place is difficult enough. Add doing it while also changing my appearance, and it was ridiculously hard. But I went for it. I had no time to mess around. Something about what Groan had said, and the way he'd changed right in front of my eyes—it somehow keyed me in to how it's done. That's the thing with the ghost world (and, I suppose, the regular world, too). Imitation is at the root of almost everything. You see it, you think you can do it, you put your head in a certain place, and *bam*. You're starting to do it. No one ever really showed me how to swing a bat—I just imitated what I'd seen other kids do, and there you go. Same with riding a bike—whatever instructions you get aren't the key, are they? Those are just words. Climbing a tree, building a house out of Lincoln Logs, talking to a girl. It's all about imitation.

So I imitated Groan's shapeshifting.

I stole his bullshit ideas, even if they'd been lies.

I got nastier than he ever could.

And it fucking worked.

There's nothing more painful than your kid dying. Flat out. By a cosmic mile. Ask anyone who's been through it. Ask anyone who has a kid and has worried about it. I saw it firsthand. It broke my family. It probably caused my mom's cancer. It cut my dad off from most of his feelings, after dragging him through the emotional equivalent of a wood chipper. The shadow of my death darkened everything else about my parents' lives. It also put all kinds of weird pressure and energy on Beth's remaining childhood.

I died right in front of them.

I'm not going to talk about most of that night, like I've said. You don't need to know anything more than this: as I was dying, I panicked, ran from the room, and tripped in the hallway, where I had horrible convulsions. I don't know why I ran. I couldn't even feel my legs at that point, but some circuit in my head just blew. Panic. Pure panic.

My folks were right there when I did it. Probably seven minutes before I died.

You see where this is going, right?

I started doing that in front of my dad. Didn't matter what room he was in. Appear. Run. Trip. Convulse. The first time I did it, I honestly thought I'd gone too far and killed him. He grabbed at his chest and staggered. But no heart attack.

And, like Groan, I took it further. I took it to a place that no decent person (ghost) would ever take something so painful. I changed my appearance to look like I'd looked as a toddler, complete with footie pajamas, and did it like that. In the kitchen. My father sat on the floor, taking in deep gulps of air. The next day, I did it again, this time in the form of a six-year-old, dressed like when I'd started first grade: rust-colored corduroys, yellow shirt with a collar, small sneakers, glasses and flesh-colored eye patch over my right eye (my left had started turning in, the lazy thing). I even gave myself the terrible haircut I'd had, with goofy bangs. Run. Drop. Seizure. This time, Dad cried out. I'd never heard him make a sound like that before.

It was so bad that I wondered if I'd be able to keep doing it.

But I knew that I had to, or Groan would get him. So I kept it up, as often as I could. I did it as a baby wearing a diaper (proud of myself for pulling that one off, ashamed at how horrid I was for doing it). I did it as a ten-year-old, wearing my Star Wars pajamas. I did it in every incarnation of my childhood that I could think of, digging deep to remember the feeling of what it was like to stay up and watch *Welcome Back, Kotter* or *Barney Miller* with my parents, and going with those kinds of feelings, those kinds of moments. I pulled out memories, like going down to a local duck pond as a four-year-old, and used the image of the weird little jumper they dressed me in. Manifesting that image of myself, I'd run, trip, and die in front of my dad.

This was no fun for me, I hope you understand.

I'm not bragging here.

Each time I did it, I felt a terrible pang of grief, summoning up those snapshots of my childhood. My life. Back before it all came down around me—around us. Life was a dream, as I looked back. A spell that was broken. An illusion that faded. The hope and promise, ripped away in a single evening. And it's not like I didn't know what I'd lost, because I did. When you're stuck (forever) in your childhood home, alone with your thoughts, you feel it. Every day. Sometimes every minute. I could see my friends, remember. My sister. I saw them all sailing down that river, mostly unaware of how far and how fast it went. I don't blame them. That's how it goes. I never thought about it once when I was a kid, and those fourteen years—holy shit, they seemed to pass in like ten minutes, looking back at them. All those moments I tapped into were more beautiful and precious than anything you could buy. Really. Not just being lame here. It's true. Playing in the sunshine at a duck pond with your parents when you're little? Come on.

So I found dozens of sweet moments like that from my life and stabbed each one in the heart, right in front of my elderly father.

What a guy I was.

Dad didn't last long. Beth knew something was wrong right away. The first night I started doing it, twenty seconds into their phone call. Still, Dad dodged her sniffing around, claiming that he just hadn't slept well the night before. I had an appearance all lined up in the chute. Me in the stupid suit and clip-on tie that I'd had to wear to my grandfather's funeral (he'd had a heart attack when

I'd been seven, a doctor who smoked, if you can believe it—but I guess that was just how they did it, back then). I couldn't do it, couldn't get any traction on it, right then. I blamed Beth for getting Dad to put all his barriers up against her questions. I needed a clear shot at his emotions to really pull it off, and with his defenses up, it was a no go.

Annoying little sister.

But the next day, I did it. He sat at the kitchen table, absently staring at the mail. When I manifested, I could tell it was more vivid than I'd managed before. I heaved and spasmed, the apparition strong. Poor Dad just collapsed into his chair at the table and sobbed, letting loose these awful cries, like something he'd kept locked up had finally broken free.

That scared me.

Again, I worried that I was killing him. Or snapping his mind. It was almost enough for me to knock the whole thing off.

Until I thought about that son-of-a-bitch Groan ever getting his filthy hands on my dad's mind.

There are things in life (and death, apparently) that you just have to do, no matter how painful or appalling they are.

So I kept it rolling.

My second-grade class picture. The plaid swimming trunks and diving mask I'd taken to Pomp's Pond every day during the summer between fifth and sixth grade. Oh, and here's another winner: me, in the suit they'd buried me in. Seriously, I can barely tell you any of this without wanting to disappear, forever.

And finally me, with the Curious George hospital gown I'd worn when I'd had my tonsils taken out when I was eight. Clutching the stuffed orange dog they'd brought me while I recuperated at Bon Secours Hospital over in Methuen.

For whatever reason, that's the one that broke him.

No big sobs. He just went still. He looked terrible. He hadn't been eating much. Hadn't shaved in a few days. An old man. He didn't pace. He didn't make a list. He didn't wander the house. He just went to the phone, and dialed Beth's number. It was the middle of the afternoon, so when she answered the phone, her voice was full of concern. I leaned in close.

"Dad?"

"Everything's fine," my dad said, "but listen—I'm going to take you up on it."

"You're what?"

"Florida. I want to come down to Florida. For good."

Beth was silent for a second. "Seriously?"

"Yes. I'm ready."

"Oh, God, Dad—that's great. I'm so happy. The kids and Ron will be so happy. Really?"

"Yes, sweetheart. Really." He put a smile into his voice, but held his hand over his brow and had his eyes closed.

"When?"

"How about I fly down tomorrow?"

"Tomorrow?"

"Is that too soon?"

"Uh—no, no that's fine," she said, "but you don't need more time to get your stuff ready? What about your bank, and your prescriptions? Your doctor?"

"I can do it in the morning. Or by phone. You have phones in Florida."

"You have a ticket?"

"I'll get one as soon as we hang up."

"That'll be expensive."

"That's fine. I can go stand-by. Or afford it. Either way."

Beth was stunned into silence. I knew her well enough to guess at the battle going on in her head: it was a doozy. If there was a Goddess of Common Sense, Beth worshipped her. Or maybe *was* her. Common Sense wasn't about buying expensive airline tickets at the last minute, or leaving medical records un-dealt-with, or the million other little details that the Goddess of Common Sense could no doubt point out on a moment's notice

—so I knew for a fact that it took everything in Beth's power to hold back from harassing my dad about it. Getting Dad down to Florida had been a campaign that she'd been waging for more years than World War II, and suddenly it looked like V Day.

Good for her, she shoved Common Sense aside (surely just for a while, until Dad was safely down in the Sunshine State). She shoved aside all the other Beth-type questions that were no doubt percolating unstoppably in her mind at that moment: *Why now? What's happened? Are you feeling okay? Have you had some kind of accident? Crashed your car? Did you try to date Mrs. Winters like I've been pushing you to? How are we going to deal with the house? The furniture? The photographs? Computer, safe deposit box, cemetery plot, car, insurance, oil delivery, shoes, change of address forms, Medicare?* Probably a lot more than that, knowing Beth.

But I'd done my part, and now she did hers.

"That's great, Dad," she said. "Really great. Do you want me to get the ticket for you?"

PART III

12

DEBORAH LANDI MOVES FAST. WITHIN THE WEEK, A CREW IN A BIG pickup truck and trailer shows up and cleans the yard, trims the hedges. Seven o'clock the next morning, she leads a different crew around the house, pointing out everything that needs to be done. The workers follow her, holding Styrofoam coffee cups, joking around here and there. After she leaves, they have at the place. A couple of them start taking out the cabinets in the kitchen, while some of the others lug in equipment to take the wallpaper off, these big steamers.

It's kind of horrible, but also kind of cool.

Horrible, because imagine someone coming into your childhood home and ripping it all apart. As the cabinets come out, I think of taking out bowls and cereal as a kid. Plopping down in front of the TV for cartoons on Saturday mornings. Learning to stack a chair near the counter, climbing up, and being able to reach a bag of marshmallows. The shelf where we used to keep the collectible fast food glasses with cartoons on them. In less than an hour, those cabinets of my childhood are gone, stacked in a pile in the breezeway. Watching it all happen—well, it feels like the beginning of something.

And then I take it in a bad direction.

Today it's the cabinets and the wallpaper, a few lights. Ten years from now? Maybe they knock down some walls, add some new rooms. Fifty years from now? Maybe they knock down the house and put in some weird Jetsons future bubble. A hundred years? Five hundred years? A thousand? The thought crashes down on me, a giant wave, an avalanche, a twenty-ton ACME weight. What will happen when there is no one left alive who knows me? Will it be like this, with me nothing but a shadow, a hidden observer, stuck fast to this spot, unable to do anything at all but float around, hiding from Groan?

I look out the windows toward the woods beyond the back-yard. Are there ghosts out there right now, ghosts of natives who died a thousand years ago, no longer stuck in their crumbled and disintegrated teepees or lodges, but haunting an empty patch of boulders, dirt, and trees? Year after year, century after century? Probably insane beyond any measure of insanity?

I need to calm down, because I'm starting to panic.

I'll be honest, a part of me kind of likes seeing the demolition in the kitchen. I'm a fourteen-year-old boy, and destruction, in most every form, is perfect. If they want to plant dynamite, use blow torches, bring in jackhammers—yes, please.

Once the cabinets are out, it's time for the wallpaper steam-ers. Pretty soon, every bit of wallpaper is coming down, filling the house with the smell of hot glue and heat, steam and warm paper. The hardest one for me is my own room, when they take down the wallpaper I'd wanted so badly when I was ten. It starts out sky blue at the bottom, and rises darker and darker until stars and planets reveal themselves at the top, by the ceiling. I'd later added to the effect by putting glow-in-the-dark stars along the top edge and on the ceiling. My room was the coolest place. I'd lie in bed, staring at the glowing stars on the walls and ceiling, imagining everything that lay beyond the ceiling, the roof, the house. All that beauty. As the glow slowly faded, I'd fall asleep. Everything where it was supposed to be.

As the guys take down the wallpaper, I weep.

Aside from that, it's not so bad having them around. There's suddenly more going on in the house than I can remember. As the week goes by, the house transforms. The bones are still the same, I guess, but the skin and muscle and face are different. The rooms feel bigger, the walls barer. The floors are stripped, sanded, refinished. Once they get the walls painted, it's really like a different house. White walls in some rooms. A light green, like moss, in others. A warm yellow in my old room. Really? Yellow? Still, I have to admit it makes everything look fresh. Inviting.

The workers themselves aren't all that interesting. They work. Seems like every single person in the world has a computer-phone-thing, because that's what they do whenever they have a break. Take out their phones and start looking at stuff. Some of them even use them as phones. One guy named Emiliano calls his wife every chance he can. Sounds like she's about to have a baby, and he keeps checking on her. He speaks half-English and half-Spanish, which I think is kind of cool. The rest mostly stare at their phones.

I enjoy watching them work. We used to have a dog named Bailey, a terrier mix. That dog was just fascinated by any human industry. Anything I'd do, he come over and watch, interested— tying my shoes, emptying the dryer, organizing my painted miniatures. He'd be there. That's what I feel like with the workers. Time to cut corners on some trim? I'm there. Time to tape off some molding before painting? I'm right there, checking out the nuances. Stripping the wires in the ceiling to get them ready for

the new lights? You'd think I'm watching the world's chess cham-
pionship or something.

Which is probably why I lose track of time, and suddenly
realize it's Halloween.

13

So, Halloween.

Used to be my favorite time of the year, until it was the day I died horribly—so I'd say I have mixed feelings. Very mixed. There's something that happens to your head when something terrible happens. It basically says, *That was the worst thing ever, and I'm going to be on the lookout for anything, anything at all, that reminds me of that, forever.* And that's what happened to me. It starts with the shifting daylight, as I've already mentioned. When the days get shorter and the arc of the sun drifts farther south, I start feeling it again. It's in the way the sky looks. It's in the way the air smells. It's in the sound of dry leaves skidding along the driveway on a breeze. It's in the color of the sunset through the woods in back of the house.

Before 1981, all of those things were great. They would zap my head with energy unique from any other time of the year. Halloween. Even the word did something. Maybe before electricity and television, every night had felt like that: alive, run through with spirits, a night where bigger currents sweep through the darkness and chill. As a kid, it scared me, a little, that energy. Then, add dressing up in costumes and running around your neighborhood at night, and it was the best. Just the best.

Until it was the worst.

A perfect night for Groan to torture me. But, here's one thing about Groan: he's kind of an idiot. I don't think he knows how to read a calendar. He might not even know what Halloween even is, or anything about it. I've come to believe that when he possessed Eleanor Gracie, he didn't realize what would happen when he got her to put the poison in the cookies. Maybe he thought she'd eat them herself. He just saw an opportunity to do something awful and he took it. Those first couple of Halloweens after I died, he didn't show up at the house. Oh, he showed up other times, plenty of other times. If anything, more frequently than he does now, in some random nonpattern.

If you're curious, the most he ever came by was eleven horrible nights in a row. The longest he stayed away was for thirty-eight days in 1996 (I'd started hoping I'd seen the last of him, which is always a mistake with Groan, because he somehow picked up on that—or just guessed it—and gave me nothing but grief about it for another couple of years). While we're on the topic, I have no idea why he never shows up during the day, or where he goes when he's not harassing me at night. I've come up with a few theories. The first is that he's always there, and his absence is just another angle of how he tortures me. If I don't see or sense him, it's because he's hiding from me. In the woods. On the roof. Just below the windows. Out in the night nearby. I suppose that's the most flattering kind of theory—it's all connected to me.

But it's wrong.

I figured that out because, as I said, Groan is a dumbass.

Here's one of his stupid games: he taunts me, lures me into some reaction or another, and then jumps all over me about it, usually ending up with him about to kill me (again). Or actually killing me (again), which is worse.

What tipped me off was him wanting me to say goodnight out the window of my old bedroom to him every night. Kind of a bastard move, although I don't think he realized it was as hurtful as it really was. When I was little, part of my bedtime routine had been going to the window with my mom or dad and saying goodnight to the world. Adorable when you're five, annoying when you're fourteen and a demon is making you do it. But in this case, it was just a typical brain fart of his, cruel and humiliating, but kind of generic. We had to go through this stupid routine, and it pretty much went nowhere, as was usually the case with him.

But then he did it again, like a year and a half later. Same thing, but as if he'd just come up with it, no mention of the earlier time. He'd forgotten we'd danced that dance before, which told me he wasn't always paying attention like he claimed, which told me he wasn't thinking about me all of the time.

I started to poke around at night, outside the closet. At first, I was totally terrified. Again, the mind has a habit of looking for patterns—particularly patterns that scare you so much that hiding in a closet every night for decades seems like a perfectly rational thing to do. As I made my way around the house, I held my breath, sneaking. I'd watch a window from ten feet away, barely able to do it without turning my head or closing my eyes. A minute would pass. Two. Ten. An hour. No Groan.

A little one night. A little more the next. Of course, I started getting more worried the longer I'd gone since last seeing him, since that meant he was more likely to show up. But it also meant that after he *did* show up, I felt a little more confident for the next couple of nights—and eventually for the next couple of weeks. He rarely did multiple nights in a row. Also, the gaps grew longer. Groan wasn't always around, and when he was gone, he wasn't paying any thought or attention to me at all.

So where does he go?

I have no idea.

But I know two things for certain: Groan is a bully, and Groan is easily bored. What does a bored bully usually do? Find someone else to make miserable. That's one idea that makes sense to me. Maybe he's out there, harassing someone else. Maybe not even someone in Andover. Or in America. He's a demon, and doesn't seem to obey any particular rules of physics. He could be here one second, and gone the next. So maybe he's chasing some stuck ghost in Alberta. Or Stratford-upon-Avon. Or Tokyo. Who knows? Maybe he's traveling, a jet-setting dickhead.

Or, maybe, he's getting bullied himself, and is just taking it out on me. I think about that a lot. The scenario is that he can only get so much time away from Hell. I mean, demons are vile creations of darkness and torment, cursed to burn for an eternity. Something like that. So maybe Groan is a low-level guard in Hell who manages to sneak off every now and then and work out his frustrations at not getting promoted (because he's an idiot) on me, the one person he actually managed to kill and keeps as a prisoner. I'm basically a kidnapping victim in this scenario, locked away in a basement that Groan hasn't told anyone about.

The third possibility, the one I fear most, is that I'm doing it myself.

In this one, Groan is a figment of my own imagination. Some kind of mental block keeping me from moving on, from letting go. That makes a certain kind of sense, right? I'd died suddenly, and young. Right at the delicate transition age of fourteen. Still dependent on my family, but old enough to have to do certain things on my own. Like, if I'd been eight, I'd have been gently whisked up to Heaven. Or if I'd been seventeen, I'd have known where to go. But instead, I'm stuck in the middle somehow, unable to work it out on my own. So I've invented this demonic captor as a mental block. A delusion that embodies my fears and gives me the perfect excuse to never move on.

But it can't be. Because that means I'm both dead and insane, a truly horrible possibility. I try to stay away from that particular rabbit hole.

And stick to the rabbit hole with the demon inside it.

I put him out of my mind. Not easy to do on Halloween. Especially on this Halloween—because I also get the idea stuck in my head that it's my *last* Halloween in the house. It already feels like a different place because of all the work. Not just the paint. Not just the new cabinets, new doorknobs, new blinds. Not just because pretty much every last sign of the Lane family is gone. Something just feels *different*.

I try not to get carried away. But still, as I float down the hallways, the feeling won't go away: when the house sells, I'm free. I won't see another Halloween nightfall from the entryway. Or the kitchen windows facing west. I won't hear the sounds of kids outside, laughing and calling out as they hurry from one house to the next, lugging a bag or plastic pumpkin getting heavier with candy, their parents hanging back, bundled against the chill.

It's the perfect night for me to disappear, of course. Most of my friends will think of me at some point. Beth and my dad, for sure. Some Halloweens, I've been able to hop, skip, and jump my way around half the country, checking in. Santa Cruz, California —Craig. Mainesville, Ohio—Hugh. Strafford, Vermont—Andy. Fort Meyers, Florida—Beth, and now Dad. Half a dozen other places, too—just the tickles of memories from kids I'd known back in junior high and elementary school. As the sun nears the horizon, silhouetting the maples hung with gold, orange, and cranberry-red leaves, I feel the tug. All I need to do is step into the closet and let it take hold.

But I don't. Something's bugging me. I go to the living room windows, the ones that look out over the front yard. Across the way, to the left, the buildings of the college where my dad taught chemistry wear the setting sunlight on their peaks. The blue sky deepens behind them. A clutch of trick-or-treaters is already making its way down the street, a pair of moms trailing them, chatting.

Fresh-baked cookies. Ugh. I still remember the smile on poor Eleanor Gracie's face as she held out the tray for us to each take a few.

The trick-or-treaters hit the stretch of sidewalk in front of my house and keep on going, the For Sale sign and blank windows making clear our "no candy" status. If it's like most Halloweens, there'll be a few unbelievers who need to ring the doorbell, anyway. Stand there. Ring again. Turn and hurry back to the sidewalk, disappointed.

For obvious reasons, my parents couldn't handle being in the house on Halloween after 1981. Beth would stay with a friend. They'd get a room up in Newburyport. Or Portsmouth. Or down in Boston. Never blamed them. After Mom died, Dad thought he could handle it—which, to his credit, he pretty much did. Couple of bags of candy from CVS in one of the silver mixing bowls. He'd crack open the door, put a smile on his face, share a bad joke or two with the kids, give a wink or a wave to the parents, let the kids grab a handful of candy, normal as could be. Then, he'd shut the door, slump a little, and the light would go out of his eyes a little more. The first years were the worst. After that, he could put up with it well enough—though he never looked happy at the end of the night as he turned off the porch lights and put whatever candy was left on the kitchen counter.

In those in-between years, I was left in the house on my own every Halloween. Just like this year.

My last year.

No, I can't let myself start thinking that way.

The sunlight fades from the highest trees and the buildings across the street, so I turn, deciding to check in with my friends after all.

"Trick or treat." Groan's leaning against the closet door, half a dozen paces behind me, draped in a dirty white sheet with two holes cut out for his bloodshot, obsidian eyes. He stands a good seven feet tall, the shape of his horns, ears, and weird head clear enough under the fabric. "Maybe I'll just take the trick, on second thought."

He doesn't move, aside from a shrug. I kick myself for not paying closer attention to the time—damn days are getting shorter every evening. I step back, staying by the windows.

"Glad I caught you outside of your masturbatorium, Timothy," he says. "I think we need to have a talk."

"Nice costume."

"Not as dorky on me as it would be on you, true." He straightens up. His hand swings up from his knee to the top of his head. As it does, the sheet disappears, replaced with a swarm of insects, crawling all over him: centipedes, scorpions, pale spiders, hairy spiders, earwigs, ticks. A clump of them drop off his elbow and hit the floor, scurrying off. The sound of buzzing and clicking hums from the shifting mass of bugs. "This was my other idea. Pretty sure it's better than anything you could ever come up with. You like? You can try it on, if you want."

He reaches up with a frown and flicks at the back of his ear. A bunch of wasps turn and circle in the air.

"What do you want?" I'm ready to dart off, wary of his every move.

"Why do you have to say it like that? You always make it sound like I'm such a drag. I can't just come over for Halloween? I thought it was our little thing. Or am I wrong? No—don't answer. I'm probably wrong. I'm always getting you wrong, aren't I?"

I force myself to keep my gaze away from the hundreds of insects crawling across his skin, watching his eyes instead. He's watching mine.

"It's not my fault," I say.

"What's not your fault?"

"This."

"What the hell are you talking about?"

"The house."

"Oh, you mean the thing I specifically asked you to make sure didn't happen? How's that not your fault?"

"I can't stop them."

"Sure you can. You just didn't. You just suck at being a ghost. Like, really suck." He pulls a wriggling centipede the color of a tarnished penny from his cheek and grinds it against the wall until it doesn't look like more than a stain covered in loose eyelashes. "The ghost of that bug, Timothy, is a better ghost than you. It could have kept your tasty little booby lady out of this place, no problem. Think of all the places a creeping ghost bug like that might creep. You probably already have, you creep. But that's your problem. Too much thinky-thinky, too little scary-scary."

"I tried."

"Did you try pulling down your pants? That might have scared her off. Speaking of mosquitos and other insignificant wiggling things."

"What happens when it sells?"

"It's not going to sell." He takes a step forward.

I take a step back. "It might."

"Why are you trying to annoy me?"

"I can't do anything about it. You can't do anything about it. It'll sell."

"Half right. You can't. I can. It won't."

"So as long as it doesn't, I'm stuck here?"

"Look at you with the questions." He starts wiping the bugs off his arms, flinging them across the darkening floor. Some grab on and he has to pinch them off with his pale fingers. "Listen, Dimothy. You're not going anywhere. I'm not going anywhere. Haven't you been paying attention for the last hundred and thirty-nine years—or whatever it is since you sicked up all my tasty cookies and flopped around the floor like a spaz? Are you really that—no, I'm not going to ask that question again. Unlike you, I *have* been paying attention. Trust me."

As the bugs drop off Groan, they skitter toward me. I step sideways, keeping out of their way, all the while hoping Groan will get far enough away from the closet so I can dive into it. He keeps himself between it and me.

"You're not tired of this?" I say.

He rips the back two legs off a clinging tarantula. "Please tell me you didn't just ask me if I'm tired of this? Why would I be tired of this? Don't you realize how fun you are? How your stupid questions and gurgling orange-juice voice just sound better and better to me every decade I'm forced to hear those sputtering brain farts exit your stupid mouth hole? How you never listen to the simple requests I ask of you? How you never—not once, not ever—light up even a little when I stop by, trying to do something nice for you? Like trick-or-treating? Spending a little time and effort coming up with a cool costume, just to hang out with a friend, as a friend, for once?" Yanking off the rest of the spider, he flings the shuddering body and remaining legs at my head. "Why would you think I'd ever get tired of so much never-ending fun and companionship?"

I duck. The hissing spider hits the side of the front door and drops to the threshold, its remaining legs scrabbling on the wood.

"You could just let me go," I say as I sidestep the horrible thing.

"Pardon?"

"You just said how much you hate me. Fine. Let me go."

"You're not going anywhere."

"Why not?" I keep my distance.

"I don't like this new attitude of yours," he growls.

"You go your way. I go mine."

"Oh, is that how this is working now? We're negotiating?" He straightens, the tops of his horns grazing the ceiling. "I don't think so. Besides—you'd miss me too much."

"I wouldn't miss you for a sec—" is all I manage to get out before he's got me pinned up against the wall, his cold fingers clamped around my throat, squeezing.

"Let me stop you before you say something you'll really regret," he says into my face. Curled worms drop from his lips, half-chewed, still wriggling. His breath smells like a load of diarrhea someone barfed up. He squeezes. His nails dig into my skin. Excruciating. "You're mine, little fella. No one's getting away from anybody. Ever. You're staying put. Not a foot—not a toe—outside these doors. You put so much as the tip of your nose outside and I'm going to camp out here every night for the next ten years." His claws puncture my esophagus. Blood bursts out in a gushing stream, running down his arm, down my chest. He squeezes harder. "Because the one thing I actually *would* miss is this." He grimaces, yellowed teeth showing behind his gray lips. "Killing you is the best, buddy."

As the world starts to fade in a crashing wave of pain and popping flashes of black in the corners of my sight, he draws back his other fist and clobbers me in the jaw, which shatters. My teeth roll around in my mouth. I slide down the wall, choking on my own blood. He doesn't loosen his grip. He hits me again, this time in the forehead, blinding me as my skull caves in.

Just before I die, Groan wrenches me up and whispers in my ear, "Happy Halloween, dipshit."

14

THE WORKMEN TAKE ANOTHER WEEK OR SO TO FINISH UP. TOUCH-UP painting. New faceplates for light switches. A final sweep of all the plaster dust, crinkled tape with streaks of paint, stray nails. Deb Landi takes a walk-through with the contractor. She approves. As do I.

The place looks good. Really good. It isn't a big house—but at least it doesn't look like a house stuck in a smeared stretch of time from 1969 to 1989. It looks fresh, different. Clean. Light. Every memory and sign of my life, gone from every surface. They've even changed the inside of the closet I hide in each night from a dusty and uneven baby blue to a neat white.

Maybe I'm making too much of it—wouldn't be the first time —but the thought that keeps going through my head is: *Purified for the transition.* Stupid, yes, but you get the idea. On one level I'm building up hope without having as much as a dust mote's worth of evidence to support the idea that I'm closer to moving on. Still, that doesn't stop the thought burbling around in my mind. There's truly something about the empty rooms and the bright colors that makes me think of heaven. The way the rooms hold the daylight, the way they glow when the sun hits the walls come late afternoon or early morning.

Okay, so the house looks sharp. Check. Open house. Check. Probably two dozen people come by. The way they look at it, I see immediately Deb was right. No one's looking at the nasty wallpaper—instead, they're thinking about how good their couch would look across from the fireplace. I stay out of the way. And Deb turns on the charm. With Joe Papadakis, she'd been all business, never cracked anything more than a fake smile. But with people who might buy the house, she's as charming as the vase of yellow flowers she put in the kitchen. She finds a way to make them feel at ease, waving them in, giving them compliments, asking their names. She's good.

Pretty soon, there's seventeen people in the house at the same time. I can't remember the last time that happened—maybe after Mom's funeral? I look everyone over with a critical eye: Do they look like jerks? Are there horrible little kids who'll fill the house with the stink of diapers and apple juice? One guy has a red face and a flattop. Both his boys have flattops, too. I follow the kids around and decide to give them some nasty smells. I whip each one out like an overeager first grader determined to use *all* the colors in the crayon box: farts, hotdog burp, feet, and classic dog turd. It doesn't do much. With all the people in the house—and the weird mix of energies they bring with them—I can't get a strong blast of anything to happen. What's hilarious is every time I manage to squeeze a tiny smell out, the older kid turns and shoves the younger one, telling him to quit it. The younger one complains he's not doing anything. The older one turns and pinches him. Seriously. The dad turns around and—after glancing around to make sure no one's nearby—puts a hand on each of their shoulders and tells them if they don't knock it off, they'd each earn themselves ten seconds of "belt time," whatever exactly that is. Nothing good, I guess from the looks on their faces. A haircut really does say a lot.

. . .

Groan blames me for the whole business.

It infuriates him. He threatens me nightly. You can believe I don't let myself get caught outside of the closet after sundown. Not by a minute. Not by a second. He comes by as soon as the sun dips below the horizon. Or, he doesn't come by until about three minutes before sunrise to see if he can catch me that way. A few nights ago, he traipsed through the house giving me an earful about how I'd betrayed him, how I'd hurt him, how I was keeping him from his rest, how lousy a friend I am, how I've signed myself up for the platinum package for pain. Last night he came stomping through the house, complained, complained, complained, pretended to slam the door on his way out. But he'd actually stayed hidden just outside the closet door for another hour. After I'd convinced myself he'd left, he jammed his horrible fingers under the door, screaming so loud he might have been a jet engine. Fucker almost gave me a heart attack.

I don't engage him. I don't talk back. I don't answer his stupid questions. I'm giving him the silent treatment, which he's correctly interpreted: *Fuck you.* But I'm counting on his short attention span. After my dad finally left, he went berserk for weeks on end, a total shit show. Banging, scraping, kicking, filling the closet with thick, gagging stenches for eight, ten hours at a stretch. But, eventually, his white-hot fury cooled off, and he resumed his regular programming.

We'll see.

15

———

Two days after the open house, Deb unlocks the door and steps inside, midafternoon. A deep cold sweeps in with her. The old thermometer mounted outside the kitchen window reads 11°F. She's wearing a padded down jacket, black and glossy, which matches the black of her boots. Cream knit hat, tight black gloves, cream scarf. The cold shows on her cheeks and she looks great. Yes, I've developed a little thing for her.

After all, she's making the *Transition* happen. She has the blond hair of a game show assistant and the figure of a Roman statue. Also, I haven't seen more than a handful of women who weren't my sister or my mom in thirty-seven years. And, no, I'm not gross about it. Not too gross. Maybe I enjoy the smell of her shampoo. Maybe during one of her walk-throughs I hover up in the air a bit for a better perspective on her cleavage. But I don't do anything creepy, like try to touch her, or try to put my eyes through her clothes to see what's going on underneath them.

Think about it.

Could.

Don't.

So she comes by, takes off her jacket and gloves, hangs them over the end of the bannister, and looks around. A minivan pulls into the driveway. A minute later, a family gets out: two parents, two kids. One kid is young, climbing out from a pink seat in the back, the other is probably high-school aged. They follow the walkway to the front door, which Deb opens for them.

"Hi," Deb says, smiling. "Come in, come in. Freezing out there."

They all step into the entry area, bringing the scent of winter with them. Once they're inside, I recognize the parents from the open house. He's tall, dark hair. The woman is pretty. The two kids are both girls. When I get a good look at the older girl, I pause.

Wow.

She's beautiful, with long dark hair streaming out beneath a blue hat, light bronze skin, and chestnut-brown eyes. She has a phone in her hand (naturally) and looks like she might even be sixteen. I can't picture someone that good-looking living in my house. The younger daughter, maybe nine or ten, is bundled up in a thick jacket. She looks like her sister, but younger, with darker eyes and a rounder face. She holds up a stuffed toy, a mouse in overalls. She lifts him and points him at the stairs, then the hallway. "Look, Widge," she says in a cute voice. "A new housey."

The older sister rolls her eyes.

"Who's that?" Deb says, leaning down and taking a serious look.

"I'm Jacinta," the girl says. "This is Widge."

"Widge?"

"Widge. Ridge is at home."

Whatever that meant.

"Nice to meet you, Widge," Deb says.

Jacinta pushes the mouse up until it brushes Deb's cheek. "He kissed you."

Deb smiles. "Well, he's very sweet." She straightens while the girl starts talking to the mouse in a squeaky voice. Deb turns to the parents. "The whole family wants to see it—how exciting."

"It's perfect," the woman says. "The schools. The street."

Jacinta holds out her hand like she's casting a spell. "I'm a wizard."

"You are?" Deb says.

"I'm going to the *real* Hogwarts. When I'm older."

The older daughter wanders off, passing into the dining room and peeking into the kitchen.

"Jacinta," the father says, "how about we take a look at what could be your room?"

"I get to pick first," the older daughter calls from the kitchen.

"I don't mind," Jacinta says. "I'm still a wizard." She holds the mouse aloft, like it's Gandalf's staff or something.

I float behind them as they head upstairs to look at the bedrooms. The big room on the right is for the parents, obviously. The two others are at the end of the hallway, my old room on the left, Beth's straight ahead. Beth's is smaller, so I guess which way things are headed. The older daughter only needs a two-second survey of both rooms to step into my old room and declare, "Mine."

Jacinta sprints into the other room and runs in circles around it, waving the mouse up and down and laughing. "Our new room, Widgie! For bedtime and playtime and making hospitals and playgrounds."

"She's super sweet," the mother says. "She's just her own person."

Deb smiles—and not her fake Realtor smile, either. "Of course she is. She's adorable."

They take the girls through the whole house and out into the backyard. It's a weird thing for me. I've been waiting for something like this to happen for months and months—but now that it looks like something might actually happen, I start freaking out. What if it doesn't work? What if selling the house doesn't change a single thing for me? What if I have to watch this family move in, grow up, move out—and wash, rinse, repeat for another hundred years? Five hundred? I try to calm myself down. Focus on one thing at a time. Stay quiet. Let Deb work her magic.

As Deb leads them back in, describing how great the neighborhood is—*Just watch out for the cookies!*—the wife gives the husband a look. "It's perfect for us," she says. "Emiliano was right."

Emiliano? I've heard the name before—and then I see it: the guy on the work crew whose wife was expecting the baby looks so much like the husband that I'm surprised I didn't see that they're brothers right away.

"I want to go play in my room now," Jacinta says.

"Alyssa, go with her while we talk," the father says.

The older girl looks annoyed, but follows her sister to the stairs. The husband and wife look at each other. He rubs his hands together and nods. "We'd like to make an offer."

16

—————

It goes quiet after that. Really quiet. For a month. The first big snow comes, half a foot of big, fluffy stuff that muffles the sound of the outside even more. Groan hasn't been by since the open house. I try not to read too much into it—but of course part of my mind decides it's because the process is starting. First Groan leaves, then I do. Of course by now, I'm seeing everything as having meaning. The clean, empty rooms. The winter sunlight swinging through, the arc of the sun lower at this time of year. The silence.

A few times, I hang around outside the closet after sunset. Nothing. Just the sky over the woods going gold and red, fading as the stars come out on the other side of the sky. I watch the sunset disappear from the window at the end of the hallway before going to the closet. A big tide of nostalgia hits me. I miss the old wallpaper, all the old furniture, everything my family lived in and around my whole life. I walk through the house, overlaying as best I can the memories of what happened where.

The faded oriental rug in the living room I'd crawled across as a baby. Opening Christmas presents in a great pile of torn paper, ribbons, and boxes on that same rug, the air sharp with the scent of the spruce tree in the corner. The table with the ends of the legs carved into lion's paws—I remember playing with my Micronauts underneath it. A drawer in the big hutch in the dining room where I'd found the Halloween candy my parents tried to keep out of sight before the big day (years before it became my death day); I'd opened a package of flavored Tootsie Rolls and eaten myself sick from them. Even stupid things get to me. The place where a metal rack had held a set of spatulas. The corner of the counter where a ceramic cookie jar shaped like a safe with a mean bulldog sitting on top of it had lived. The weird brown, yellow, and white flower vinyl wallpaper that had been in the kitchen before the blue stuff the crew had steamed off. The spot our Siamese cat, Sampson, had staked out as his own on top of the fridge—from where he'd swat any passing head that came his way.

Every room. Every wall. Every corner. The details become myths. All the little moments—they were mine. My time in the sunshine, my time underneath the stars. Being teased for wearing a patch over my eye in first grade and the way it made me feel different and flawed for the first time—that was part of my mythology. Ancient, formative history. The crazy things I did in school, same thing—the young hero, testing his strength. The memories of running through the woods, burning things, climbing things. The games we played in the humid evenings of August, or on the freezing, clear winter afternoons. Olympics. The trench warfare of junior high, so much bigger than elementary school, the schoolwork so much harder, thrown together with all these strange kids from other elementary schools. Inching closer to adulthood, getting a glimpse of something bigger.

And always, home.

I'm not sad about it. It's a different feeling, remembering. I'm okay with it.

·   ·   ·

It must be December by now. The snow melts away with a weird week of warm weather. Neighbors put lights up, so I know Christmas is coming. I try to check in with Beth.

She wasn't always tough. Just a kid who lost her older brother and didn't really understand at the time what it meant. As she grew up, it turned her into, let's just say, a bit of a control freak. The only time she was able to lose herself and get away from her real and imagined responsibilities to the family after I'd died was when she ran—so she ran. A lot. Track, from junior high through her college years. And that turned into a whole thing about what she would eat, and how much sleep she needed, and how much water she needed. She would time things. She would block out her days to optimize her productivity. She nailed all of her schoolwork. Her underwear was always folded and sorted by type. All of it, every little bit of her life, she was able to put into boxes, check them off. It's not like that's a bad thing, necessarily. Teachers loved her, then bosses. Her friends could always count on her. But it also turned into never being able to find a boyfriend who was good enough for her, focused enough for her, serious enough for her. So to all of the poor suckers who never really had any chance at all with Beth no matter how promising it looked at first, because I'd died: Sorry, guys.

When I reach out, I'm right—she's been thinking about me. I let the pull take me. I see Beth and Dad in her living room. Warm sunshine falls through a wide window. My nieces and nephew flit about, decorating a Christmas tree. Beth holds a painted ceramic tree that looks like a badly made holiday cookie, dark blue and red glaze smeared across it. Carved into the back—with a tooth-pick—are the initials TCL. Timothy Carey Lane. I'd made it in first-grade art, back in 1973. (The art teacher, Ms. Donovan, always wore dresses with bright colors and flowers on them and had long blond hair—I thought she was beautiful, the first time I'd ever thought that about a teacher.) It'd always been a tradition that each year I hung it on the tree, while Beth hung a similar ornament (of her small handprint, forever caught in clay and painted green). The rest of the decorations changed with time, but not those. When my dad stopped putting up a tree after Mom died, Beth took those two ornaments back with her to Florida one year and kept up the tradition with her own family. It was sweet. This year, they both well up with tears. And I get to watch. Beth looks up from my art project from another era and smiles at Dad.

"Tomorrow," Beth says. "It's weird, isn't it?"

He nods. Not a man of many words when emotions run thick. He clears his throat.

Tomorrow.

"It's the right thing to do," Beth says.

"I know, I know." His voice wavers. He reaches over and takes my ornament. He runs a thumb over the smooth surface of the front. He turns to my youngest niece. "Here, hang this up for Grampy. It's a special one, so be careful."

I pull myself back into the house, and the silence. Being able to see into the world of the living is sometimes the one thing that keeps me sane.

And sometimes it hurts too much.

17

THIS IS IT. MY LAST DAY IN MY HOUSE. MY DAY TO MOVE ON. I'M ready. Beyond ready.

The afternoon lengthens. I just want to get on with it. I float down the hallway. Through the kitchen. Up the stairs. The last light of day turns the white walls gold. Nothing from Groan since the offer was made. Not a single pass through. Not one stupid move to scare me. Nothing.

What if I'm already free?

The thought hits me like a brick to the back of the head. Hanging around in the house when I don't need to anymore, waiting for some invitation that won't come? I glance out the window then back at the hallway.

Is this it?

Okay, confession.

I suddenly don't want to leave. I suddenly *can't* leave. This is my home. My family. My childhood. My life—and my death. How can I leave it all behind? Instead of steadying myself, I have a little (okay, maybe not so little) freak-out. I fly into my room, fast as I can, as if I'm being chased by every memory I ever had. I even manage to slam the door. I can't face it. Leaving. Anything. I just want it all to go away. Everything. I want to be back in my room. Alive. With my family around. My bed. My blankets. My records. My old toys. My books. My future. The life I was supposed to have. I want it *all* back.

I fall apart. Embarrassing.

But I get it out of my system. By the time I get myself together again, evening's here and I'm in the dusk shadows of my room, in my silent house.

And I'm ready to leave. It's time.

One last look around. Closet. Drawers built into the wall.

Goodbye, room.

I slip through the door, casting one last glance around the hallway, into the growing darkness of my parents' room. Beth's room. I float downstairs and do one quick circuit of the living room, the den, the kitchen, the dining room. The trees out back are blue silhouettes against the fading crimson of sunset.

Okay.

I pass through the kitchen door, pausing for a moment in the breezeway. I think of our old dogs—Bessie, Trixie, Jessie, JoJo, Bailey, Bomber—running back and forth out there.

Okay.

Through the screen door. Outside. The unseasonably warm weather held. It's up in the midthirties, which is cold, but not December cold.

Okay.

A half-moon hangs above the houses across the street. I look up at the window to my room. Dark. I start down the driveway, quickly reaching the point where the pull normally keeps me tethered.

I don't feel it. I reach the end of the driveway.

Holy shit.

I turn, looking back at the house. The sky is down to a deep red shining through the woods out back. Twilight shades the yard and the house. I step out onto the sidewalk.

And feel the familiar tug.

At first, I think I'm imagining it, the way you might imagine you're starting to itch after passing through what *might* have been poison ivy. But I take another step and there it is, cinching around my waist and shoulders, making it hard to move forward. It doesn't make any sense. I've never gotten this far from the house in thirty-eight years. A few cars come down the road, their brilliant white headlights bathing the street in light. Lights are on in the neighboring houses, too. The sharp colors of big televisions are visible here and there through windows.

I don't give in. Instead, I dig in, willing myself forward. Straining. I can't get more than a few steps. All my weight holds me back, a harness stretching to its limit.

"Well, look at this."

The familiar voice comes from the little brook running out from beneath the sidewalk. Groan stands in the gurgling water, his pale face showing in the darkness. He reaches out with white hands and lifts himself over the lip of the concrete culvert, pushing through the hemlock branches. I back into the street, but I'm caught by the tether. Groan lifts one long leg over the fence, then the other, moving with the jerky motions of a marionette. His clothes are dark and tattered, a high collar, a ratty vest, a rounded bowler hat covering up his horns and ears.

"You don't think you can just leave, do you?" he says. "Sneak off? Break out? Tunnel away? Saunter forth?"

"Get away."

Groan stops, frowning. "Let me spell this out for you, Timothy. *You're. Never. Leaving.* Because I won't let you. Don't you understand that yet? Do you really need another thirty years to figure it out?"

He leaps at me, knocking me to the road. A car speeds past,

inches away. Groan kneels on me, crushing me with his bony knees.

He leans down into my face. "What in the hell are you thinking?" he bellows. Ripe breath chokes me. He puts his cold, maggoty fingers around my throat. With a squeeze, he pulls me up until our noses touch. "You're mine—and there's no way you're ever going to walk out on me. You made a commitment when you ate all my cookies. A commitment. Com-mit-ment. Find a dictionary."

He gets to his feet, tightening his grip. A brown delivery truck passes through us, leaving me with exhaust fumes filling my head. Groan lifts me by my throat. He raises me to the limit of his arms, and I'm six feet in the air before I know it.

"This little tango of ours is only getting started, you sick, little dipshit." He crushes me against his chest. I smell must and rot, putrescence and pus. "And I'm leading, not you."

He takes me by the wrist and swings me around, as if in a dance twirl. I cry out in pain—he doesn't let go of my wrist and the bones are straining. He stops. He leans over, his mouth turned down in mock concern. "Oh, stupid me. I could've broken your wrist with that move. Like this."

His other hand clamps down on my forearm and he wrenches my hand clockwise so hard all the bones in my wrist splinter. I scream. He kicks me in the middle of my chest and sends me flying back into the yard. I scramble away but he takes a couple of long strides and before I know it he's looming over me again.

"It's a drag you're a moron," he says. "You don't listen. You don't respect what I tell you. You don't *think*, Timothy. You don't think *at all*. What did I tell you about letting people into the house?"

He steps on me, his heel grinding into my crotch, squeezing my nuts so hard I pass out for a second in a white haze. He slaps my face, bringing me back. "*Don't let anyone in.* That was your promise to me. And now look." He points one scarecrow arm to the blue sign that reads Sale Pending in white letters across the top. His bloodless finger extends. "Blah, blah, blah, it says." He presses down with his boot each time he says "blah." "The problem is you don't respect me. I don't care that you apparently can't understand basic words. I'm used to that—tired of it, but used to it. You people make me crazy—but it's the lack of respect that hurts."

His smile is madness, long and crooked, his eyes gleaming from the darkness beneath his hat. "I don't forget your broken promises. And I'm not in the mood to dance anymore."

He shakes me with a brutal jerk. My teeth clack and my neck whiplashes. "Here's the easy part—are you listening?" Another shake. "Really, really listening?" Harder shake. "Come on. I'm waiting on an answer, Dimothy."

"Yes," I whisper.

He pulls me forward until his face mashes against mine. "Oh, goodie." The feel of his lips revolts me, like roadkill on my cheeks. "He speaks. But does he understand?"

"Yes."

He shoves me. I crash into the front steps.

"Ahem—I haven't even told you what I'm going to tell you, so how do you possibly understand, idiot?"

My spine is broken, everything below my waist numb. Electric pain shoots up through my upper back and neck, so strong I almost pass out again.

"Rule number one," Groan says, squatting down in front of me like he's talking to a child, tilting his hat back. "Just because I'm not here doesn't mean I'm not here. I'm always here. Always. Rule number two: don't set foot outside your house again, especially when you promise not to." He puts a hand around my neck and sits me upright. I try to punch him with my good hand, but he catches my wrist without even glancing at it. "Rule number three: no hitting." He crushes the wrist with a snapping crack. I moan, nothing but pain. "Other rule number three: no one moves into this fucking house."

"I can't do anything about it." I grit the words out through the pain.

"Well then, you'd better think of something, Mr. I-can't-do-anything-about-it. I'm tired of excuses, you know that. You *should* know that. Oh, who am I kidding? You're too dumb to know that." He sits back. "Where was I? Rules. One. Two. A couple of threes. Oh. Duh. Yeah. Rule number four: if you ignore the other rule number three like you ignored my other polite-yet-firm request about letting people into the house, your father is going to kill himself—right after he murders your skinny-lipped sister, her flaccid artist husband, and their three little whelps."

He rolls out his hand like a magician directing the audience to a trick. "To whit." My dad suddenly appears, standing next to Groan, clear in the growing moonlight. He flinches, seeing Groan.

"No, no," Groan says to him. "Don't look away. You tell him. Tell your dummy son, just like we practiced. Do it."

My dad looks at Groan, then at me. When he speaks, his voice is hoarse. "Do what he says, Timothy. Please. You can't stop him. None of us can. Do everything he says—I'm begging you." Dad takes a step forward. "I'm so sorry—"

Groan shakes his head and lets out a *Meh* and waves his hand. Dad vanishes.

Groan turns to me. "Are we clear as a tear?"

I stare at him.

He whispers, "Just nod if you understand."

I nod. Anything to get him to stop.

Groan sighs, relieved. A genuine smile comes up on his face. "Finally. Honestly, it feels like we're taking this thing to a new level." Standing, he extends a hand down to me. "Come on, champ. Let's get you back inside. Sorry about the wrists and stuff." He wags his hand again.

My arm throbs as I lift it.

"Duh." Groan smacks my broken wrist. He shoves my arms aside and grabs my head in both hands. He bashes it against the concrete steps, again and again, until my skull cracks and caves in with an explosion of pain, killing me.

Again.

18

—————

WHEN I RETURN TO CONSCIOUSNESS, I SEE WE'VE GOTTEN MORE
snow. It softens the edges. Sketches things I normally don't
notice. Power lines. Street lamps. Mailboxes. The branches of the
big sugar maple. Over the brook, the tips of the hemlocks droop
under the weight of the snow.

I'm sitting on the roof, my back against the chimney. The sun
arcs down. In the backyard, shadows of the old fence stretch out
blue across the snow. Little whorls of fine powder spin up off
edges, skitter along surfaces. It's all white, soft, quiet.

Life turns into memories. How many? A hundred? A thousand? Maybe a thousand more if I really try? All getting buried
underneath time, like the yard is buried beneath snow. Actually,
it's worse. The snow will melt. Spring will come. The sun will
wake up the ground and eventually feel warm on skin again.

No such luck for me.

Life is more like a spill of soda. It dries slowly, leaving a sticky
residue for dust and cobwebs to cling to, eventually becoming no
more than the ghost of a stain.

I'm not in a good place.

If only I could wink myself out of existence. Into stillness. Into silence. There's nothing left—except a long, lonely, depressing road. Maybe I'll just do nothing. Spend every day up here on the roof. Watch the seasons pass. Watch the sun shift its curve through the sky. Time will pass.

Can I make forever pass?

I don't bother asking the question I've asked myself a hundred thousand times: What did I do to deserve this? There's no answer. *Frustration* doesn't begin to describe it. I need a new word. A word that blends *frustration* with *Hell*. But I never took Latin. That would have been ninth grade—which I never reached, and never will.

I'm clueless. Totally fucking clueless. Always have been.

I've never been able to figure things out. Everyone else seemed to get it, whatever it was. Spelling. Handwriting. Dating. Haircuts. Baseball. Homework. Not losing things. Moving on in the afterlife. Maybe they had better parents, or older siblings to show them the way. Maybe they were all better mimics than I was. Maybe they thought more than I did. Or less. Deep down, I always felt like everyone else got a manual that laid out all the rules in big, basic blocks. Maps, diagrams, charts, tables.

Sorry, Tim—we're one manual short. Good luck, have at it.

So I'd cut my own hair the day before our first-grade class pictures. Badly. And there I was, jagged bangs, thick glasses, skin-colored patch over my right eye. I'd thrown a dirt clod at Kimberly Carter at recess, because I'd liked her. I'd still wanted to play with G.I. Joes while all the other boys left them behind and started sports. I'd sworn at Mrs. Kristoff, the gym teacher, because she'd smirked at my futile attempt to pull myself up a rope. I'd answered questions when it wasn't cool to answer questions. I'd not answered questions when I should have. I'd laughed too loud. I'd said anything that popped into my head. Everyone else knew how to do it right. Not me.

And the most frustrating part? I am, technically, a genius. Seriously. A genius. In third or fourth grade, they gave us IQ tests.

I scored 154. Twice. I'm not bragging here, because I think I've laid out a pretty good case that I'm actually an idiot.

But, yeah. 154.

Whatever. Just more memories.

An old patch of soda, gathering dust. Eventually I'll be no more than a ghost of a stain.

Yeah. Not in a good place.

19

———

The afternoon grows long as I wallow. I'm about to head down to the closet—after the way Groan killed me last time, I'm not going to spend a single second outside the closet after nightfall for a while—when I glance to the south. The brook runs along that side of the yard, a black ribbon cutting between snowbanks, winding into a stretch of woods. Three houses past it, another street, Field Drive, opens up to the right.

A fall of snow drops through the branches of one of the hemlocks, dragging curlicues of fresh powder through the late sunlight. Because the branches are weighted down with snow, I can see a few of the houses on Field Drive. One of them, a white Cape Cod, has someone on the roof.

At first, I figure it's a trick of the light. Sun getting lower, dragging the shadows out longer, painting the snow with strange patterns. But as I look more closely, I make out a little kid, dressed in red and blue, walking carefully through the snow at the very top of the roof, from the chimney to the corner and back again. Arms lifted, then down. Up again, down again. Like they're conducting an orchestra. Every time they get close to the edge, I cringe.

There's no one else around. Even if there was—what could I do? Yell? Wave my arms? Warn them about a kid on a roof? The kid's about to slide off the snowy roof and break his neck. He swings his arms and looks to the west where the sun is sinking through the trees. And then he walks right through the bricks of the chimney and disappears.

My jaw drops. I float up above the roof, as far as I can (which isn't far, maybe another three feet or so), but can't see the kid anymore. He's not on the other side of the chimney. I also notice what else is missing: footsteps. The snow on the roof is as smooth and undisturbed as vanilla frosting on a cake.

Holy shit. I think I've just seen a ghost.

20

MAN, I TURN IT OVER IN MY HEAD ABOUT SEVENTEEN THOUSAND
times while I pass the night in the closet. Had I imagined it? My
state of mind is, like I said, not good. Maybe I'm delusional?

But, no. I saw the kid.

As soon as morning comes, I do exactly what Groan told me
not to do and hike in the direction of the kid's house, to see how
close I can get. Or if I can see anything. The sunshine reflecting
off the snow nearly blinds me. By the time I reach the brook, I'm
paying a lot more attention. The tether never let me closer than
six feet from it, but suddenly I'm on the other side, the gurgling
water behind me. I explore every inch of the limit and find some
variation. From where I stand, I can make out a couple humps of
snow that suggest outside furniture—a table, maybe a firepit. A
small deck overhangs a stack of firewood, visible beneath a blue
tarp. I spot dog prints and patches of yellow snow.

I lean toward the house and yell "Hey!" as loud as I can.

At least two different families have lived there since I died. At
one point, one of them had been big on the Fourth of July, filling
the yard with mosquito candles, tiki torches, and, of course,

illegal fireworks. Nothing huge—firecrackers, a few Roman candles, bottle rockets.

Gazing at the roofline, I don't see any ghost.

"Hello!" I shout. "Are you there?"

The windows don't reveal any ghostly faces. Nothing stirs. I assume a ghost can hear a ghost. Groan and I have our idiotic conversations, so why not? I stand there shouting for an hour or so, until I reach the point of feeling stupid. No one answers and I start to wonder, again, if I'd imagined the whole thing.

21

I HEAD CLOCKWISE, FEELING MY WAY ALONG THE EDGE OF THE
tether. Maybe there's an opening I've missed. I glide through
prickly bushes. A fence marks the edge of the property in the
back of my house. I come out looking at a green house that had
looked modern in the 1970s, but now looks worn. Beyond, I see
the cul-de-sac where we'd all played as kids. Snow forts and
snowball fights. Sledding. Skidding contests with our bikes.
Races along the paths we'd cut in the woods that bordered the
circle, with its old stone wall that snaked along a ridge carpeted
in decades of pine needles. A big field beyond the stone wall,
perfect for staging allied assaults in the tall grass that turned
golden in the summer and left us pulling ticks off our corduroy
pants. Seeing it all again is like stepping into a time machine.

Pushing forward gets me nowhere, so I cut through the fence
at another spot and climb up a low, wooded rise separating that
yard from mine. I trek north toward where the circle runs down
from Chestnut Street, into the yard of the gray house next door. I
almost reach the scraggly crab apple tree that smells like autumn
when the hard little fruit darken and drop off to go soft on the
ground. The branches are bare, gnarled, the color of pencil lead,

frosted with snow. Following the circumference, I edge along the narrow stretch of trees and boulders rising next to a gray house on the side of my yard opposite the brook. I don't see anyone inside, but the possibility is exciting. I keep walking, leaning into the limit. No breaks. No openings. No weakening. And before long, I'm back in front of my house, back to where I started.

Okay.

The boundary has shifted by a good fifteen, twenty feet. Recently. It's not like I've been making a scientific survey of it at regular intervals, but I'm sure I bumped up against the old limit at some point during the year since Dad left. Last spring? I have a vague memory of walking backward away from the house, trying to get as far away as I could out of sheer boredom.

So it's changed.

I will humbly submit that however much of an idiot I can be, I'm no moron.

In fact, this last time Groan killed me has actually given me the one thing he tried to extinguish.

Hope.

The boundary that's held me back hasn't changed by a single inch *the entire time* I've been dead.

Groan can threaten me all he wants. He can tell me to stay inside all he wants. He can tell as many lies as his corpse-lips can flap at me. He can claim he and I are going to tango for another thirty years. Or forever.

But I'm standing farther from my house than I've gotten since dying. Ever.

Something has shifted.

Let me say that again.

Something has shifted.

PART IV

22

———

They've moved in.

It's late morning and I make a loop through the house. Shocked. The rooms hold all new stuff. Boxes everywhere, packing bubbles, random piles of stuff. New couch in the living room, plush and deep. The TV is giant, and half an inch thick. Rugs in cool patterns, bright colors. Slim lamps and lights, not the squat ceramic ones I'd grown up with.

The father—Alejandro—is wrestling with an exercise machine in the cellar. The mother is in the kitchen loading up the new cabinets. She puts a bunch of pill bottles in a cabinet over the stove. As she reaches up—she's not tall, and is on her tiptoes to do it—I see the resemblance to the daughters. Same face shape and eyes. They got their skin color from their dad.

I drift upstairs, past a mirror they've hung. (And, no—I can't see my reflection. It's a weird thing and I avoid it. Like I need more reminders I'm not here.) The daughters are in the bedrooms. Jacinta sits squat-legged in the middle of her floor on a circular purple rug. She's surrounded by a dozen stuffed animals, mostly mice and rats, but also two squirrels, a weasel, and a pig. A crayon sits in front of each one. She's got a book open in front of her, something about a lemonade stand.

"When is snack?" she says in a squeaking voice, moving one of the rats.

She sits back. "Reading corner first. Then drawing. Then snack." She grabs one of the squirrels. "Nee nant nacks! Nee nant nacks!"

We want snacks?

"Mom?" she yells. "Mom?"

From downstairs, her mother answers, "Yes?"

"Can I bring a snack to my room? Just this once? Please?"

"You want to what?"

Jacinta turns to the assembled animals and holds up her hand. "Wait here. Teacher will be right back. Find your calm spots." She runs out of the room, clomps down the stairs, and repeats her question about the snack. I look over the room. White bunk bed, the top bunk layered deep in worn-looking stuffed animals of all species. White dresser. Stuffed chair against the wall with the little window. Stacks of little kid books. Clothes scattered everywhere, already.

I slide through the wall into my room. Alyssa sits at an unfinished pine desk in the corner, a thin silver computer open like a briefcase in front of her. The binder I hauled around in school was twice as thick, so I take a minute just staring at this computer. She already has posters up on all the walls—a move that impresses me, since I understand that sort of priority. Most are women and they all look kind of strange, but awesome. One has purple-gray hair and a guitar. Another has huge red boots and suspenders, shorts, and hair like someone from the Ramones. Another pair look like they're straight out of the '70s with long hair and golden dresses. Not exactly the KISS posters I'd plastered the walls with back in 1977—sweaty Gene drooling blood, Ace with his mouth open, his guitar billowing smoke from the pickup—but I give her credit nonetheless.

Music comes out of her computer. Alyssa sings along, typing on the keys built into the computer. Her dark hair is pulled back and kind of piled on her head. She's in sweatpants and a T-shirt. Looking over her shoulder, I notice she smells amazing. Like candy and flowers, spice. (And while I'm on the topic, how is it true that from back when I was in junior high to now, girls in school always smell awesome, while guys smell like Italian subs and dirty laundry?) Anyhow, she clacks away on the keys as I peer at the screen. Colored bubbles hold words. A *bloop* noise goes off and another bubble appears.

I'm jealous ;-) When can I see?

Alyssa types, fast. *You can come over tonight. Pizza?*

Another bubble. *Yes. I'll get Darien to drive me. Ride home?*

Alyssa types, *We'll drive you home.*

K. 5.30?

syt, Alyssa types.

First of all, how awesome? Second, what in the hell are they typing? Code? A new language? It blows my mind. If my friends and I'd had something like that, we'd never have stopped. Seriously. Amazing. With music playing. No wonder none of my friends think about me much anymore.

Jacinta bursts into the room holding some kind of food bar and a bowl of dry cereal. She walks into Alyssa, bumping her with the bowl, already talking. "Can you come over and play preschool with me? It's snack time and I have to feed everyone, and then it's story time some more, and then nap time. Little cutie squirrel misses his mommy, but he's excited about the clay barrel."

"I'm busy," Alyssa says, not taking her eyes from the screen.

"You said you would. Little cutie squirrel—"

"Later."

Jacinta starts to cry, loud. Sounds fake. "Mom!" she yells. "Alyssa won't play with me and she said she would."

"Don't spill any of that in here," Alyssa warns her.

Jacinta marches to the door and hollers, "Mom, she said she'd play with me! Now she's not playing with me, and I want to play preschool with her!"

The mom comes up the stairs. "What's the matter?"

"Alyssa won't play with me and she said she *would*. It's *snack* time for the preschoolers, and then *nap* time, and little cutie squirrel misses his *mommy*—and nobody understands!"

The mom leans into the room, eyeing Alyssa. "Can't you just play with your sister for a while? I'm right in the middle of getting the kitchen in shape."

"I'm in the middle of something."

"What are you in the middle of?"

"Things." She looks at her mom. "Separate rooms, remember?"

The mom purses her lips, twisting them to the side. She looks at Jacinta. "Jacinta, why don't you bring the preschoolers on a field trip, downstairs to the kitchen?"

"Because it's almost nap time."

The mom sighs, then nods. "Fine, I'll play with you, and the kitchen will wait. Your sister will help me with that when we're through."

Alyssa's eyebrows go up. "How is that fair?"

"Pick your battles."

"Can I get a lock on my door?"

"No, you cannot get a lock on your door."

The mom leads Jacinta into the other room, and that sing-song voice starts up again. I swear I'd had the same—and I mean *the same*—conversation with my mom about a lock on that door. It'd been about Beth, of course, and forty-some years earlier, but still.

Talk about haunting.

.   .   .

I hit the roof every few hours, hoping to catch a glimpse of the ghost again.

Nothing. Zero. Zilch.

Also, Groan doesn't show up that night, or the next. No frothing. No bashing me to death. I keep to the closet. Course, now it's full of winter coats, boots, and a vacuum cleaner, and smells like leather and suede. But I creep out the next night. Playing with fire, yes. Groan's on a tear. Whatever else he has on his to-do list, *Terrorize Tim* is surely a box waiting to be checked off again. So that's coming. At some point.

But something's off.

Why isn't Groan all over me after his latest warning? The Cruz family (I spotted their last name on a stack of mail they put on the counter) is *in* the house. Fully and obviously. He should be coming after me every night. But he isn't. One night goes by without him. Then another. Soon enough, I haven't seen him in over a week. Nothing. Not a peek. Not a boo. Not a bash. I decide to make the rounds while everyone's asleep.

The silence—even when they're all asleep—is different from before. Maybe it's the rugs or the furniture. Maybe it's the subtle sounds: breathing, heartbeats, shifting in bed. Maybe it's the vibration the living radiate. A nightlight in the bathroom emits a pale green glow. I float into the bedrooms. It feels a little weird, yes. But if I'm going to be stuck with these people for the next whatever, I can't really give them their privacy even though it's the polite thing to do.

I'm a ghost. Different rules, as far as I'm concerned.

The parents' room is fairly plain, so far. Big bed, nothing fancy. A pair of dressers, a stand-up mirror. A digital clock showing thin blue numbers, 12:41. Alejandro sleeps on his back, his mouth open, not exactly snoring, but not exactly quiet. She sleeps on her side, the rise of her hips and shoulders forming a valley under the blankets. Her hair is tied back. She's wearing a loose T-shirt. It occurs to me that they're younger than I would have been if I were alive.

But what does that even mean?

As I've watched my friends grow up, in bits and pieces, I've seen them do things I never got to do. Driving. Having sex. Getting paid. Moving out. Not wearing sneakers all the time. Giving up posters. Exercising. Dating. Getting married. Getting stressed out. Working too hard. Going to concerts. *Not* going to concerts. Getting fat. Losing hair. Drinking for fun. Drinking to relax. Drinking to get by. Saving money. Getting dogs. Buying houses. Having kids. Did that make them adults? Some of my friends did *all* those things, but I still see the same person I'd rolled character scores with, climbed trees with.

What if becoming an adult is different? What if it's thinking—really thinking—about life and death? Struggling to understand your own family. Making peace with who they really are, not who you want them to be. Coming to grips with the nature of time. With possibilities—those still open, those closed forever. Knowing a hundred different kinds of winter light. Realizing just how little time other people spend thinking about you. Learning that home isn't, after all, yours. Not forever.

So I watch those children—Alejandro and Lilibeth—sleep in the dark as the moonlight slides along the floor.

I look in on the girls, too. My old room has a familiar glow of moonlight bleeding in around the closed shades. Alyssa is a collection of curves under the soft waves of her blankets. Her hair a dark spill. Hint of a nose. A slender arm escaping from the blanket only to jam itself back underneath her pillow. I don't hang around too long. I slide through the wall. The cold plaster gives me a chill as it scrapes inside me. In Beth's room, Jacinta isn't asleep. Her blankets glow, a tent around her head as she sits up in bed, a flashlight under the covers. She's whispering in silly voices. I make out the shapes of toy squirrels.

She giggles. "No, no, no, Squirrelly. The marshmallows go on the stick, not into the campfire, you silly. Here, I'll show you."

She sings. After a second, the blanket bangs around, Jacinta making a high-pitched squeal. "Shhhh," she whispers. "You'll be all right, you just got a burney on your paw. We'll find some Band-Aids. Or tapey."

The covers fly off. A circle of her stuffed animals is set up around some plastic rocks and the flashlight. She grabs the flashlight and climbs off her bed. Her pajamas have cartoon girls on them. She quietly opens her door and sneaks out into the hallway, then the bathroom, where she opens the medicine cabinet and spots a box of bandages on the top shelf. She has to stand on the lid of the toilet to reach it. I instinctively step closer since she's leaning so far over, but she doesn't slip. When she gets down, she accidently knocks the flashlight against the sink, then scurries back to her room. She closes the door slowly. When it's shut, she jumps on her bed.

"Now give me your paw, cutie-pie." She opens the box of bandages. The squirrel whimpers, with her help.

Then the door to her room opens. Lilibeth comes in, squinting, wearing a long T-shirt and baggy undershorts. "Jacinta." She sounds exasperated.

Jacinta snaps off the flashlight. "I had to pee."

"You were playing. I heard."

"But Mommy, the cutie-pies had a campout, and Squirrelly burned his paw when he was trying to make s'mores."

"The cutie-pies should be sleeping." Lilibeth sits down next to Jacinta, reaching over and stroking her hair. "So should this cutie-pie."

"But they've always wanted to have a campout."

"They can do that tomorrow, not now. It's late."

"But we're on vacation."

"Quit but-butting."

Jacinta giggled. "You have a big butt."

"I do not." Lilibeth smiles.

"Butt, butt, butt."

"Hey."

"Fart butt."

"All right, how about you get *your* fart-butt back under your blankets. No more playing tonight, okay. Do you need to pee?"

"I did a while ago."

"You're sure?"

"I'm sure."

Lilibeth moves the stuffed animals to the floor.

"Not Squirrelly," Jacinta protests.

"Jacinta."

"I won't play. He's just scared because of his burney."

Lilibeth sighs. "Fine. Just promise to sleep, okay?"

Jacinta jumps into bed, scooching around, snuggling the stuffed squirrel, while Lilibeth tucks the sheet and blankets over her.

"You like your new room?"

"I love it. The cuties do, too."

"Well, I'm glad the cuties like it. And the house?"

"I love it. I never want to leave."

"Good." Lilibeth leans in and kisses Jacinta's forehead. "Because I never want to go through another move again. Good-night, cute stuff."

"Nighty-nighty." Jacinta makes the squirrel wave goodnight.

"Everybody sleep, please. Goodnight." She leaves the room, cracking the door open a handbreadth. Jacinta adjusts the blankets, then looks at me.

"You must love this house, too," she whispers. She smiles. "I have to go to sleep now, or I'll be in trouble. Goodnight, ghost boy."

She waves at me, then rolls over and starts singing softly to herself.

23

———

I FLY DOWN TO THE CLOSET, FAST AS I CAN, RIDING A WAVE OF PURE panic and confusion.

What the hell was that?

That's never happened. Ever. Nothing like it. Aside from one psychotic demon, not a single person has communicated with me in thirty-eight years. I pace back and forth inside the closet, slipping through coats and the vacuum cleaner, ignoring the sensations tickling my insides. I consider the possibility that I'm hallucinating the entire thing—the sale of the house, the Cruz family, everything. Maybe I've been alone too long. Maybe instead of going lose-your-mind-and-drool insane, I've done something more insidious: imagine-a-new-life insane.

I stop myself. Look around. A woman's coat hangs in front of me. Velvety, maroon, with a fluffy collar of lighter shades of pink and white. How could I make that up? I'm not that talented.

Okay, fine. I haven't invented the Cruz family. They're real. They live here.

Jacinta saw me.

Spoke to me.

I don't understand.

So, logic. Some people are more sensitive to me than others. Especially if they knew me, or had some connection. That's not Jacinta. Also, no sensitive person has ever actually *seen* me. It's not like that. No apparition. A subtler perception. A chill. A feeling of being watched. A flicker of unease. And when they responded to me, it wasn't like they saw me standing there and waved at me. No. If I moved closer, they'd move away, not quite knowing why. Like magnets with the same poles pointing at each other. None of them ever mentioned anything to my parents or Beth. Probably because when sane people who aren't looking for attention or anything start to get freaked out, they usually keep it to themselves.

So why did this kid look at me as if I'd been standing right in front of her?

The next morning, I wait until the line underneath the closet door lights up with the dawn before I step out. Too much on my mind to risk an ambush by Groan. The house is quiet. Seeing all the furniture in the growing daylight calms me down. Even as a ghost, the light of day has an amazing power to chase away the crazy thoughts the long hours of night can spur on. I look for Jacinta and find her scooting around the house in her pajamas, playing and singing. Lilibeth turns on the radio in the kitchen, weather and local news. She makes pancakes. Soon, Jacinta sits at the table playing with a couple of tiny dolls. She doesn't look at me, doesn't point me out to her mom. I stand in the corner. Watching.

"Use your fork, please," Lilibeth says.

Jacinta ignores the fork and picks up a hot pancake and lays it in her palm, blowing on it before biting it gingerly, maple syrup running on her fingers.

"Fork."

"More fun this way," Jacinta says.

I go over to the table, right across from her. She doesn't look at me, but makes the dark-haired doll wave at me. I wave back. She makes the doll wave again, then picks up another pancake.

"Can you hear me?" I say.

She gives me a quick glance, but nothing else.

"Hello?" Nothing. "Can I have one of those pancakes?" Nothing again.

I back out of the kitchen through the wall, out into the breezeway. I go around to the front and slide back in on the other side of the kitchen. Jacinta is back to playing with her dolls—apparently seeing a ghost isn't terribly concerning for her. My dad sure hadn't reacted that way, but who knows. She's got her back to me so I glide across the floor, coming up behind her. She keeps playing.

"Hey!" I shout, ghost style, right behind her.

Nothing. She doesn't flinch, doesn't startle. Doesn't hear me.

I get closer until I'm an inch from her. She doesn't react at all. I reach out and put my hand right into her shoulder, feeling the strange static-like warmth of passing through someone alive (which I generally avoid doing because it seems weird). Jacinta smiles. She makes one of her dolls run away from me, then stops her, turns her around slowly and makes her wave at me.

Okay, so she can see me. Can't hear me. Can't feel me. But she can, without a doubt, see me.

Amazing.

I wonder if it's hereditary, so I wait for Alyssa to wake up. And wait. That girl doesn't even stir until after ten o'clock. The first thing she does is check her phone, sitting on the edge of her bed, her hair tossed and unkempt over her shoulder, her face sleepy. She's wearing a tank top and underwear.

I kind of forget where I am for a minute. Sorry.

I look up from her body and snap out of it. Her thumbs jump all over the screen of her phone. A quick smile crosses her face.

I stand right in front of her, waving my arms.

"Schuyler, nooo." She shakes her head. More typing. I get closer and, as usual, I may as well have not been there. She doesn't see me. While I'm close, I look at her phone.

Ur too good for him. I'm telling you. Believe.

From the expression on her face, you'd think she's negotiating a nuclear arms treaty with the Soviets. It's the same accountant-assassin look Beth used to get when she decided it was time to break up with a guy. Alyssa makes an exasperated sound and puts the phone to her ear. Waits a second, then says, "You're insane."

I hear a fast voice on the other end. Alyssa walks over to her desk, where an oval, white-framed mirror stands. She squints at herself, using her free hand to rub the sleep from her lashes. "Yeah, he's just saying that."

More fast talk.

"He said the same thing to Rachel, remember?"

I get in front of her, between her and the mirror. *Hey there, friendly ghost watching you walk around in your underwear, don't worry, this used to be my room, so we're cool.*

Nothing. She doesn't blink. Doesn't wave. Doesn't see me at all.

Like most pretty girls, *rimshot.*

Later that afternoon, Lilibeth takes Jacinta out and Alejandro takes the other car to I guess run some errands, so I'm left with Alyssa, who takes the opportunity of there being no one else in the house (except me) to film herself. She sits down in front of her thin briefcase computer and starts reviewing a book. She's pretty creative about it, filming segments in the kitchen, in the living room, one part while holding a toy swan, one part sitting in the empty bathtub. She wears glasses, which I find irresistible.

She raises one eyebrow. She playfully places a fingertip on her chin. Talks fast.

She's apparently got a TV station inside the computer. She adjusts lights. Frames shots. She knows what she's doing. Once she filmed everything, she plunks down on a giant stuffed pillow that makes a *shhhhh*ing sound and starts editing all the stuff she filmed. I'm not sure what the computer *can't* do. I swear, if she pushes a button and a pancake slides out a side door, I won't be surprised. As she's working, she's listening to music, of course from the computer.

Her taste in music: questionable.

Not being a music snob here, but—really. What the hell's happened to music? Where are the guitars? Worse, when the song ends, she makes it repeat. It doesn't sound any better the second time through. Annoyed, I look over her shoulder and see the name of a band and the name of the song. She listens to it probably fifteen times in a row as she works on her little movie. Okay, fair enough. I'm sure I made my family listen to "Shock Me" by KISS at about the same pace back in 1977. When you love a song, you love a song.

I don't love *this* song.

It's catchy, all right—catchy the way poison ivy is catchy. Catchy the way a commercial jingle is catchy.

The phone rings. On her computer, because of course. And bang, there's a girl, same age, long reddish hair, apparently staring into her own computer. Without preamble, they're talking girl stuff. More of the drama involving a guy named Tyler, a senior at the school Alyssa went to before they moved. He's interested in Schuyler, who's lapping it up. Alyssa is worried about her, because she's her friend, and she knows Tyler is already in tight with Sophia, she's also heard he's been with a girl named Jasmine, who's apparently something of a slut, as well as a girl named Sadie, and it all might be tied to a pact Tyler and some of the other guys on the football team had made about the off-season and the last half of senior year called "notches on the belt," which is exactly what you think it is. Alyssa has dutifully collected more evidence since the morning. Schuyler isn't buying it, she thinks there's something really there.

It goes back and forth like that until I'm convinced everything ought to be clear enough to both of them that more talk isn't necessary.

I'm wrong.

Alyssa reaches over and grabs this other thing, like a big flat book made of glass, and turns it on. Another magic device, like a phone, but bigger. The size of the chalk slates we used in kindergarten. I wonder if she's going to hold it to her head and make a call. Instead, she slides her finger around and plays a song on it.

Guess which one.

I almost turn around and float out.

"Oh my God, I love that song," Schuyler says.

"Me too."

Of course.

I look more closely at the giant phone slate thing. The song is driving me insane. I'd watched how she got the music to play. No buttons. Just touching the screen. In the corner, I see rewind, pause, and fast-forward symbols. Just like on my old tape recorder. Not really thinking about it, I reach over and tap the triangles pointing to the right. I don't expect anything to happen —I'm just sick of the song. I expect my finger to slip right through the glass and out the other side. Which it does, kind of. But as my finger makes contact with the surface, I feel the lightest whisper of a touch, a tiny pulse. Close to what I'd feel if I'd stuck my finger into a person. A little charge.

And suddenly, the song changed.

What?

Alyssa looks over. She looks at it and hits the other triangles, once, twice. My least favorite song is back, from the beginning.

I tap it again. It goes to the next song.

"Annoying." Alyssa frowns and picks up the giant phone thing. She rubs her sleeve across the glass surface, then taps the button again.

Oh, really? I tap fast-forward again. The song changes again.

"Why are you doing that?" Schuyler asks.

"I'm not. It's doing it on its own." She taps the screen.

"How old is that?"

"Kind of old. The year before last."

I change the song again.

She puts the phone thing aside. "Whatever."

Whatever? No—this isn't whatever.

I pause the music, then start it. I pick another song on the list and tap the screen. New song (still gross). Alyssa gives it an annoyed look, then reaches over and shuts it off. I look at the dark screen. Tap it. Nothing. I look closer and see a weird, real button. I push it—or, rather, I push my finger right through it. It doesn't move. I have no feel for it, no connection.

"Maybe I need an update or something," Alyssa says.

"I could call Tyler—see if he can swing by and help."

"Stop it."

"Jealous."

"Yeah, so jealous."

And, et cetera. They go on like that. Meanwhile, I try a dozen different ways to turn the thing on, but no go. I try tapping the screen of the computer they're talking on, but nothing happens there. Zero. I try pushing some of the keys, but, again, my finger goes right through. Everything I can think of, I try, but it's no different than anything else around me. Solid and empty, at the same time.

24

IT DOESN'T TAKE ME LONG TO FIGURE OUT THAT WHAT WORKS FOR
that tablet thing also works for phones. Which means that
everyone in the family has some kind of machine I can do something to. And they stare at them all the time. So whenever
someone pulls one out, I'm there, right in their space, learning.
Parts of me slip into parts of them, which is unnerving and
uncomfortable. Like chewing on felt, but they seem oblivious. I
hold back on doing that with Jacinta. She'd see me.

It's all about tapping. Sliding fingers. Little teeny arrows. Little
teeny keyboards. Making things bigger. Moving them around.
Going from one thing to another. Every now and then, I reach in
and do something, just to see if I can do it with everything they
open. Tapping some extra letters. Hitting a bright square. Making
stuff disappear. Boy, they hate that.

The next time Alyssa is home alone, I try something. The
parents went shopping, taking Jacinta with them. Alyssa makes a
drink in the blender: an orange, a banana, plain yogurt, almond
milk. While she's drinking it she—guess what—turns on her
slate thing. I'm right there. Before she can turn on that horrifying
song again (please, no more) I sneak a finger in and hit the little

candy-looking thing that looks like a yellow notepad. She pauses, hand over the screen.

I tap. Typewriter keys come up.

Hi there. Each letter makes a little clack when I hit it.

She stares at the screen, mouth open. She looks around the kitchen. Back down at the screen. "What?"

Don't be afraid.

Maybe that's the wrong thing to type because she suddenly looks afraid as she puts her glass down on the counter.

Okay. I have her attention.

Now what?

Now that I have actual words at my disposal, actual words, as specific as I want them to be—

I can't think of what to say.

I lived her—

That's all I manage before she hits the button and turns it off. After a second, she turns it back on. She opens a couple of apps —I heard her call them that, talking with Alejandro—and frowns. Shakes her head. "Crap." She goes over to the table and sits, opening up the briefcase computer.

Great. I can't type on that one.

She starts typing. I lean over her shoulder.

iPad hacking is what she types. A whole list of topics fills the screen. I can't make sense of what it's saying. Hacking? DFU mode? Passcode? Jailbreak? Alyssa starts clicking and reading. One thing I notice: she's moving the little arrow around by sliding her finger on a silver rectangle between her palms. I'd been so busy looking at the screen before that I didn't notice. I reach between her hands and drag my finger along the metal. The arrow moves. She lifts her hands, sitting up straight. The arrow follows my movements (so that's how they do it). I can't seem to do much with it, but suddenly the movie she made about the book fills half the screen.

"No, no, no." She reaches over and shuts the screen, sending my hands right through it.

The kitchen door opens and Jacinta walks in, bundled in a pink winter jacket and a red hat, a pom-pom hanging over her shoulder. Her cheeks are flushed with the cold. Lilibeth and Alejandro are next, carrying brown grocery bags. Jacinta walks over to Alyssa, pushing some space-age container with bright colors all over it right into her face.

"Banana-blueberry yogurt," she says. "Try some. It's delicious."

Alyssa leans back. "No, please."

"But it's delicious."

"Jacinta."

"Mom, she won't try it."

Lilibeth puts two bags on the floor next to the counter. "She doesn't have to try it."

"I think I got hacked," Alyssa says, ignoring the yogurt drink still thrust in her face. "Our network is locked, isn't it?"

"Maybe someone found the key," Jacinta offers.

"It's set up fine. It's locked," Alejandro says.

"Can't you check, anyway?" Lilibeth says. "My phone's been acting weird, too."

"Maybe there's something off," Alejandro says. He sighs as he puts the other grocery bags on the counter. "I'll do it."

"You noticed it, too," Lilibeth says. "Why are you being that way?"

"I'm not being any way," Alejandro says.

"Don't be mad, Daddy." Jacinta walks over and gives him a hug, an Oompa-Loompa in her big coat. She leaves a smear of yogurt from her cheek on his jacket.

"I'm not mad," he says. I hear the exasperation. He pats Jacinta on the head.

She lifts her drink. "Do you want to try this?"

"Maybe later. Everyone should change their passwords."

"Oh, great," Alyssa says. "I've got like twenty places I need to change now."

"Don't use the same one everywhere."

"No, really?" she says, putting a finger sarcastically to her chin.

"I do that. Sometimes," Lilibeth says.

"That's probably how they got in," Alyssa says.

Lilibeth puts a bunch of celery into a drawer in the fridge, followed by a bag of little carrots. "Says the person who spends ninety percent of her waking hours online."

"At least I use different passwords."

"Listen," Alejandro says. "Let's just deal with it. Check our main accounts, change our passwords. And she's right—use different passwords."

Lilibeth shuts the vegetable drawer. "I get it. Stop blaming."

"Maybe he did it." Jacinta points at where I'm standing, in the doorway to the dining room.

"Who?" Lilibeth says.

"The boy who lives here. He's right there."

Alyssa snaps her head around to look at her sister. The parents exchange a look. No one says anything. In the silence, Jacinta waves at me. I nod and wave back, wiggling my fingers and smiling.

"Jacinta," Lilibeth says. "What did we talk about?"

Alyssa crosses her arms in front of her chest. "Are we going to have to deal with this again?"

"Alyssa," Alejandro snaps.

She rolls her eyes, takes her computer, and leaves the kitchen.

"He's friendly." Jacinta holds the yogurt drink in my direction. "Want some?"

I shake my head.

"He doesn't want any, either," she says. "But it's delicious."

"Do you remember what we talked about, honey?" Lilibeth says.

Jacinta nods her head.

"No more imaginary friends, right?" Lilibeth continues.

"He's not my friend. He just lives here."

"Well, we're not going to set places for him, okay? No bunk bed. No extra stories."

Jacinta stares at me. "But what if he's hungry?"

"Jacinta, come on," Alejandro says. "No more. You agreed."

Jacinta looks away from me, pouting. Curious, I walk over to her, try to catch her eye. She keeps looking away. "Fine."

"Go take your coat off and hang it up," Lilibeth says. "Boots, too. Don't just leave it all on the floor."

"Can I have some cheese?" Jacinta says.

"If you put your stuff away properly."

Jacinta clomps off in her winter boots, still holding that drink.

When she's out of the kitchen, Lilibeth quietly says, "Oh, joy."

"We'll tell Doctor Cohen at her next appointment. It's Saturday," Alejandro says.

"I'll bring her, then."

He puts a bunch of bananas on top of the fridge. "I'm perfectly capable of explaining the situation."

"Well then, maybe we should both go."

"Fine. You just take her."

"Why are you being that way?" She folds up one of the empty grocery bags, staring at him.

"Because you don't trust me to tell her the right way."

"You minimize things. Sometimes."

"What's to minimize?"

"Okay, okay. You take her. I'm sorry." She puts the folded bag next to the stove.

"I'll finish this." He nods at the rest of the groceries. "You go change your passwords."

"Fine."

"Passwords," he says, emphasizing the plural.

"Got it," she says. "How about butthead123? Or maybe assface98? Stubbornjerk12? Those'll work, right?"

Alejandro smiles.

"This is easy." She smiles to herself. "I can think of dozens."

"There you go," he calls after her as she heads to the other room. "I use the same technique. I've got hundreds."

Soon enough, the sun is close to setting, the windows on the west side of the house lighting up in an orange winter wash. I feel it then: Groan. Just an inkling, a shadow of a thought. Early on, I'd have missed this little itch. Not now—I've got a refined feel for his nasty presence. I speed to the closet. Hunkering down, I strain, listening for him. Sniffing for him. Nothing. I hear the parents in the kitchen, making dinner. Someone, probably Alyssa, goes up the stairs. A door upstairs closes. Jacinta runs by the closet a few times, either singing or talking to herself.

But no Groan.

After a while, I don't feel him any longer. Still, I'm cautious when I step out of the closet. It's full dark. A flickering blue comes from the living room while the kitchen is lit only by the little fluorescent light over the sink. Down the end of the hall, the dining room is dark. The upstairs bathroom light is on. I take a few steps, eyeing the ceiling, the windows. No sign of Groan anymore. Pretty sure he came by just long enough to make himself felt, then split. Head game.

It's probably around eight o'clock. Lilibeth turns off the TV to get Jacinta ready for bed. It's a big routine, with Jacinta talking pretty much nonstop, getting goofier, rolling on the floor, doing little dances. Lilibeth is patient—but not quite enough and eventually stops urging and starts demanding. Takes a while, but eventually the kid is in bed. Lilibeth sings her a couple of songs then leaves. I hear Jacinta singing softly to herself for a while, then she goes quiet.

Alejandro and Lilibeth head to bed not long after, taking turns in the bathroom and then shutting their door. The house grows quiet. A light shines beneath the door to my old room. Before I go in, I take a circuit of the house. Groan isn't anywhere to be found.

Still keeping my antennae out for him, I go back upstairs. Alyssa is on her bed, computer on her lap. Some TV show or movie is playing. Her slate thing is on the desk, the screen black. No good. I turn back to her computer. I reach over, feeling kind of weird about it because it's like I'm reaching for her crotch. Minding my manners, I run my finger along the surface. The black arrow shifts. I drag my finger in circles. Her gaze lands on the arrow and follows it. She lifts her hands from the computer. The show she's watching pauses.

"Damn it," she whispers. She moves her finger along the silver rectangle, bringing the arrow up to the left side. I drag it back down. She sighs and swipes more quickly. We have a little war going on for a couple of seconds.

"Stop it," she says.

I stop, giving her full control again. She gets up and brings it to her desk. Taking a little piece of a sticky note, she covers the middle of the top edge of the screen with it. I don't touch anything. She makes a bunch of boxes show up on the screen and clicks one that says *Turn Wi-Fi Off*. She sits back, looking at it. I reach over and slide my finger across the rectangle again. Alyssa flinches. She double checks that the Wi-Fi is off.

I make the arrow go up and down three times. Then pause a second. Then three more times, up and down. A clear pattern. She puts her hand to her mouth, touching her lips with her fingers.

I repeat the pattern. She looks around the room.

"Can you hear me?" she whispers.

I almost float up to the ceiling, I'm so excited. I bounce the arrow, fast. *Yes, yes, yes.* Alyssa keeps her fingers on her lips. She stands. Looks at the computer, looks around. Paces to the door, then back. She takes a long breath. Looks at the screen.

"Are you . . . a ghost?" Her voice is quiet, like she's surprised she's asking it.

It's hard to explain what this feels like. This isn't a person *remembering* me. This is a person—a real, living, breathing, nondemonic person—*talking* to me. Directly. In real time. Expecting an answer.

This hasn't happened since October 31, 1981.

Yes, yes, yes.

25

____

I can tell she's freaked out. Honestly, I'm freaked out, too. But here we are.

Alyssa stays right where she is, about five feet from her desk. "You're in the room? Right now?"

Yes, yes, yes.

She folds her arms in front of her chest. Nods. Frowns. Turns for the door, stops herself.

"What do you want?" she whispers.

What do I want? Jeez, where to start? I want to move on, to leave the house I've been trapped in since I died. I want my family safe. I want to never see Groan again. I want not to be a ghost anymore. The joke of my afterlife has gotten stale. Still, not exactly a yes or no question. I don't touch the rectangle on her briefcase computer.

"Still there?" she says.

Yes, yes, yes.

"Can you type?"

I slide the arrow back and forth horizontally, once to the left, once to the right: *no, no.*

"But you did earlier." Her gaze snaps over to her slate thing. "On my iPad?"

It's the word she typed earlier. I think I get it. I type: *Yes, yes, yes.*

"But not on my laptop?"

Laptop makes more sense. Clever.

No, no.

She shakes her head. "This is insane."

Yes, yes, yes.

"Should I—"

Yes, yes, yes.

She hesitates for a split second, then gets the iPad. She fiddles with it, turning off the Wi-Fi, which by now I figure is like radio waves. Or TV waves.

"Notepad?" she says.

Yes, yes, yes.

The yellow jewel with blue lines opens into what looks like a sheet of paper. At the bottom, the letters. Alyssa places it down on her desk. "Type?"

I can type on this. Yes. The soft clacking accompanying each letter sounds more real, more concrete, than any sound I've heard in decades.

Her eyes widen. "Holy shit."

Holy shit, yes. I did it. Unbelievable. I don't even know what to type.

Words. I can type words.

Bingo. You said it.

She laughs a nervous, not-quite-believing-it laugh. I think I do, too.

"You're a ghost."

I am.

"Are you evil?"

No. Not at all.

"Which is what an evil ghost would say."

Not an evil ghost. Just a regular ghost.

"Did my sister see you?"

That was me. Yes.

"Oh my God. She really saw you. She really can see dead people."

She can see dead people?

"No—I mean, I guess. This is insane." She stops herself, holds out her hands as if checking she's not dreaming. "She always has imaginary friends. Some of them seemed so weird—I started joking with my parents that she's seeing dead people. Like in that movie."

Movie?

"Because you're a hundred or something? I mean, you died that long ago?"

1981.

"That's before I was born. Way before."

Thanks.

"I don't mean it like that." She looks around the room. The window shades are down. Closet closed. Door closed. She looks at the corners, her dresser, the computer. "This really isn't a setup? It has to be a setup."

No setup. I'm not that smart.

"Can you *prove* you're a ghost?"

I pause, looking at her. *I'm typing on your thing. Standing here. Invisible. So a ghost.*

She reads along as I type. She lifts the bottom edge of her sweatshirt, sticks her hand underneath it. "How many fingers am I holding up?"

Maybe I could poke my face through her shirt to find out, but no.

How do you think ghosts work? I type.

"What am I thinking?"

I don't know.

"This is crazy. This is *crazy*." She paces, looking at all the spots she's already looked at. "What's your name?"

I go to type it—but my fingers pass right through the surface of the screen, through the letters. Nothing happens. No click, nothing on the screen. What the hell? I try again. Again, nothing. I focus. My fingers slip through it like they'd slip through anything else. Panic sweeps over me.

"Your name," Alyssa prompts.

I try my last name. Nothing. Middle name. Initials. Nothing. I try to spell it backward, still no go. Anything I try that has to do with my name: nothing. It's insane. What the hell kind of afterlife rule is this?

I can't tell you. At least I can still type other things. Okay, I can breathe again.

"Why not?"

Don't know. It won't let me.

"What do you mean, it won't let you?"

I can't type it.

"What about your last name?"

Already tried. Middle, too. Backward. Nothing works.

"Then how are you typing this?"

I don't know. I've never done this before.

I wish I'd spent less time goofing around in seventh-grade typing class, because doing this two-finger-chicken-pickin' is slow.

"Are you a man or a woman? Er—*were* you?"

Man.

"How old were you when you died?"

I'm so stupid. I could tell her the truth: fourteen. Simplest thing in the world to tell the truth. But, no. I'm a dillweed. I have to *impress* her.

Seventeen.

"Oh my God—you were so young."

Young? I'm older than her. Kind of. You know what I mean.

"How come I can't see you? Can you appear?"

I doubt it. Unless you knew me.

"Try."

First of all, I'm pretty sure it won't work. Secondly, I don't exactly look seventeen, so I feel like an idiot for having lied. I consider pretending to just then notice I'd mistyped my age—silly me, whoops, har har—but it'll only make me look worse. Why am I even worrying about this? You'd think nonsense would fall away. But, nope. Awkwardness follows through the grave. So there's a thought to cheer you up.

I give it a shot. I'll have to live with the embarrassment (get it?). I'm kind of curious. Maybe something else has changed since I chased Dad out.

OK, hold on. I stand by the desk, reaching out with my mind, looking for little currents of energy, thin as a spider's strand, potent as the sparks off the giant Tesla-coil I'd seen as a kid at Boston's Museum of Science. Hard to explain. Reaching out, reaching out.

Nothing. I'm as insubstantial as a box of air.

Alyssa looks around the room. "I don't see anything."

I try harder. I think about my family. What the room had looked like when it'd been mine. Nope, nothing. I turn to the iPad. *Sorry. Doesn't work.*

"But Jacinta sees you."

I have no idea why.

"Can she always see you?"

Not sure. Ask her.

She shakes her head. "That won't go over well. We had a *huge* problem with her invisible friends. For years. She didn't want to play with other kids. She talked to them at preschool and kindergarten. In stores. Everywhere."

Look who's talking with a ghost now.

She closes her mouth. Goes to the window and opens it,

getting the old storm window up. Freezing air pours in. She inhales deeply.

What are you doing?

She glances over, groans, puts her head out the window again, breathing deep. After about ten seconds, she looks back at the desk.

I'm not a gas leak, if that's what you're thinking.

"I've lost it."

Not really.

"This is how it starts."

How what starts?

"Insanity."

You're not insane.

"I'm having a conversation with my iPad. How is that *not* insane?"

Try being a ghost for 38 years. Then let's talk about sanity.

She shivers, puts her arms in front of her chest, then reaches over and closes the window.

If there was a gas leak, those alarms would go off. I'd watched the construction guys put up a bunch of smoke and carbon monoxide alarms, and I'd watched Andover's Fire Inspector test each one of them.

"No alarm would go off if I were going insane. Or, it'd be like this. *This* would be the alarm."

Sure, this is crazy—but do you feel insane?

"At the moment, yes."

Seriously, though. Insane?

She points at the iPad, where my words just appeared. She raises one eyebrow.

You know your name? Who the president is? The year? What 6 x 7 is? Those aren't what crazy people know.

"I should get my parents," she says.

I doubt an insane person would do that. Go ahead.

She gets up, paces some more, glancing at the iPad every few seconds. Okay, so it's a shock for her. For me, too. But here we are. I'd be happy about her parents communicating with me. I'd be happy if they were to bring in a news crew. I haven't really thought that far ahead on any of this stuff. I just see an opportunity, and I'm taking it.

Just like Groan sees an opportunity. The bastard.

26

———

HE MUST HAVE BEEN WATCHING FOR A WHILE. I WAS SO EXCITED about tapping out my thoughts to Alyssa I didn't notice the fumes of Groan seeping in, building up, all around me.

"Oh, isn't this precious," he says.

I spin around and there he is in the corner of the room, tall and lanky, skin pale above his funeral garb, his horrible eyes shining from their dark orbits.

He shakes his head. "What did I tell you, dumbass?"

Before I can do anything—answer, take off for the closet—he disappears. Less than a blink later, he pokes his torso out from the ceiling, right above my head.

"Yeah," Alyssa says, no idea Groan is there. "But would a sane person stand around talking with a ghost? What if *I'm* the one typing all that. Just blanking it all out?"

Groan grabs me by the head, digging his claws into the soft flesh of my face. Blood runs down my chin. "Aren't you going to answer her? Cat got your tongue?"

He headbutts me from above and dives down, wrapping me with his limbs, my ankles in his hands, my head locked with his legs. He drags me down through the floor. On my own, I can pass through walls and other solids without feeling too much, like I've said—but when Groan has me in his grip, I rip apart, torn through the actual floor and walls. My skin peels, my joints dislocate, everything breaks and ruptures inside me. Even the scream that bursts out of me gets mangled as my jaw, teeth, and skull crash through the floor and ceiling below.

Groan doesn't stop. He slams me through the first floor, too, right down into the dark basement. I hit the concrete floor by the furnace and lie there, wrecked. Suffocating, too stunned, empty, and broken to even suck in a gasp. My heart jumps around crazily in my chest, about ready to give out.

"Patient in distress!" Groan stands over me. "Nurse, bring the crash cart, stat!"

I'm slipping over the barrier again, the border between life and death (or death and death). Stepping off a ledge. Sinking below the surface.

"Nope, nope, nope," Groan says, his voice growing distant. "Nope you don't."

As if from a distance, I feel twin stabs of pain, one in each nostril. He lifts me off the floor, two fingers up my nose, his nails driving into my sinuses. He breathes into my face. Foul air, laced with some other force, washes over me, carrying me back from the black.

"Jeez," he says. "Suck it up."

He yanks his fingers from my nose and grabs my shoulders, leaning me against the furnace. It thrums with heat, filling that corner of the cellar with its muffled roar. I collapse, but Groan catches me, his hand grinding my broken sternum and ribs. He pushes me upright. Kneels in front of me.

"Cute little trick you pulled up there," he says. "But I'm not angry. Sorry about the whole drag-you-squealing-through-the-house thing." He smiles at me like it's all some hilarious misunderstanding, shaking his head at the nuttiness of it. "I just don't want you to get hurt, is all."

He keeps me pressed against the furnace. "You're young. Inexperienced. Virgin. Take it from me, Timothy—you don't want to get your heart broken by a vixen like that. I know it's hard for you. When you watch her slipping her panties on. When you stare at her sliding her firm, soft cupcakes into a lacy bra, getting them nice and settled."

I try to move, but feel only pain and broken circuits. Nothing works right.

"And now you think she's going to be hot for you, her little ghost boyfriend?" His tone is gentle. "You're only setting yourself up for disappointment, buddy. She's not going to be hot for you. Nope. She's going to spend her days like any other hot girl, picking and choosing exactly what she wants, and pretty much getting it. Just like that. And she'll get older, and sexier, and you'll still be nothing but a little pervert, ogling her from the corner of the bathroom. Right up until she moves out and leaves you here. The younger sister will do the same. She's a piece of work, though. Right? La la la. Singing songs. Looking around. All kinds of stuff going on with her. Don't you think?"

White noise fills my head and Groan's voice sounds echoey. He notices and breathes at me again, bringing me back.

"But you need to know your place. Really. I'm not kidding. Listen to me. Your place is here—with me. I'm your only friend. I'm the one who's going to be here for you, like I am right now. I'm the one who's going to watch out for you. Save you from yourself." He sits back on his heels. "Maybe we've gotten off to a bad start. Probably my fault, mostly. I've got impulse control issues—and, believe it or not, you kind of help me with that. You test me. A lot. And that helps. I'd like to think I can help you. Like I'm doing right now. The two of us need to work harder to make this friendship work. Because that's all we've got. Friendship."

He smiles at me. Looks at the way I'm sitting. "Man, I did a number on you tonight. Sorry. Let me help."

I flinch.

"Hey, hey," he says softly. "See? That's what I mean. You don't trust me. What's friendship without trust?" He touches my right arm. It's torn open, the wrist dislocated, the elbow broken into tiny pieces. He raises his long, white finger over it and moves it back and forth. I feel heat. The flesh begins sealing itself together. The bones contract, slipping back into place with knuckle-crack clicks.

"Does that feel better?" Groan's expression is serious.

I nod.

"There you go," he says. "Sometimes you need to rely on your friends."

He moves his hands to my other arm, which isn't quite as bad, save for the long strip of skin that peeled down like a loose sleeve, bloody and curled. Again, I feel warmth as the skin straightens out, rolling up my arm, knitting itself back together with a tingle.

"Honestly," Groan says as he starts fixing my legs. "I'm seeing things in a new light. I really am. And I'm gonna have to apologize because a lot of this is my fault. I don't know how to act most of the time." He gives me a quick grin. "I didn't exactly have the best childhood."

My legs, broken at horrifying angles, straighten as he works his magic on them.

"Why won't you leave me alone?" I say. It's the pain talking.

"Gee, thanks," he says, not looking at me. "I tell you I want a fresh start and the first thing you say is something hurtful." He yanks my left leg, hard, straightening it. I bite back a scream. He pauses, his gray lips turned down in a frown. He inhales, forces a smile onto his face again.

I look him right in the eye. "Why do you keep doing this to me? How do I deserve any of it?"

"See? You're testing me. Just like I said. And I'm going to have to respect you for that. It's what you do. I can't control that, right? I can only control how I react. No one can make anyone else really do anything, or feel anything—have you noticed?" He grips my shattered ankle with both hands, and all the pieces inside wriggle like stony goldfish, finding their way back to their proper places, bringing on a terrible itching sensation.

"Why?" I repeat.

"All right, enough with the fucking questions," he growls. He grabs me by my waist and pulls me flat out on the floor. My head knocks the concrete. He pushes on my belly and sides. "I don't know why I fucking bother with you. I should just leave you here, leave your insides jelly, let you writhe in pain."

He straightens up, breathing. The air reeks with rotten flesh and decay.

"No," he says, calm again. He smiles. He's actually *more* disturbing when he smiles, as far as I'm concerned. "This is what we're going to do, buddy. We're hitting the reset button on things. On you and me. You think I'm happy with what we've become? I'm not. We're going to start over. I'm not going to lose my temper." Half his ear comes off when he leans over, landing on the floor. "Dang it."

He picks up the severed bit of ear and looks at it, then jams it into his pocket. Turning back to me, he pushes my stomach, gently. The damage inside me repairs itself.

"And you're not going to do the things that piss me off," he continues. "No wandering around outside. Ever. Not a finger. Not a toe. No communicating with that little hottie or her family— although I suppose I won't blame you if you leer at her every now and then."

He winks at me.

"Look," he says. "My advice to you is simple: sit back and enjoy the show. You're here, I'll always be around. We can compare notes. Share jokes. Maybe we could even take in a titty-show together one night—that'd be fun. All that make sense?"

He stands. His jacket is tattered. The bottom of his left ear, the one that tore off, is blackened and rotting. A row of scabs trails around to the back of his neck, thick as nickels.

"Because this is a serious time for us," he says. "A time when we can be serious with each other. And I'm serious about what I've said."

He extends a hand for me. I just stare. He nods. Reluctantly, I reach up and grab his wrist. He grabs mine and pulls me upright. The feel of his skin is both cold and hot, repulsive. My injuries are gone, but everything is sore and unsteady. He smiles, looming above me by a good foot and a half.

"See? I'm here for you," he says. "But just so we keep it on the up and up: No more typing with your new friends. No more anything. They're here. You're here. That's all. If I catch you doing it again, I'll be here every single night, angry. All my self-control won't help. I'll fucking tear you apart, again and again. You get what I'm saying, Timothy? Don't think I won't."

"Fine," I say.

"Fine what?"

"Fine—I won't do anything."

"Not a word?"

"No."

"Not a letter?"

"Nothing."

"So how hard was that?" He breaks into a ghastly smile. "This is us, working things out. I'm kind of getting a feel for it. You?"

"Sure," I say.

"Great." He claps me on the shoulder. "We're good?"

"We're good," I say.

"Cool. I've got to run now, leave you to do your thing. Probably swing by tomorrow night. Maybe even later tonight, who knows. Busy night. We'll play it by ear, okay?"

"Okay."

He makes double pistols out of his fingers and clicks them at me with a wink. Then, he turns and walks through the cellar wall. I slump back, looking around. I lift myself to the corner of the ceiling just below the hall closet when Groan's hand catches me by my belt.

"Whoops." He pulls me back down and gets me into a headlock, then whispers into my ear, "Forgot one thing, buddy. Just for old time's sake."

He tears my head, excruciatingly, from my shoulders.

27

I DON'T FADE AWAY, LIKE USUAL. NORMALLY, I'D BE OUT OF THE blue and into the black for at least a couple of days before returning. Instead, I come to in the closet, my neck and head aching from having been decapitated by Groan. That's also strange. I usually don't feel a thing by the time I'm back. When I peek out past the closet door, I see Alyssa walk by, holding her iPad and looking around. Whispering. Is she looking for me? Sure looks like it. She's wearing the same black tights and sweatshirt as earlier.

Not feeling Groan, I take a chance and step out a little farther. Everything looks the same. For a second, I think about trying to get in touch with Alyssa again. But then I figure that's exactly what Groan expects me to do, in spite of his warning. So maybe it's a trap. He's probably lurking around outside waiting for me to do it. Not keen on getting killed again tonight, I hesitate. I slide across the entryway to the outside wall. Poke my head through it.

The night is clear the way it only gets in winter, the snow catching the light of the crisp stars and slender moon. I look down the length of the house in both directions. No Groan. Curious, I continue along the house, with just my head outside it. The snow-covered shrubs gather shadows beneath them. No demon that I can see. At the corner of the garage, it strikes me that this is a bad idea. Maybe I'm regaining my senses after Groan's mauling. Either way, I'm about to duck back inside and hurry to my closet when a movement off to my left catches my attention.

Through the line of backyards past the brook, on the roof of the house: the figure I'd seen before, clear against the snow, bright beneath the midnight heavens. The kid. I watch. He's waving his arms around again. I look around the yard for Groan.

No wandering around outside. Ever. Not a finger. Not a toe.

Man, I might be as stupid as Groan says I am.

I try not to overthink it. Or even really think it, apparently—because the next minute I'm hauling ass toward the brook, heading to the spot that gets me closest to that other house. Running like all the demons of Hell are on my trail. Or one in particular. You get the point. I bound across the gurgling water, the brook itself looking black like the river Styx. At the boundary —well, at the boundary something weird happens.

Expecting the tug to hold me back, I hurl myself forward. But nothing stops me, and in between the extra effort and meeting no resistance at all, I'm tumbling feet over head, crashing through the snow until I slide halfway into the tarp-covered stack of cord-wood behind the kid's house. I right myself.

How? Why? The questions jackknife in my mind, causing a twenty-car collision.

This is impossible.

I look back. My house is dark, except for the window in my old room, which shines with the pale light of a computer screen. Each window pane. Each shingle. Each angle. The trees. The brook. The fence out back. I know them all—but they look so strange to me. Miniature.

I haven't seen them from this far away in almost forty years.

"That's really stupid," a voice says.

I leap backward, sure that Groan's caught me, that he'd set it all up to trap me. Flinching, I raise my arms above my head. But when I look up, I don't see Groan anywhere. Instead, I see the head and shoulders of the kid sticking out over the edge of the roof of the house I'm next to. He's staring at me. We lock gazes for a second.

"Who are you?" I say.

His eyes widen. He yelps and scurries back, disappearing through the snow and roof. The snow is undisturbed.

"Wait!" I call.

What the hell?

"No, you don't," I mutter. I don't give myself time to think about what I do next.

Which is to walk in through the wall of the house.

The slightest pull of the tether registers, so I'm pretty sure I can't just go *anywhere*, but here I am. Somewhere else. Another house.

I'm not going to faint. I'm not hyperventilating. I'm not wondering if I'm dreaming. I should be doing all of that. Instead I feel the opposite. I feel as close as I've felt to being alive since I died. I'm not in my house anymore. You might think: well, you're standing in another house, big deal.

No. No. Most definitely, no.

I'm here. I'm seeing things I've never seen. Space beyond the edge. Electric, that's what it is. Even though I'm standing in a corner of a basement—a weird one with rough fieldstone walls and a cement floor—every detail shouts at me. The pipes. The pegboard hung with tools in front of a work bench. The white five-gallon bucket beneath a leaking spigot at the side of a slanting washbasin beside the dryer. A pair of rubber boots. A collection of yard tools, including a hoe, two rakes that have seen better days, a curved saw for trimming branches, all nice and rusty. A circuit-box. A wheelbarrow.

And me.

I feel a weird tingle behind me. I turn, just catching the quick glimpse of the top of a head yanking back through the wall near the stairs.

"Wait—come back," I call. "I know what you are."

No go. The kid doesn't show himself. So I go looking for him. I dive through the wall he slid through and find myself in a narrow stairwell, much nicer than the rough basement. White walls. Cream-colored carpet on the steps. I follow them up to the far end of a dining area. To the left, a set of sliding doors opens onto a wooden deck. Next to the doors is an elevated nook strewn with pillows. The rest of the room has a dark wooden floor. A dining room table, a kitchen beyond it. To the left of the counter, another room opens up. Beyond the fridge is a hallway that goes all the way to the front door. I see the kid slip off to the side in that entry area.

"Hey, get over here." It's weird, but I feel self-conscious about raising my voice inside some strangers' house. Until I remember I'm a ghost. "Don't run away. I'm not—going to hurt you. Okay, that sounds lame. But I'm not."

There's nothing but silence. I feel the living, slumbering. The energy is there. Not like my family. Not like the Cruz family. A different vibration, or whatever it is. I figure the kid is ducking to the left, so instead of going after him that way, I cut through a small room, some kind of den with a TV in it, then through the opening into the living room. A long couch lines the opposite wall, windows look out on the quiet street, a hulking woodstove stands tucked into a corner in front of the chimney. The kid is in the corner, next to an old stereo set in a built-in bookshelf. He's in the shadows—the room is dark, after all—but I catch some of his features. He's shorter than me by a foot and a half. Round head, red hair like a brand-new penny. He's maybe nine years old. He's wearing pajamas, red and blue, matching tops and bottoms. He also looks terrified.

I lift my hands. "Don't take off."

He takes off, flying through the ceiling and disappearing again.

"Damn it." I shoot up after him. I pass into a bedroom. A couple is asleep in a huge bed between two sets of windows. The room is neat, not too much furniture. A sleek dresser. Big mirror. Matching nightstands. Grown-ups, for sure. The kid's bare feet slip through the ceiling of that room as well. I follow him and emerge in the attic. One lone window at the end looks down on the street. The inside of the roof is bare wood, old and full of nails poking through. Rafters and joists show. All the nooks and corners where the ceiling is low are stuffed with suitcases, storage trunks, plastic bins full of papers, other stuff. A seamstress mannequin stands in one corner. Skis rest across the beams overhead. A dartboard near the window is surrounded by a hundred pinholes where near misses landed. A brick chimney rises from floor to roof about halfway through the space. Mismatched carpet lines the floor. Past the chimney is a set of stairs leading down, painted white, a rickety-looking railing along the top. A small room is walled off to the right of the stairs. Above it is a small loft, a space about the size of a medium tent.

The kid looks at me from there.

"Look, I'm not here to hurt you or anything," I say. "I'm like you. I'm a ghost."

His face screws down like he's debating whether to bolt again.

"I'll just follow you," I say. "I can keep playing like this all night long. All day. All week. But let's not, okay?"

"Why'd you trip across my yard? Into the woodpile?" His voice is high, like a girl's.

I pause for a second. "*That's* what you want to ask me?"

"It looked weird."

"Says the kid who was up on his roof conducting an orchestra."

"I wasn't—conducting."

"And I wasn't tripping. Not exactly."

"It looked really weird."

"Fine. I get it." I stay where I am. "How about—gee, who are you, fellow ghost? Where did you come from? Not even a little curious?"

"Maybe."

"I'm Tim. I live"—I figure out the direction relative to the street—"over there. The brown house."

"I thought you said you're a ghost."

"I am. I—you know what I mean."

"How come I've never seen you?"

"How come *I've* never seen *you*?"

He shakes his head. His eyes are wide, like he still can't quite believe he's talking with me. I wonder if my own eyes are doing the same thing, because that's sure as hell how I'm feeling. I think I'm probably scaring him.

"Okay, ignore that," I say. "This is all a little weird for me. And for you, I'm guessing."

He grants me a faint nod.

"What's your name?"

"Kyle."

"Hi, Kyle. I'm Tim. When did you—well, how long have you been here? Like this?"

"I'm not sure."

"What do you mean you're not sure?"

"I can't really tell time."

"Were you born before clocks?"

He frowns, keeping away from the edge of the loft. "No."

"Then when did you die?"

"A long time ago."

"Like, years?"

"Years."

"A hundred?" I step closer. He flinches, so I stop.

"I don't know."

"How can you not know?"

"I don't know. Please stop yelling at me."

Am I yelling? I guess I'm a little overstimulated. I take a long breath, trying to calm down. "Okay, I'm sorry. Didn't mean to. It's just that this—I don't know—it's never happened. And I've been here a long time."

"Here?"

"Well, not *here*. But a ghost. Over there." I point again. "At my parents' house. I died on Halloween in 1981."

"You're lying."

"What?"

"You're lying."

"No—I heard you. I'm not. Why would you think I am?"

"This is a trick."

"What kind of trick?"

He shakes his head, giving me a hard look.

I take another step closer. "It's not a—hold it. Do you think I'm Mr. Groan?"

"What?"

"Groan."

"Groan? Why?"

"Not you. Groaning. *Mr.* Groan."

"I don't understand."

"The demon."

"Are you him?"

"Groan?"

"A—demon."

"No, I'm not—wait. You know a demon, right?" I glance around at the attic, picturing Groan flying up through the rough boards.

"*You* said demon."

"Fine. Yes. I said demon. Do you know one?"

He looks away. "I don't want to say."

"Why not?"

"You're yelling again."

I take another deep breath. "Sorry, Kyle. Do you know a demon?"

"I don't want to say his name."

"So you do."

Another barely perceptible nod. He looks around again.

"Why don't you want to say his name?"

"It might make him show up."

Now, I'd thought that same thing about Groan often enough. Especially in the beginning. The idea that even *thinking* about him would summon His Dickishness. The kid looks like he's about to cry.

"Okay," I say. "Don't say it. I get it. What's he look like?"

He shakes his head. Doesn't want to even say that. "Have you seen Karen?"

"Have I—what?"

"Karen."

"Who's Karen?"

He points in the direction opposite my house. "A girl. She lives at the corner. Karen."

"No, I don't—wait. Is she alive? Or a ghost?"

"Ghost."

"Another? How do you know?"

"She comes over."

I go to the window facing the street. Up at the corner, I see the house I think he's talking about, a few lights shining in the darkness. "Comes over? Here?"

"She visits. She's nice."

"You're sure?"

He leans down, like he wants to make sure I'm looking at the right house. "What do you mean, am I sure?"

"She's not a demon?"

"She's Karen."

"But Karen's not the demon."

"Are you dumb?" The kid's giving me a look without guile.

He's not giving me the business—he's genuinely asking.

"No. I'm not dumb." *Not usually.* "I just don't understand."

"Karen comes to make sure I'm okay. Except she hasn't in a while. Almost a week, maybe."

I cross my arms. "How often does she come over?"

"Every other night. At least."

"She just waltzes over—wait. Did you say *night*?"

"Yes."

"She comes at night?"

"That's when she can reach here."

"What do you mean?"

"She can't reach during the day."

"But she can at night?"

"It changes at night."

It changes at night? *It changes at night.* I stare at him, probably with my mouth hanging open.

I am dumb.

In fact, maybe I'm the biggest idiot who ever died. *It changes at night.* Unbelievable. In thirty-eight years I never thought to test if the boundary changed at night. I checked it *thousands* of times during the day, different times of day, different times of year, dawn, dusk. Backward, forward, sideways. Eyes closed. Eyes open. Humming. Silent. Praying. Not praying. Crawling. Leaping. Sprinting. Tumbling.

But never—not once—at night.

I am such an idiot.

"Of course," I say. "Right. I meant, how does she avoid, you know—the demon?"

"She only comes when he's busy."

I turn from the window. "Busy?"

"Yeah. Busy."

"She knows when he's busy?"

"She figured it out."

"How?"

He shut his eyes, thinking. "A pattern."

"There's a pattern?"

"Mostly. Not always. Do you think he caught her?"

"Why would you think that?"

"She's not there during the day."

"I thought she can only come at night."

"We signal during the day."

"How?"

"Karen taught me."

"Wait a minute—is that what you were doing on the roof the other day?"

"Sort of."

"How sort of?"

"Usually it's from the top bedroom. But since I didn't see her, I tried the roof."

"And the two of you have a system? Of signals?"

"And Andy."

"Andy? Who's Andy?"

"Andy Van Etten."

"Who's Andy Van Etten?"

"He's only four. His house is across Chestnut Street."

I look out the window again. "And he's a ghost?"

"Yes."

"Hold it." Things click together in my head. Unbelievable. I stare out at the neighborhood. "And Karen's right there?"

"Right across the street here. At the corner," Kyle says, pointing again.

Then I get it—bam. How did I not get it? "It was Halloween, wasn't it?"

"I don't want to talk about it."

"1981. Halloween. Cookies."

He clams up.

I put my hand on my chest. "Same here, Kyle. I died from Mrs.

Gracie's cookies. That's what happened to you and Karen and Andy, right? I'm not trying to trick you."

Nod.

"And you've all been communicating since then. Even Andy knows the signals?"

"Yes." He chews the corner of his lip. "Maybe she's been *there* all week?"

"Maybe she's inventing a telephone for ghosts. Next logical step."

"What?"

"Never mind. How old is she?"

"Old."

"Like how old?"

"Twelve."

I lower my head. Twelve. A twelve-year-old girl left me in the dust.

Fine. I take the mantle: I am the dumbest ghost.

"When was the last time—" Before I get any further, Kyle looks toward the stairs, fear on his face. He looks back at me and waves his hand, fast. Shooing me away.

"He's coming," he whispers, panic in his voice. "Go. You have to go!"

I don't need to ask who *he* is. Even I—the dumbest ghost in the Chestnut Street region, apparently—sense the strands of dread suddenly trailing through the air like the venomous tentacles of a poisonous jellyfish. A demon. I look from the door to the attic back up to Kyle. "I'll be back."

He scoots back into the loft crawlspace, out of sight. I don't hesitate, sprinting into the wall facing my house. In a moment, I'm through the slats and nails, suspended out over the side-roof, spinning my legs like in a cartoon. I swan-dive down, coming up short enough to avoid moving through the ground. I fly over the moonlit snow, across the yard, through the patch of trees, over the brook and back into my garage. I dart into the closet. Come to a stop. At least I'm safe. Mind completely, utterly, permanently blown—but safe.

The house around me is silent. Even the light in my old room was off when I approached.

Safe.

After a moment, I step out from the closet. Listen. Nothing. Feel—nothing. No Groan. Not a whiff of his subtle stank. Not a tickle of his galling malice. He's not here. But he's somewhere— and there's a pattern to it.

Karen is a genius.

28

I DON'T KNOW HOW YOU ARE, BUT WHEN I DO SOMETHING SUPER dumb, I dwell on it. Like, it engulfs me. And I'm dwelling on it now. I'm forty feet away from the front door to the house, past the other side of the street. The moon is high, cold. The snowdrifts lining the road are speckled with frozen slush and road salt. So, yes. I'm forty feet from the house, which is twenty feet farther than I'd ever thought possible before tonight. Because I never checked at night. Duh.

How many nights have I spent in the closet? I can't count that high. All my investigations of the barrier—daytime. Every one of them. Too many to count.

Without question, I am the dumbest fourteen-year-old who ever died.

There. Happy?

Because I'm not.

I feel my way around the limits of the tether. It's still there. It *feels* the same as when I've leaned into it in the daytime, but I'm twice as far from the house, maybe a little more. So it changes at night. I wonder if the nighttime boundary has shifted lately, too.

I guess I'd better ask Karen.

· · ·

Come morning, I see I'm not the only one questioning. Alyssa keeps her iPad with her, looking for opportunities to reach out to me. I ignore her. She's bringing up the notepad thing and whispering, "Hello? Are you there?" whenever no one else is around. One time, she does it in the living room and Jacinta, who's playing with plastic horses on the floor behind the couch, says "I'm right here." Alyssa shakes her head and leaves the room, only to be trailed by her sister for the next ten minutes.

It takes everything I have to not answer Alyssa. Think about it. She's a living, breathing, gorgeous girl. She wants to talk to me. She *can* talk to me.

But I have to ignore her because of Groan.

Will he be able to tell if I answer Alyssa? I doubt it—but maybe. I don't want to give him any excuses to come by every night, to break his pattern. To give me a chance to figure out what the hell is going on. So I tread carefully. I stay quiet, out of sight. It's easy to do that with Jacinta. She's loud. Often singing. Always talking. Stomps around without any grace.

But as I'm trying to keep a low profile, Alyssa seems more determined to make contact with me. She goes full speed. After an hour or two of quietly trying to get me to talk to her, she plants herself down in front of her briefcase computer, watching little movies and shows about ghosts. She types in: *ghosts, ghosts and iPads, making contact with the dead.* Variations on those themes. Pretty soon, she's watching clips about people claiming they'd contacted their dead mother on their computer. How people discovered their new houses were full of *EMF activity.* How to record voices of the dead with their phones.

Scientists, they aren't. Just regular folks sitting in their laundry rooms under fluorescent lights talking into cameras they're holding in their own hands. I watch over Alyssa's shoulder. In fact, I probably watch more of them than she does, because she's going back and forth with Schuyler and her other friends about whatever random thing is the hot topic.

As far as the ghost movies go, no one has any idea what they're talking about. It's not just that their theories don't make sense to me, an actual ghost—it's that I wouldn't trust a single one of them on much basic knowledge, let alone claims about the supernatural.

Bad haircuts. Too much makeup on the ladies. Not a lot of logic. Way too much certainty. I don't think they're exactly lying. Unless you count not being honest with yourself about why you're willing to believe something. Is that lying? It's clear they all have some other reason for claiming to believe in ghosts, most of which have nothing to do with ghosts. Desperately wanting to believe in the afterlife because of some specific death in their lives. One woman claims the ghost of a young girl contacted her in her new house. By the way, that woman also mentions how she lost her sister to leukemia when they'd been young. Desperately wanting to appear to be an expert or authority on the subject (despite clearly *not* being particularly educated). Desperately trying to prop up their religious views (because God, or maybe Satan, is looking out for—or is challenging—them). Stuff like that. Transparent.

The depressing part? I didn't see a single second that makes me think the ghosts they talked about were real. Not a single one. None.

29

BY LATE MORNING, ALYSSA HAS THE HOUSE TO HERSELF AGAIN.
Alejandro and Lilibeth took Jacinta to a birthday party where
there are going to be trampolines, which made Jacinta nervous, a
point she brought up about fifty times. A car pulls up out front
and drops Schuyler off. She bops over to the door, shivering. I've
seen her on the computer and phone, but seeing her in person is
different. She's got reddish hair, longish. Definitely a pretty girl,
even though she has sort of pop-out eyes. Not quite Marty Feld-
man, but noticeable. She's wearing black tights, a deep blue
sweatshirt, and boots she kicks off in the entryway. The two of
them head to the kitchen.

"You eat?" Alyssa says.

"I had a bar a while ago."

Alyssa opens the fridge. "There's pizza from last night."

"Sure." Schuyler leans against the counter as Alyssa puts a
pair of slices on a plate and slips it into the microwave. She looks
around. "I like it."

"I have my own room. Finally."

"You don't miss the toy rats?"

"I do not miss the toy rats."

Schuyler steps into the doorway of the dining room.

"Look around," Alyssa says.

"I feel a presence."

I look at her. So does Alyssa.

"Seriously?" Alyssa says.

"The presence of a sexy guy who hangs out in the bathroom when you're showering."

"Don't need that image, thanks."

Schuyler purses her lips. "It doesn't make you just the tiniest bit hot?"

"Not even the tiniest."

The microwave beeps. Alyssa takes out the bubbling slices of pizza and drags one onto another plate for Schuyler.

"Maybe he's watching you get off," Schuyler says. "Now that you have your own room."

"Getting off? That's where your mind goes? And thanks for the thought."

"Well, it's probably true."

It's not.

"I doubt he would," Alyssa says.

Thank you.

Schuyler smiles. "Oh, ho—so it's crossed your mind."

"I keep the lights out."

"Ghosts see in the dark."

"He doesn't seem like the kind of guy who would do that."

"All guys are that kind of guy."

They walk through the dining room to the living room.

"*He doesn't seem like the kind of guy*," Schuyler says. "You're already turning him into an Alyssa kind of guy."

I don't think a girl's ever turned me into *any* kind of guy, so this is getting interesting.

"I'm not turning him into anything."

"I can tell."

"You're just jealous I have a ghost."

"I *am* jealous, true. I've also figured out what you need to do."

"Thank God. I can sleep easy."

Ditto.

"I'm serious."

"Are you?"

"I am." Schuyler sits down on the couch and curls one leg underneath her. "Use a Ouija board."

"Like *The Exorcist*? Isn't that exactly the worst idea?"

"Not an actual board. An app. They have them, I looked."

"Why would I need a Ouija board app when he can type in Notepad?"

"Not the same thing."

"You're an expert?"

"I've *listened* to the experts," Schuyler says. "Spirits have to respond to the Ouija. It's like a command."

She's wrong.

"I don't think that's a rule," Alyssa says.

"Now *you're* an expert?"

"Okay, so we're *both* not experts."

"Then we should trust the people who are," Schuyler says. "Come on, it'll be fun."

"I never should have told you."

"I'll pretend you didn't just say that. Where's your iPad?"

"Fine." Alyssa puts her plate down on the end table. "Wait."

She leaves the room and goes up the stairs. Schuyler looks around the living room. "Can you hear me?"

"Yeah, I'm right here," I answer loudly.

"Are you here?" she whispers.

"Right in front of you, Schuyler."

Nothing. She can't hear me, of course. Curious, I reach over and put my finger on her shoulder. The tip goes in, just a little. She shifts. I pull my finger back, then do it again. She shifts again, this time putting her plate down. I hear Alyssa on the stairs. I try to manifest a chill, just to see if I can. When Alyssa comes in holding her iPad, she looks at Schuyler's plate.

"Want more?"

"The weirdest thing just happened," Schuyler says. "I got a chill."

Alyssa gives her a look. "Yeah, right."

"I'm not kidding."

"Seriously?"

"Seriously. It's creepy."

"Were you getting off?" Alyssa bites her lip.

"Yeah, because that's what I do in other people's living rooms."

"So you're messing with me."

"No. It was weird."

"Weird like what?"

"Weird like I wasn't alone."

"Stop it."

"I'm telling you the truth."

As they look around the room—made brighter by the snow on a sunny day—I do a little dance and take a bow. Nice to be appreciated.

"If you're trying to freak me out," Alyssa says, "please don't."

"I'm not." Schuyler says it so plainly it makes an impact, given how over-the-top she's seemed every time they've talked.

"You still want to do this?" Alyssa puts the iPad down on the coffee table.

"Yes." Schuyler doesn't sound quite as sure of herself as earlier. "Go to the app store."

Alyssa looks at a display of little squares, all colored and cool looking.

"Which one?" she says.

"I looked at that one this morning," Schuyler says, pointing to one on the top row. It looks like a tiny Ouija board.

"Okay." Alyssa taps the screen, a little bar fills up, and she has the Ouija board open. It fills the screen. She places the iPad on the table and kneels on the floor opposite Schuyler. "So how does it work?"

"We put our fingers on the thing and it moves. On its own."

"Or one of us moves it."

"No. The point is that we don't."

Alyssa touches the screen with the fingertips of her index and middle fingers, on the planchette. She wiggles it back and forth, moving it across the screen, getting a feel for it.

She looks up at Schuyler. "You better not."

"I won't. Don't you."

"I won't."

"Fine."

Schuyler reaches over and puts her fingers across from Alyssa's. The two of them slide the planchette around in a tiny circle and bring it to a stop.

"We just keep our fingers on it?" Alyssa says.

"We ask questions, and after a while it should move."

"Okay. What do we ask?"

"We have to concentrate first," Schuyler says. They look at each other. They close their eyes. I don't sense anything changing, or different at all.

I'm pretty sure I could reach over and move the planchette, but I think of Groan so I don't.

People have tried to talk to me with Ouija boards before, and it doesn't work. Craig and I fooled around with one once during that summer between sixth and seventh grade. We used the old version we found in his parents' collection of games and managed to creep ourselves out, somehow inventing an entity called Old Man Creak. I'd definitely been pushing the planchette. Craig, too.

And then about two years after I'd died, the guys tried to summon my ghost with that same Ouija board. Tenth grade, high school. It'd been the last year the three of them had still been really tight. After that, Craig started carrying his guitar to school all the time, growing his hair out, and using that sensitive artist schtick to impress girls. Mark was pretty much still Mark, focused on whatever weird thing obsessed him that week, but increasingly left behind as Craig waded ashore onto the foreign land of girls. Hugh's family bought a campground up in Maine, and they moved up there full-time. Friendship felt so permanent, but it wasn't.

The three of them pulled out the Ouija board and had at it. It wasn't at a sleepover—those had by then disappeared in the rearview mirror—but after school one afternoon. It was autumn, though not my death anniversary. Close to it. They did it in Craig's kitchen (his parents both worked, so they had the house to themselves). I give them credit for trying—I'm sure I'd have done the same thing. I'd known they were doing it not because of some ghostly summoning, but because they'd all been thinking about me. In fact, it was the most intense time I'd been able to blink into friends' lives, because they'd all been thinking about me at the same time. It was awesome and horrible at once. Awesome because I was out of my house for a while, and horrible because it reminded me of all I was missing. And would always miss. Forever.

The worst part about dying isn't that you're dead—it's that life goes on without you. All those moments and days and years and seasons, the sights and sounds that aren't for you anymore.

So I'd watched my best friends try to contact me. Could I move the planchette? No. Did it call to me in some supernatural way? No. Was there some channel of communication opened into the spirit world? No. Just three teenage boys, scaring themselves and exploring the edges of their grief. Oh, and they came up with answers. According to their Ouija session, I revealed to them that I was fine. That there was music in heaven (better than Rush, which amazed them). That I still thought Halloween was good. That I could see their futures—but wouldn't reveal them, other than to say that they were all destined for cool things. That being dead wasn't really that bad, in fact it was pretty awesome. Among other goofy nonsense.

See what I mean?

So what if it was bullshit. Those guys had faced the reality of death before they were ready for it (as if anyone's ready for it, but you get my point), and they'd hung together, for a while at least, and tried to find a way to explain it to themselves. Tested what their bonds of friendship were really made of. Those friendships didn't go on for all that much longer, sadly. But at least they'd helped each other through that first real patch of whitewater life showed them. Helped each other after childhood was truly and harshly ripped away.

I loved them. They were the best friends I ever had.

Alyssa and Schuyler hunch over the Ouija, intent on reaching out to the other side.

"What do we ask him?" Alyssa asks. Their fingertips nearly touch.

"Are you here?"

"Okay."

"You ask."

"Why me?"

"It's your house."

"I don't think that matters."

"It might. Just ask."

"Fine." Alyssa inhales, then speaks. "Are you here?"

After a few seconds, the planchette moves. Schuyler gives a little yelp. Both girls look at each other. Neither says it aloud, but both wear expressions that say: *you're doing that.* Then they look down again. The planchette moves to the word *Yes.* It's not me doing it.

"Schuyler," Alyssa says.

"Not me."

"I can see you doing it."

"I'm not doing it."

"You're leading it."

"I wasn't. I swear to God. Let's just keep asking things."

"I don't want to do this if you're just trying to scare me."

"I'm not."

"Okay." Alyssa closes her eyes, then opens them. "Are you the spirit that communicated with me before?"

The planchette moves again, drifting from the middle of the board to the word *Yes*. From my vantage, I can't tell who's moving it. I'm pretty sure they both are.

"Ask him if he watches you in the shower." Schuyler drags the planchette back to the center.

"I'm not asking that."

"I'll ask him."

"I thought we were being serious with this?"

"We are."

"How is that serious?"

"We need to have a conversation, get the words flowing."

"About me showering."

"It's communication, isn't it? And it's a thing, isn't it? You must have wondered. Just let me ask."

"I thought I'm supposed to ask him."

"We should investigate that."

"Changing your tune. Agenda."

Schuyler laughs. "Come on, let me just ask."

"Fine but annoying."

"He might be an annoying ghost. You should know." Schuyler clears her throat. "Do you watch Alyssa soaping up her sexy body?"

Alyssa shakes her head. The planchette slides up to the *Yes*.

Great.

There's no way I'm going to let her think I'm spying on her. I reach down between them and put my fingers on the planchette. The subtle sensation of contact is there. I swoop the planchette from *Yes* over to *No*. I couldn't have done that with a real Ouija board. Their fingers follow it.

"Did you feel that?" Schuyler says.

"That was weird."

"Were you doing that?"

"No."

They both sit back.

"Okay, he's not a perv," Alyssa says.

Schuyler looks around, then she puts her fingers back on the centered planchette. "Ghosts can lie."

"Not with a Ouija board."

"Since when?"

Alyssa smiles.

"My question next," Schuyler says. They put their fingers back.

"You just went."

"I have a follow-up."

"Fine. Go ahead."

"Spirit, are you gay?" Schuyler said.

Alyssa laughs.

Schuyler smiles, and continues. "Do you watch Mr. Cruz soaping up his body in the shower, reaching back to—"

"Gross." Alyssa takes her hands off the screen.

"Okay, okay. We'll just ask him if he's gay. He might be."

Alyssa puts her fingertips back onto the screen. "Fine."

"You ask."

"All right. Spirit, are you gay?"

I really don't want to get drawn into their Ouija session. Honestly. But, come on. I have no idea if any guy in my grade when I'd been in school had actually been gay. Possible, I guess. But I do know every guy in my grade lived in ever-present fear of being *called* gay. Things have clearly changed since then. It hasn't taken more than a few hours of watching TV with the Cruzes to see that. But as the planchette heads to *Yes* I reach in and bring it smoothly to *No.* Okay. I said my piece. I'm not going to jump in again.

"Maybe you're not his type," Schuyler says.

"Yeah, he'd definitely watch you. Over me."

"Maybe he would. Maybe blondes are his thing."

"Let's ask," Alyssa says. "Are blondes your thing?"

"No, ask him if he'd watch me in the shower."

Fingers on the planchette.

"Spirit," Alyssa says. "Would you watch Schuyler in the shower?"

"Don't just ask it that way," Schuyler says. "Here, I'll do it. Spirit, would you watch my tight, firm bod as I slowly caress each and every curve?"

Alyssa shakes her head. The planchette darts up to *Yes.* Wasn't me.

"Gee, the *spirit* seems pretty definitive on that," Alyssa says.

"I'm hot. I'd watch me, too," Schuyler says.

"Yes, great. Firmly established. Now can we get on to more serious questions?"

"It's still moving," Schuyler says.

The planchette moves down to the arc or letters that spanned the screen, landing on the *E.*

"Yeah, because you're moving it."

It shifts sideways.

"I'm not."

It stops on the *A.*

"Yes, you are."

Schuyler lifts her fingers from the screen. Alyssa's stay on it and the planchette moves again, with a jerk. It slides across the screen and stops at the *T.*

"Nice," Schuyler says. "*Eat.* And, busted."

Alyssa takes her hands off the screen. The planchette stops. "I wasn't doing that."

The planchette jerks across the screen and both girls gasp.

Neither one of them is touching the iPad. It isn't me—I'm not touching it.

"Oh my God," Schuyler says.

The planchette stops at the *Y*.

"How is that doing that?"

"It's the ghost."

The planchette slides to the left, stopping on *O*. Both girls look around the room. It's creeping me out, too.

"This is creeping me out," Schuyler says.

"I told you."

The planchette shifts slowly to the left, landing on the *U*.

"*Eat you*," Alyssa says. She and Schuyler look at each other. "Well, I guess we know who he prefers."

"I *am* pretty hot." Schuyler's voice has lost the playful tone, and it comes out as unconvincing.

I stand still and feel around the room. It's obnoxious. It has to be Groan. But—it's daytime. That doesn't happen. Also, I'm pretty sure he can't spell. I don't know why I'm sure of that—it's not like I've ever put that theory to the test. Sure, he's a genius at torment, but I've also heard him say stupid things often enough to give me what I think is a pretty solid peek behind the curtain.

"Okay," Alyssa says. "We didn't just imagine that, right?"

"We *definitely* didn't imagine it."

"I want to turn it off."

"No, don't." Schuyler puts her hand out. "This is what you want. Contact. Ask him his name."

"I don't think he can answer it—he couldn't before."

"With the Ouija, he probably can. Let's try."

They both stare at the screen. The planchette is still.

"What's your name?" Alyssa asks.

It doesn't move. A minute drags out. The three of us watch the screen.

"Maybe we need to be touching it," Schuyler says.

"We didn't before."

"No, we were touching it to start with." She has a point. Maybe I underestimated her.

I step back, suddenly wondering if Groan is using me as some sort of relay device.

"Fingers down, come on." Schuyler put her fingertips on the planchette. I float over to the far side of the living room, next to the doorway to the front hall. My closet is just on the other side of the wall, so as a way to test my idea, I slide backward through the wall, passing into the closet, keeping nothing but my face in the living room. If Groan is somehow using me to channel this energy into the Ouija board, maybe I can use the protection of the closet to shield myself, to stop him from being able to do anything. Of course, now I can't really see the screen.

Alyssa touches the screen, carefully, as though she thinks it might open into jaws and bite her hands off. Schuyler nods at her.

"What's your name?" Alyssa says.

They stiffen as the planchette moves. Their hands move in synchrony.

"*D*," Alyssa says.

D? What is that? I don't have a *D* in my name. I think about Groan, and guess he's going for any number of names for me: dickhead, dillweed, dipshit, dumbass, dogshit-breath, Dimothy.

"What's that?" Schuyler says.

"It's mostly on the *S*."

"I think it's mostly on the *T*."

"I can't tell."

"DT? DS? I don't get it."

"Those are his initials?" Alyssa says.

"It's still moving."

They go silent, watching. Schuyler frowns.

"Not even a letter," she says.

"Let's try it with our fingers off," Alyssa says.

They both lift their hands from the screen. After a few moments, they look at each other.

"Nope," Schuyler says.

Great. Groan is using *me* to channel his nasty self into the iPad. How? I have no idea—but it's clear that without me being right next to it, nothing's happening. I don't like it. And the more I think about it, the more uneasy I am.

He warned me not to so much as tap a screen again. I wonder if this counts.

30

———

I DON'T WANT TO GIVE GROAN ANOTHER CHANCE TO USE ME TO GET any kind of bead on them, so I leave the house and head out past the edge of the property, across the brook. The tether holds me back—but I think I'm farther than I've gotten before. (During the day, duh. Don't remind me.) Maybe by a yard? A little more?

"Kyle!"

I yell his name until his face shows up in the window of the back door, near the woodpile. The kid looks terrified. I motion for him to come outside. It takes him probably thirty seconds to screw up his courage. He slips through the door. Still looks hesitant.

"It's me," I say.

"How do I know?"

"It's daytime. And I look like me. Not like Groan."

"Who?"

"The demon."

"Scary Eyes?"

"Scary Eyes? That's what you call him?"

"It's what he makes me call him."

Definitely Groan. "Is he about this tall, messed-up long chin, big ears, pale, dark eyes?" I lift my hand about a foot and a half over my head. "Crappy clothes, like old-timey? Claws on his hands?"

"No."

Was there *another* demon? Oh God—do we each get our own personal demon? Hold it, no. I've seen Groan change his shape enough times to know it's possible. "No? Then what's he look like?"

Kyle doesn't look happy talking about it. "He's only a little taller than me. But his head is big and round. Like a beach ball. And his eyes are all black and really mean. His arms and legs are short, but his fingers are long and pointy. His feet, too. And he wears black pants and a white shirt with a jagged black stripe across it."

"Is he a dick?"

His eyes widen at the word, but he nods his head. "He's bad."

I'm still thinking it's him. Groan. Just with a different look. Maybe one that better fits each of us, what we find most frightening. Groan, the genius of cruelty.

"Karen calls him a wight," Kyle says. "From a book she read."

"Which house is hers?"

He points across the street to a brown-mustard-colored house on the corner of Chestnut and Field Drive. From what I can see of the side of it, it's got a couple dormer windows, a deck out back, and a wooden fence around the edge of the yard. It's about fifty yards away from Kyle's house.

"I need to talk to her," I say. "But I can't get any closer than this. Can you reach her house? During the day?"

"No. I can't get past the edge of the street. She can only get to the backyard fence."

"What about at night?"

"We can both get all the way. Or most of the way. I can get into her house, but not all the way to the front rooms. She can almost reach back here."

"Did you tell her about me yet?"

"She hasn't come by. I'm scared."

"Scared? Why?"

The kid clams up. He's looking at me, looking back to his house. Glances over in the direction of Karen's house.

"Kyle," I say.

"I shouldn't say."

"Shouldn't say what?"

"Anything."

"You can trust me."

He squints at me. "I don't know you."

"You—what?"

"Why should I trust you?"

"What do you think I'm going to do? Kill you? Rob you?"

"Trick me."

"Listen. Kyle. I'm a ghost. Like you. I'm not going to trick you."

"Of course you'd say that."

"Do you think Karen will trust me?"

He shakes his head.

"Why not?" I say.

"Why should she?"

"Because I'm a ghost. Like the two of you. And it's the same demon we're all dealing with. And we all live within a quarter mile of each other. And we all died here on Halloween in 1981. What more could we have in common? But you still don't think you can trust me? Think what you're saying, Kyle."

He stares at the snow for a little while, frowning. "But I only just met you."

I pace back and forth. I could cut him some slack. He's probably only ten, after all. But I'm not that patient at the moment. "True. But whatever. Here we are now. Right here. The two of us." I face him and spread my arms wide. "I'm as honest as they come. The bullshit came off me a long time ago."

Kyle frowned again. "You don't need to swear."

Oh, but I want to. This kid is getting annoying. "So when was the last time you saw Karen? Let's just take it from there."

"Last week. I already said."

"Well, what did she say? Anything?"

Now it's Kyle's turn to pace. I suddenly get it: he's that kid who just *has* to tell the teacher the other kids misbehaved. The one who makes sure to remind the teacher she hasn't given out the homework assignment yet. That kid. And for the past however many decades, Karen—twelve-year-old Karen—has been his teacher. So he looks at me like I'm the kid who stayed back a few grades. And uses bad words. He wants to tell Karen about me. Wants to tell *on* me. That's his specialty. But he can't.

"Okay, fine," I say. "Let's take another swing at it. Let me talk to Karen. When she gets back."

"She should already *be* back!" Kyle spits it out, little red spots showing up on his cheeks. And are those tears clinging to his eyelids? "She said she was going to take a look. That's all. Just a look."

"Whoa, whoa—slow down, Kyle. A look at what?"

He turns and kicks his foot through the powdery snow. If he hadn't been a ghost, it would've raised a respectable spray.

"At the way out," he says.

31

———

I stare at him. "Wait. What did you say?"

His face twists up. My theory is right. This is the worst for him —he should be tattling on *me* to the teacher, not the other way around. Goes against every bone in his little do-gooder body. He crosses his arms and shakes his head.

"Kyle—did you say a way *out*?"

He stares at the snow by his feet.

"What way out?" I say.

Again, he just shakes his head. Pouting.

"Kyle?"

"I'm not supposed to say anything."

"You're not supposed to say anything to Gr—to Scary Eyes. Karen never said anything about saying something to me. Right?"

"Still."

"Still? Still nothing. You should've said something right off the bat. *What* way out?"

"I don't know."

"Of course you know. You just said."

"But I don't know where. Or how. She wouldn't tell me."

There they go again, little ghost tears burbling up in his little ghost eyes. Okay, I get it. Karen's no dummy. She didn't tell him for his own good. I mean, look how quickly I got him to spill the info. If she didn't want him spilling the beans to Groan—whatever he calls himself with Kyle, or Karen for that matter—the best way was to not tell him any details. I think I may have a new hero, this Karen. Now I just have to figure out where she is.

"All right," I say. "Don't beat yourself up."

Looks like my words just inspire him to beat himself up harder, because now he's squeezing his arms and shaking his head. "But I wasn't supposed to say anything."

"Hey, hey—don't worry. I forced it out of you. I'm an older guy. Intimidating."

He glances at me.

"Fearsome, handsome, and charming," I continue. "How could anyone resist doing my bidding. Am I right?"

The humor doesn't exactly put a smile on his face, but it snaps him out of the dark place he twisted himself into. It's never easy to go against your nature. Especially if your nature is being *that* kid. And I feel for him. He's gone through what I've gone through, except probably even worse. I'm a dillweed who never knew what half the rules were in the first place. And sort of didn't care, now that I think about it. For me, getting lost in the afterlife makes a certain kind of sense. But for Kyle, whose world was made up of firm and bright rules—well, I can only imagine the confusion and frustration of things not working the way the rules said they should have.

"You're not those things," he announces.

"Come on now, Kyle—now you're just being hurtful." Before his eyebrows raise up any farther, I add, "Kidding. Come on. We're going to figure this out."

To my surprise, I add an enthusiastic, single clap. Like my old buddy Joe Papadakis.

•   •   •

Kyle's a sharp kid, his rigidity notwithstanding. So he doesn't have much in the way of a sense of humor. Maybe he would've grown up to be an accountant or something. But once he gets used to the idea I'm not some demon in disguise—and the even bigger issue that I'm not Karen—he lets it rip, everything he knows.

He points out Andy Van Etten's house. It's across the street from Karen's, two down. A small white ranch-style house, low slanting roof. And just past it, through the leafless maples, I catch a glimpse of the roof of Eleanor Gracie's house—from which a plate of home-made cookies baked in the first year of Ronald Reagan's presidency doomed a handful of kids to haunt a quiet neighborhood, seemingly forever. A chill runs through me. I haven't seen that house since.

"Have you been there?" I ask. "At night?"

"I told you I can't get that far. But Karen can."

"Could she be there now?"

"Not in the day. She can only reach it at night."

"Have you asked Andy? If he's seen her? At night."

He shakes his head.

I have an idea. "Let's ask him."

"Scary Eyes?" He turns and gives me a look. I might as well have just suggested the two of us eat turd pizza.

"Not Scary Eyes. Andy. Let's ask Andy."

"I told you. I can't reach him. And if I can't, you can't."

"Couldn't."

"What?"

"You couldn't. Maybe you can now. Have you tried?"

After a moment he gets it. Like I said, Kyle is sharp. I'm farther away than I've been in the past, even in the daytime— which means the tethers are loosening, which means what might have been impossible in the past might not be impossible any longer.

"Is Scary Eyes coming by tonight?" I say.

Kyle shakes his head. "He shouldn't."

"Then we're going to try to reach Andy. Tonight."

32

———

BUT FIRST I HAVE TO GET THROUGH GROAN, WHO, OF COURSE, PICKS tonight to make a visit.

As the daylight fades, I'm antsy. Not just nervous because of what I'm planning—though that's plenty, really. But I'm also feeling the restless, itchy alertness that Groan brings on. He's out there. Close by. So instead of cruising past the boundary of the tether, I'm sticking near the closet.

Oh, and it's Christmas Eve.

The Cruz family brought in a fragrant Christmas tree a few days back. With the move, they did it pretty last minute, and it hadn't seemed like a big deal to anyone but Jacinta, who decorated the tree until it looked like it'd rolled down a hill where an ornament truck crashed. Still, points for enthusiasm.

Keeping one eye out for Groan, I watch the Cruz family. They're keeping it low-key. I like them. A lot of jokes go around. They like to needle each other, even Jacinta. She gets in on the action, too—usually it's pretty obvious stuff, but she does it with a twinkle in her eye, barely able to contain her own laughter, which is adorable. I can tell they all feel they've opened up their life by buying the house. That life is going their way.

Jacinta opens an odd-shaped package that looks soft—many of her gifts fall into that category—and reveals a big mouse, about a foot tall. She yells *"He's adoooooorable!"* and mashes him to her chest, rocking him back and forth. Her folks smile, no doubt having been through this routine more than once. As Jacinta runs from the room to collect more of her stuffed rodents, she holds her new friend up for me to see. She doesn't really slow, just smiles at me.

Which is how Groan catches me unawares. Sneaky bastard. His hand clamps around my ankle and snatches me off my feet, dragging me through the walls until we're out in the cold breezeway. Before I can scramble away, Groan flips me onto my back and sits on my chest, pinning me down.

"What'd you get me for Christmas, jerkoff? A racecar? A BB gun?" His face leers over me, his stench filling the air. He frowns. "Nothing? Oh, come on. Seriously. Aren't we pals? Aren't we practically family? And you didn't get me anything?"

I try to buck him off me. I knock him around a little—but he's stronger and it doesn't take much effort on his part to slam me still.

"Jesus, what're you trying to do?" he says. "Are you trying to have sex with me or something? I think you've gotten the wrong idea, buddy. I don't diddle my friends."

He smiles.

"Oh, I see." He nods toward the living room. "You've got diddling on the brain. Because of what's-her-face. She's a morsel, isn't she?"

He licks his lips, his tongue like a pale sea creature.

"You'd take a slice of that pie," he says, wiggling his eyebrows. He shakes his head. "Actually, probably not. She's too much woman for you—don't get your hopes up. The best you're ever going to get is wanking your spanker as you goggle her bending over. That's my bet, and my bets are always bull's-eyes."

"Get off," I grunt.

"You want to get off on me? You're disgusting."

"No, get off me," I squeeze out.

"But you haven't seen my present yet." He rolls his horrid eyes. "Way to ruin Christmas, you little shit. Here I was, going to make a friendly visit, a caring gesture—and you're acting like you don't even want to see me. Again." He reaches down and grabs my face, squeezing my cheeks between his thumb and fingers, forcing me to look at him. "Don't you want to see me?"

"No." I'm tired of his crap.

"Oh, you're not doing this again, are you?"

"I said no. Get off me."

"You sound like a real dick." He squeezes my face harder. "It's Christmas frigging Eve. And even though I'm busy day and night, I thought I'd take the time. Make the effort. Seriously."

I try to shake his hand free, but he clamps on.

"Get off," I say, my voice muffled by his cold hand.

"Maybe you'll stop acting like such an ungrateful jerk once you see what I got you for Christmas," he says. "Here."

He coughs, once, twice, then lifts his free hand up to his mouth as he gags. He opens his mouth wide as something crawls out of it and into his palm. A string of pale fluid spills down between his fingers. He turns his head and spits, making a face like he'd just tasted something bitter and vile. He stifles another gag. I look away. He twists my head again until I'm staring straight up.

"I got you a pet." He clears his throat, a bubbling, viscous sound. He flips his hand around, holding a large, fleshy spider, pinkish gray, almost the size of a kitten. Its legs curl and straighten. A slender stinger extends off the thing's back end, whipping back and forth. Its underside is smeared with something nasty that reminds me of the green stuff inside the backs of lobsters. "His name is Lollipop—but don't really lick him. He's poisonous."

He lowers the spider-thing down to my face. I thrash back and forth. One of its legs brushes my face. Groan drops him.

"Oops—where'd he go?" Groan says, mock surprise on his face. I hear a hissing and the slapping of wet legs as the thing scrambles off into the darkness of the breezeway. "Oh, well. He'll find you later, probably. You'll need some kind of a cage or something—he can be pretty ornery, and he's got a nasty bite. Though, really, it's the sting you have to look out for. That'll make you blind."

He scooches back until he's just crushing my legs, then pulls me up by my shoulders until I'm looking right at him.

"So what do you think?" he says. "Pretty cool, huh? I was trying to come up with the ultimate gift, and I realized a venomous spider-wasp from where I come from would be perfect. It's considered to be good luck. Kind of a compliment, too—those things are almost impossible to keep as pets, since they're so dangerous, but I think you can handle it. Do you love it?"

So far, he hasn't mentioned anything about me communicating with Alyssa. Or Kyle, for that matter. I take that as a good sign. Still, sooner he leaves, the easier I'll breathe. And the only way to get him to leave is to play along.

"Sure, yeah," I say. "It's great."

"How great? *Really* great?"

"Yeah. Really great. Thank you."

He tilts his head, smiling. "You want another one? Because I might have one more." He starts hocking up something.

"No, no—that's fine," I say. "I love it. I really love it."

"You're sure?"

I nod, fast. "Positive. I love Lollipop—he's the best."

"*He's* the best?" Groan says, narrowing his eyes.

"You're the best," I say. "You are. You give the best presents. Seriously."

He sighs, smiling. The noxious stench makes me want to puke.

"Aww," he says. "See? We *can* be friends, if we both try. That's not just the Christmas spirit talking, either. That's from right here."

He extends one long, pointy finger and jams it through his moldering shirt and jacket, puncturing his chest and causing dark blood to squirt out. His shirt soaks through fast.

"So what'd you get me?" he asks.

"I—I—" I don't know what to say.

"You didn't get me *anything*?" he says, sounding disappointed. "What the hell?"

He looks morose, all his weird features turned down—but then he breaks into a chilling smile.

"Aw, I'm messing with you, buddy," he says. "I know you couldn't get out to get me anything. I mean, we never really exchange gifts or anything, so this was totally just me, going out of my way to surprise you. Maybe next year you can get me something."

I nod.

"Yeah?" he says.

"Yes."

"What would you get me?"

"I don't know. I think—I'm not sure. What—what do you like?"

"Just guess. Name something cool. You know me pretty well. Or at least I hope you do."

I can feel his anger starting to work itself up.

"What about a record or something?" I can't think of anything.

"A record? What would I play it on? Besides, I hate music. Try again."

"How about a knife?" I'm off balance.

"Ooooh." He draws the word out, a twinkle in his eyes. "Now we're talking. A knife would be excellent. Not a kitchen knife, though, right?"

"No. Like a big knife."

"For stabbing?"

"Sure."

"For skinning and slicing?"

"Yes."

He looks at me, then nods appreciatively. "There you go. I'd *love* a stabby knife. You know me—and I was right about you, Timothy. You'd be a great gift giver. Thought that counts and everything. Nice."

He gets off of me, then extends a hand down to help me to my feet. I cringe. He's done that so many times, and each time, it turns into something horrible. He keeps his hand out, reaching closer.

Fine.

I grasp his hand and he yanks me upright. He lets go of me, looking out the storm door. He glances back at me.

"Gotta boogie," he says. "But enjoy your present. Merry Christmas. I can't wait until next year to see my knife—seriously, that'll be amazing."

I watch him, waiting for the blow that's sure to come.

"We good?" he says.

"Sure. Yeah."

"Merry what?" he says, frowning and inclining his head.

"Merry Christmas."

"Merry Christmas *who* . . ."

"Merry Christmas, Mr. Groan."

He smiles, wide and horrifying. "And Merry Christmas, Timothy." With that, he turns and walks through the wall. I watch him stride across the snowy lawn, pass underneath the glare of a streetlight, then disappear into the night. I look around, terrified of the shadows in the breezeway, the corners where Lollipop had crawled off into. I sprint back into the house, hurrying to the closet.

As soon as I'm back inside, I calm down. I think back over his whole lunatic spiel. Then I see it. I nod, relieved. He hadn't mentioned anything about my communicating with Alyssa. Nothing about the Ouija episode. Nothing about Kyle. Nothing about his earlier threats. Maybe he's saving up for something nastier—I can't discount that. But maybe he has something else on his mind, so he's not paying as close attention to me as he should. Something like: Where's Karen gone to?

If that's the case and Groan's starting to lose track of his cruel promises, I'll take it.

Because I've got work to do.

33

INSTEAD OF COWERING IN MY CLOSET FOR THE REST OF THE NIGHT, I only wait about ten minutes after Groan leaves. Because, fuck him. Also, because I think he's rattled and not keeping particularly good track of things. His pattern is off. He's improvising, giving me nothing more than a half-assed visit to keep me thinking everything's fine. If Karen figured out a system to get around at night, dodging Groan—well, then I'll take a cue from her. The yard looks empty, still underneath a clear sky, the snow on the ground and in the trees contoured and catching the starlight. The road is black, not much traffic, befitting Christmas Eve. The Cruz family is still in the living room, having fun.

Okay, here goes.

I slip through the wall. Cut through the shrubs with their crowns of snow until I'm past the garage, looking down the slope to the brook. I scan the edges of the yard for Groan. Don't see him. More importantly, I don't feel him. I pass down the yard in the shadows of the hemlocks, and cross over the black ribbon of the brook. Just like before, when I think I should be reaching the end of my tether, nothing holds me back. I still can't get used to it —it's as though I've learned how to walk up a wall, or something.

I reach Kyle's yard and pause. Could Groan be here? Kyle didn't think he was on the schedule for tonight—but I'm suddenly not sure. Groan knew it was Christmas Eve, after all. Why would he pass up an opportunity to torture the other kids the same way he did me? Hideous spider-wasps all around, ho ho ho. He could also be waiting for me to do something stupid like this.

Looking back at the house, I see the lights on. The stars glimmering overhead, silhouetting the peak of the roof, the chimney. I think of how many nights—both good and terrible—I've spent there. The best and the worst nights of my life. And death. For some reason, I think of my mom. She cried at beauty, it was one of her things. Really, she was one of those people who was pretty much *too* sensitive for the world. She would've loved the view I'm taking in. The house, cozy under the wondrous stars on Christmas Eve.

Where is she now? The stars, if they have the answer, aren't saying.

I turn back to Kyle's house.

Because I'm damn well done hiding.

Kyle sees me before I even reach the woodpile, his pale face peering out the window in the back door. He slips through.

"Where were you?" he says.

I ignore the whining tone. "Had a little hang-up. Don't worry about it. You ready?"

"I've been waiting for hours."

"At least you're not waiting for hours more. I'm here. Let's go."

"I don't think we'll reach it."

"So you've been waiting for hours to tell me we're not going to be able to do this?"

"Well, yeah."

"Did you try? While you were waiting?"

"No." He said it like it was the dumbest question he'd ever heard.

"If you have a theory, Kyle—you should test it."

"But what if—"

"Come on. I'm giving you a hard time. Look, I'm here. The theory is right over there." I sweep my arm in the direction of the main road. "Let's go test it. Right?"

"I don't think we'll reach it."

"As you've said, yes."

"I'm not going."

"So you waited for hours not only to tell me you think I'm wrong, but also that you're not doing it? So, really, you've been waiting to complain."

"Well, no."

"Come on, Kyle."

"Okay. Yes."

"What would Karen do?"

"What?"

"You heard me."

That got him. He wants to tell the other kids in class not to misbehave while the teacher's out of the room. Every instinct inside him wants that. But I just turned it back on him. Because the teacher would test the hypothesis, wouldn't she? He's standing there, basically biting his lip and frowning, caught between two powerful urges.

"Come on—you know what she'd do," I say. "Because she's already done it. She's over there, somewhere. Out there. Let's go find her. Okay?"

I get the sense that Kyle's not the type to settle his mind without overthinking the situation, so I just head off around the side of his house. Like I figured, he scoots after me a couple of moments later.

"I still don't think it's going to work," he has to add.

"You might be right. Only one way to find out. Let's do it."

As before, I feel nothing but exhilaration at being somewhere I haven't been in decades. The night grows clearer. More detailed. I even feel like I'm *thinking* more clearly. Coming around the far side of the house, I get a stunning view of Field Drive running downhill to my right, the road a soft blue-black between the snowbanks left by the plows. Houses have their lights on inside. Christmas lights—in fine, sharp blues, golds, whites; brighter and smaller than anything I'd grown up with—drape small trees, bushes. I've never seen such amazing lights. A few houses down, a giant inflatable snowman holds a six-foot-tall peppermint stick.

Holy night.

Don't get me wrong. After all I've been through, I'm not religious. Too many complaints about the management to even think there's a management. But something hits me. A feeling. There's *something* in the night. Winding in between, among, through. It was here before I was born. It remained after I died. It'll be here after *everyone* on this street who's alive and enjoying another night with their loved ones, or by themselves, is dead and gone. It's all around. In the snow. In the wind. In the stars. If that's not holy, then I don't know what is.

I bring my gaze back around to Karen's house. "Come on, Kyle. This way."

Karen's house is dark, save for two windows around front that hold single electric candles inside.

"I don't feel anything holding me back," I say. "Do you?"

"Not yet."

We go ten more paces. "Anything?"

Kyle stops. "This is where I should feel it."

"Do you?"

"No."

"Don't sound so excited, Kyle."

"But I usually can't get any farther."

"How about me? I'm farther out than you."

"I don't understand it."

"Maybe Karen's figured it out. Come on." I didn't like standing there in the open, arguing with Kyle. But so far, so good. Still, I don't feel like blowing the opportunity by being extra stupid. I step out into the street. A lone car is heading our way, from the direction of the center of town. More Christmas lights. How have I missed how amazing those have become? Andy's house is dark. No holiday lights, no candles in the windows. A wreath hangs on the door. Each step I take, I'm convinced I'm about to feel the inarguable pull of the tether. To the point where I'm practically generating the feeling on my own. But we reach the other side of the road just fine. Kyle and I exchange a look.

"See?" I say. "Rules are made to be broken, buddy."

He frowns. "Not really."

I turn my attention to the house. "Karen can reach here at night?"

"Yes."

"How much farther can she get?"

"I don't know."

I look down the street. The headlights of the approaching car come like a wave, bringing in detail as it washes over the driveways, the streetlights, the maples above the wires. "How far do you think we can get?"

"I don't know."

I want to test it—but I also want to get to Andy. "We'll figure it out later. Come on." We head up to the front door. The look on Kyle's face tells me he's surprised that he made it this far. I probably have that same kind of look, too—I was pretty sure I was right, but I've been wrong enough before to leave it an open question. Until now. A curving walkway from the driveway to the door is shoveled. Before going any farther, I scan the area for Groan, but, like before, don't see him. Don't feel him. I turn to Kyle. "See? We made it."

"What if he saw us?"

"Did Scary Eyes show up tonight?"

"Don't even talk about him."

"Well—did he?"

"No." That single word says a lot, the way Kyle drops it on me. *Would I be standing here with you if Scary Eyes had visited, probably killing me? Do you think I'd be running around outside with you if he had? How dumb are you?*

"Just checking. Relax."

Kyle pushes ahead of me and slips through the front door.

"Maybe you should go first," I say after him.

"Andy knows me."

By this point, I'm expecting Andy to be yet another Einstein on a street full of them. With their signals. Their communication. Their plans. And then there's me, the ghost who thought he was all alone for almost forty years. Good thing my pride has already been ground to dust beneath Groan's nasty foot, otherwise I'd take it personally.

I duck in after Kyle just as the car passes. I'm standing in a short entryway. On the other side is a rectangular mirror over a narrow table. A wooden bowl holds a decorative bouquet of pine cones. The entryway opens out into a wide hallway that leads back to a kitchen. To the left is a living room. A door, to the cellar, I'm guessing, is next to the kitchen. Just past it is a hallway heading off to the right. I see a couple of bedrooms.

"Andy—it's me, Kyle." Kyle heads straight back to the kitchen.

Once again, I'm awestruck at being somewhere else, in someone else's home. Everything looks interesting to me. The rugs. The collection of blue glass bottles by one of the windows. A low bookcase with a record player on it and a row of LPs filling the top shelf. A recliner. A painting of a wooded lake. I smell a hint of cedar trunk and mothballs.

"Kyle?" a faint voice calls out.

"I'm here," Kyle says.

I follow him into the kitchen. A light over the sink is on. To the right, an oval table and chairs stand before a set of sliding doors that open onto what looks like a decent-sized deck. Before I can get much of a look at the rest of the kitchen, a little kid in a Spider-Man costume crawls out through the door of one of the cabinets beneath the sink. His crazy blond hair, which looks almost white, flies away from his head like doll hair. Bangs. A style I was more than familiar with having grown up in the seventies. What kills me is that he's still wearing his Halloween costume, just like I'm still wearing the clothes I died in. All these years later. His costume.

He's getting to his feet when he spots me. His eyes go wide and he turns and jams back into the cabinet, slipping through the door.

That's where he hides?

Now I'm pissed. He's just the ghost of a little kid. Hell, even Kyle is only ten. And the look Andy gave me said it all. Can you imagine being a little kid, terrified for thirty-eight years? Hiding in a cabinet under the sink?

"Tell him I'm okay," I say to Kyle.

"Go away!" Andy yells from inside the cabinet.

"He's okay," Kyle says.

I turn to Kyle. "You could say it like you mean it."

"I said what you told me to."

"Yeah, you said it like a hostage."

"But you told me."

"Say it like *you'd* say it. Come on."

Kyle has no patience with my vague instructions. I suspect he needs an insightful lecture on the renegade freedoms enjoyed by independent thinkers such as myself—but it's not the time. I motion with my hand instead: *hurry up, before the kid gives himself a hernia.*

"Andy," Kyle says. "He's a guy from up the street. He's a ghost. Same as us."

"I want Karen!"

"Me, too. Come out, it's okay."

"I don't like him!"

"He's—not bad."

"Thanks, Kyle," I say.

Silence from beneath the sink.

"I promise," Kyle adds.

"Make him go away," Andy says. At least he's not shouting.

Kyle kind of looks like he wishes I *would* go away, but I've gotten used to that. I go over to the sink and crouch next to the cabinet door.

"Andy, my name is Timothy Lane. You can call me Tim."

Silence.

"I'm from down the street," I continue. "The brown house two down from the circle up that way."

"But I don't know you," comes the reply.

"I know. We haven't met. Because I'm kind of a dummy sometimes. Right, Kyle?"

Kyle raises his eyebrows and turns his mouth into a little sideways comma.

"Go on," I say. "I don't mind."

"He crashed into the woodpile in my yard," Kyle says.

"See, Andy?" I say. "What kind of dummy would crash into a woodpile?"

Silence. "Why'd you crash into a woodpile?"

"Because I was so excited to see Kyle that I ran as fast as the Road Runner. And I forgot to stop."

Silence. "You're as fast as the Road Runner?"

"What do you think, Kyle? Am I as fast as the Road Runner?"

"Maybe faster," Kyle says.

Good. He's catching on.

"The Road Runner is silly," Andy says after a few more beats of silence.

"I can be pretty silly. Right, Kyle?"

"No TNT near you," Kyle says.

"Good thinking," I agree.

Silence. "Because you'd blow yourself up?" *Blow* comes out sounding like *b-woe*.

"I would *totally* blow myself up. That's how silly I am. I should probably also stay away from cliffs."

"Because you'd run off them," Andy says.

"I would. And I'd better look out for giant one hundred ton weights."

"It's the coyote who usually gets the weights dropped on him," Kyle adds.

I give him an annoyed look. "See how silly I am, Andy? Good thing Kyle is around to point it out." I turn back to the cabinet. "I'm sorry it's taken me so long to say hi to you, Andy. Sometimes I'm too silly for my own good."

After a few moments, Andy leans his head out through the cabinet door, giving me a disarmingly direct look. "I want to see."

"How silly I am?"

"How you're fast like Road Runner."

"Sure thing. Check this out." I straighten up. Look around. Go flying off through the kitchen, down the hall, cutting through the living room, which circles back around to where the table is, spinning my legs as crazily as I can. When I reach the kitchen again, I tumble through the fridge and into the bathroom on the other side of it, letting out an operatic "Ohhhh, noooo!"

I poke my head back into the kitchen. "See? Told you."

Andy breaks into a smile. "Again."

So I do it again. And again. And again. Takes me about ten circuits and mock crashes before Andy decides I'm not just okay, I'm better than okay. He climbs out from under the sink. "You're funny."

"I think you're pretty funny, too," I say. "Boy, I wish we'd met sooner."

"Yeah. Sooner." Another big smile.

I want to punch Groan in his stupid fucking face. What's he

put this little kid through over the past four decades? I can only imagine.

"So you know who I really want to meet, Andy? I want to meet Karen. Kyle says she's awesome. Do you know where she is?"

Andy's brows scrunch down. "She's gone to help us."

"Gone?"

"I think he means *going*," Kyle says.

"Karen's *going* to help us?" I ask.

"Gone."

Kyle and I exchange a look.

"Which way did she go?" I say.

Andy marches to the hallway and down it. Kyle and I go after him. At the far end is a wooden trunk beneath a window. Andy climbs up on it and looks out the window. He points. "She went that way."

Kyle and I stand behind him, looking out the window. Chestnut Street heads that way, cutting a gently curving line south for a mile before it reaches downtown.

"Are you sure?" I ask.

Andy nods.

"Why that way?" Kyle says. "She can't go that way. Not far."

"She did."

"That's the way out? She said that?" I ask.

"She said she's coming back."

"Has she?"

"No. Not yet."

"But why that way?" Kyle says in his *this doesn't make sense and I'm not moving on until I make that abundantly clear* way.

"Because the sunset," Andy says.

"No." Kyle points out. "It's that way." He motions to the right with his cocked thumb.

"Karen said it was *that* way." Andy points down the length of Chestnut Street again.

"What else did she say, Andy?" I ask. "Anything?"

"That she'd seen fire."

I don't know what he means, so I turn to him. "Fire?"

"It's harder to hide it now."

"To hide—the fire?"

"And then she went that way," Andy says. He points, his hand moving through the glass.

"You watched her go?"

Kyle leans, looking out the window. "How far did she get?"

"Far."

"How far?"

Andy shrugs. "I had to stop watching. Flibber."

Flibber? I turn to Kyle.

He's staring at Andy. "He saw you?"

Andy shakes his head. "He saw Karen. He followed her." It comes out like *fa-woed*.

Kyle turns to me. *Who's Flibber?* I mouth to him. Kyle puts his hands up to his eyes and opens his fingers, big and creepy.

Scary Eyes.

Groan.

We make a little expedition, the three of us, into Andy's yard. I go first, scanning all over for Groan, aka Scary Eyes, aka Flibber. I don't see him, don't sense him. As I look off south along Chestnut Street, I wonder what he's done to Karen. If she really hasn't been back in nearly a week, that can't be good. But I'm also thinking back to how quickly he split from my house earlier in the evening. What was that all about? I take a full circuit of the yard. Back around the side of the house where Andy pointed out Karen's route, I wave the all clear. Kyle comes out first. Andy's next, looking terrified.

"You're sure she went this way?" I ask Andy.

"Yes."

"Should we try it?"

Andy shakes his head. He clearly doesn't believe the coast is clear.

"I think one of us should try it," I say. "I'll do it. You guys keep a lookout back inside."

"Is this smart?" Kyle says.

Judging from my track record, probably not. Still, gotta find out.

"Is Karen smart?" I say.

"Yes."

"Then this is the way Karen went. Worth a try?"

Kyle doesn't like that, being tugged between his urges to dismiss me and to venerate Karen. Finally, he nods, clearly not pleased.

"Look, I won't go too far. I just want to see where she went." And *why* she went this way. Oh, and *how* she went this way.

"You'll come back, right?" Kyle says.

"Don't worry. I'm not going to ditch you guys. Now get inside."

Once they're back in Andy's house, I head off, crossing the yard, staying parallel to the sidewalk and street. I pass a birdbath near the edge of the yard. A tiny strip of young trees separates Andy's yard from the one beyond. As I pass through that, I feel it —the first touches of the tether.

But Karen went this way.

I keep going. And the tether keeps getting stronger. Maybe there's some trick to it Karen figured out. Like it gives way, eventually. Snaps. Or starts lessening. Or something. But it sure doesn't seem like it. I'm not much more than halfway across the next yard when it feels like I'm climbing a good slope with a backpack filled with field stones. I keep going.

Until I can't.

And, really, I can't. I'm walking in place. I throw everything I have into it, but it's like leaning into the world's worst storm. The harder I press, the more I start to slide back. I veer to the left, then the right, looking for some gap, some exit Karen found. Nothing. Not a single thing. I can't get an inch farther.

Because the sunset. She'd seen fire.

I don't see any sunset, or any fire. What had Karen meant? What had she found? I look and think, but come up empty. No clue. No idea. No way out. Nothing but the stars overhead as the world tumbles through another Christmas Eve.

Hopefully, the swear word I let rip into the night doesn't change Andy's newfound opinion of me as a funny guy.

34

———

Come morning I have a lot on my mind.

But the first thing I do is search the house for Lollipop the spider-wasp. Merry freaking Christmas, right? I want—no, *need*—to know that Lollipop faded with daylight. While I'm searching, the Cruz family makes pancakes and opens presents. I leave them to it, not wanting to fend off memories of all the Christmases I spent in that very room with my family, back when all of us had been alive and mindlessly happy. I don't need the reminder.

So to cheer myself up I search for a spider from Hell.

And I search everywhere. Under every piece of furniture. In every corner. Inside the walls. In the eaves. Down in the cellar. Up in the crawlspace attic. I'm as thorough as possible, and I don't find a sign of it, so that's encouraging. Just another one of Groan's torture sessions, hopefully.

By the time I'm done, the presents are opened, the torn paper picked up and crumpled into the trash, ribbons saved, cards stacked on the end table. The kitchen smells like fresh coffee as Alejandro helps Jacinta assemble some kind of dollhouse that looks like it has about five hundred pieces (and when I say *help*, I mean *does it all* in the face of her constant incorrect suggestions as to how to do it). I find Alyssa up in her room. On her computer, surprise. She's messing around with a bracelet, connecting it to her computer. She's got her iPad open. It's got instructions.

Because the sunset. She'd seen fire.

I hesitate for a minute. Maybe Groan's playing some kind of clever long game. Classic misdirection. Waiting to catch me in another misstep. But my questions aren't going to answer themselves. I reach over Alyssa's shoulder and tap the yellow notepad thing. She gasps and sits back.

I type, *Sorry, didn't mean to startle you.*

She pushes her chair back, looking at the desk, the air above it, then back at what I typed.

"Timothy?" she whispers.

Now it's my turn to gasp. I go to type, then pause. Then settle on hitting the question mark.

"You're the ghost, aren't you? Timothy Lane?"

How do you know? I type.

"I did some research. You're one of the ones from that Halloween, right? Back in 1981?"

I am.

"And we talked to you on the Ouija?"

Kind of. That wasn't all me. I didn't say the rude thing.

"Eat me."

That's it.

"Then who said it?"

A demon.

She turns and paces the room, shaking her head. "Okay, that's bad."

A little bit worse, actually.

"Oh, God."

He can't hurt you. Only me.

"What does that mean?"

It's complicated. I'm not even really sure—but he can't do anything to most living people. Only dead people.

"I've never heard that."

Me, either, but take my word for it.

"How do I know you're not a demon? Isn't this exactly what a demon would do? They're sneaky. I've watched videos."

Maybe there's a test? I don't know.

"Then why can't you tell me your name?" she says, turning to the iPad. "That's the mark of a demon."

Had I ever asked Groan if that was his *real* name? I don't think I ever had, no. I always assumed his real name wasn't really a name, I guess. Does a great white shark have a name? Because that's what I think of Groan, when it comes down to it. He isn't a person, he's a predator. As for my name—well, I'd been able to tell Kyle and Andy.

I think it might be the mark of a ghost. Like they can't tell the living.

"Why?"

Great question. I don't know. I don't have a lot of answers.

She nods slowly, taking a deep breath. "Okay. Let's start at the beginning. You were fourteen when you died, weren't you?"

The stab of shame I feel takes me by surprise. Busted. Fine. I'm not going to dig myself any deeper into a lie.

Yes.

She folds her hands in her lap. Purses her lips. "Why'd you tell me seventeen?"

Because I'm an idiot. Trying to show off.

"I'm not sure how that's showing off," she says after making me squirm for a little bit.

I'm an idiot, like I said. Look, I never got fluent in *girl*. Further explanations will only garble the issue.

"All right, fine. Don't worry about it. You lived here?"

Yes.

"And you died here?"

Yes.

"In this room?"

No. I died just outside the bathroom. And no, I don't hang around in there. Watching or anything. When anyone is doing...anything. Your friend is wrong.

"But you could," she asks.

I could, I guess. But I wouldn't.

She doesn't look one hundred percent convinced, and I can't blame her.

"Not your type?" she says, with a cautious smile.

Ha ha. Your friend is wrong. I don't know.

I have no idea what I'm typing. I hadn't known how to talk with girls when I was alive. Somehow I haven't gotten any better in four decades of wandering around my childhood home, alone. Alyssa stares at the iPad.

But you're pretty. That's not what I don't know.

Again. I am an idiot.

I'll stop typing right now.

She waves her hand and shakes her head. I can't tell if she's upset or maybe a little pleased. She looks around the room.

"Have you tried to leave?"

Duh—why didn't I think of that?

"Oh, of course." A little blush creeps up her throat. "Sorry."

No, it's fine. I can only get a little ways down the street. Then I can't go any farther.

"And you were poisoned."

Murdered.

"By the old lady. Mrs. Gracie."

No. By the demon. He took her over—it's the one thing demons can do to the living, I think. And they have to be going senile or something.

"Oh my God. Hold it—is it the same one who did the thing with the Ouija?"

Yes.

"Why's it still here?"

That's a great question.

"It's been here the whole time?"

He comes and goes.

"That's horrifying."

You get used to it.

"Seriously?"

Seriously.

"Can you get rid of it?"

He pretty much does what he wants.

"It's a *he*?"

Yeah, I think so. I mean, he looks like a he—but he's pretty much a monster.

"There's got to be something you can do," she said.

I've tried everything.

"Praying?"

Yes.

"What about your death anniversary? Or your birthday?"

?

"I mean, maybe there's a certain time when you can leave?"

Yes. Tried those. Don't work.

"Can you banish him or something? Like an exorcism?"

Never tried. I doubt it.

"What if a priest could?"

Not sure. I have my doubts. My mother's cousin was a Roman Catholic priest, and he'd been over at the house a half dozen times over the years when she'd still been alive, visiting from Rochester. He wasn't any more sensitive to me than anyone else. Maybe even less sensitive, because I'd tried to get his attention. He'd been more into the wine. And there was no special glow about him, he wasn't brighter in the spirit world, his collar didn't blaze like a beacon. Even when he'd been saying grace before a meal, no special magic was going on. So, yeah. Doubts.

Alyssa shudders. "Is he here right now?"

No. He only shows up at night.

"But we didn't use the Ouija board app at night?"

I know. That was weird. That's never happened before.

"So is he getting stronger?"

I don't know. I don't think so.

She's no dummy, those are good questions. I don't know. That's the maddening thing about this chess game I'm playing with Groan. I can't see the pieces until they strike. Half the time, I can't even see the board.

But maybe now I have an advantage I never had before.

Listen, I type. *What else did you find out?*

"About you dying?"

About the other kids who died.

"Oh, yeah." She sits down in front of her computer, giving a couple of wary glances around. She clicks here and there until she brings up a recording of a show. "I found this."

When she sets it to playing, it shows a guy with a beard and tattoos—and, holy shit, he's standing in front of Karen's house. It's sunset. The guy looks at the camera. "If you grew up any time since the 1980s, you probably never got anything for Halloween that wasn't wrapped, sealed, and protected. The reason for that is along this stretch of Chestnut Street in Andover, Massachusetts, where in 1981, four children died after eating cookies accidentally poisoned by an elderly neighbor . . ."

The show cuts to a montage of footage from the news at the time. Headlines from the *Boston Globe*. Grainy Instamatic pictures of Kyle, Andy, a dark-haired girl who has to be Karen—and a horrible picture of me holding a shark jaw from when I'd gone on my fifth-grade field trip to Cape Cod. The footage cuts to modern-day shots of the street, including my house. Looks like it was filmed in the autumn, naturally, but I spot my dad's old Toyota in the driveway, which meant it was filmed at least six years ago, because Beth made him get rid of it after the front end got clipped by a snow plow (he'd been convinced it was still perfectly fine, even missing half the front bumper and with one headlight shining walleyed to the right).

And then there's a picture of Mrs. Eleanor Gracie along with footage of her house.

"Is this one of the most haunted neighborhoods in America?" says the host, now standing on Mrs. Gracie's front steps. "We're going to take a look and find out."

Okay, so I immediately don't like this guy. First of all, who has that many tattoos? And his baseball cap has a completely flat brim. But really, it's his smug attitude. Like he's the first person to guess my street might be haunted.

Is this where you got my name from? I type.

"No," Alyssa says. "You're just mentioned as like 'two others' or something. But this led me to the other stuff. I found articles from the time. There's even a Wikipedia page about it. It's crazy."

Wikipedia? I have no clue—but she makes it sound important. The show is still playing. Looks like tattoo guy spent the night in Karen's house during a stretch of time it wasn't occupied. Seems like a lot of nonsense. Shaky cameras. Night-vision filming. Shots of dark doorways and cellar stairs.

"Can you imagine how brave this guy is?" Alyssa says. "Going into the most haunted places in America like that? At night. Actually looking for demons and ghosts."

Uh, excuse me—I've been, apparently, living in one of America's most haunted neighborhoods for thirty-eight years. With a demon. A real one, not some little fart of distortion on some recording. How brave does that make me?

Don't answer that.

The show's only twenty-something minutes long, with the commercials. A lot of questions, not a lot of answers. And brave tattoo guy ends it with some dumb cracks about Halloween, like he's just done something daring—but not so daring that he's lost his sense of humor. It's not like I learn anything.

What else did you find? I type.

Alyssa flicks through some other squares. "This is where I found your name."

The article she shows me gives a decent overview of what happened, nothing terribly surprising. But it does list our names and ages. There's me. Then Karen Jarvis, 12. Kyle O'Brien, 10. Andy Van Etten, 4.

Are there street addresses? I type.

"Um, I think so. Somewhere. No, I definitely saw them, because that's where I saw the address for this house," Alyssa says. "I should probably get in touch with Tony."

Tony?

"Tony Eagleton. From the show."

Sure. I can give him some advice on baseball caps.

"You're funny," she says absently as she types. I look back at the frozen ending of Tony the ghost master's show. It's weird to have seen it. The one thing that got to me was a short clip of news footage from that night back in 1981. Three seconds, that's all. Maybe not even. From one of the local Boston TV stations. It showed ambulances on the street. One in front of Karen's house, another in front of Andy's. A few police cars block the road and fire trucks are parked up on the sidewalk.

How had I forgotten about the ambulances?

And the fires.

Because the sunset. She'd seen fire.

35

OKAY, I HAVE TO TELL YOU WHAT HAPPENED ON HALLOWEEN IN
1981, the night I died.

It's not pretty, so don't say I'm not warning you. If you're the
type who's easily upset, skip it. Seriously. You can pick things up
after this. All you need to know is that I died a horrible, grue-
some, terrifying death, and in the midst of it, I noticed something
I misinterpreted at the time, and haven't thought of since then.

Move on now if you don't want to hear this.

Those of you left—are we good? We're gonna do this?

Okay. I'm ready. Deep breath. Here goes.

It was a lark. A goof. The year before, we'd all decided we were
done trick-or-treating. Not that it was a bad Halloween. No, we
were thirteen and had fun. But the next day, word had come
down from the most popular kids of our school that trick-or-
treating was for kids. Little kids. Definitely not cool for junior
high. Parties were cool, snagging candy was not. And it's hard to
ignore that kind of thing when you're that age. It's like a tiny little

poop in the punch—you can't really drink around it. So much for the punch.

By the time Halloween rolls around the next year, we're cynical fourteen-year-olds. World-weary. Much too sophisticated for that childish nonsense. Of course, no one invited us to a cool Halloween party, either, so we were left to our own devices, as usual.

The genius idea of dressing up again and trick-or-treating was mine.

What a terrible idea.

To be fair, I wanted to help Mark. A week earlier, his parents had sat him down and told him they were getting divorced. They did the whole song and dance: it's not you, honey, it's us; we're still going to be a family; and, hey, you'll have two houses to live in now—how fun is that? All in all, a too-cheerful way of saying, *Sorry, kid, but we're blowing up the only life you've ever known because one of us cheated on the other—oh, didn't you know real life is like that? Don't worry. You'll figure it out. And by the way—never fully trust anyone again! Thanks, we love you, signed Mom & Dad.*

Couldn't have happened to a more vulnerable guy. He already worried about everything. Perfectionist. Cried when he got frustrated. Turned beet red whenever he spoke in class. Was short for his age and had a weird birthmark on the side of his face.

His stance on the whole divorce was simple: I hate them both. Which is fine to say, unless you're Mark, who actually loved them so much it was a little odd. Half the time, he wouldn't hang out with us for some stupid reason like he was playing Monopoly with his parents. Or going to the library with them. Or going to the gardening store over in Lawrence with them. Or going caroling around Christmas with them.

The divorce left him shell-shocked. Didn't know up from down. It was hard to watch him screwing his face up and saying how much he hated them while at the same time tears trembled in the corners of his eyes and his cheeks burned hot pink.

So I thought I'd do him a solid and get his mind off of it by taking the four of us on a wacky nostalgia trip back in time to when we'd been but a tender thirteen years of age. Three hundred and sixty-five days earlier. Nothing like helping a buddy out. Taking his mind off the worst tragedy to befall his life up until then.

By dying.

Sorry, Mark!

(Well, at least your parents' divorce didn't seem quite so terrible after that, right?)

The night was brisk, just the right amount of chill in the air. Clear sky, bright stars, Venus shining over the horizon when the sun went down, sliver of a moon coming up through the trees. We all went as that old standby: hobos. Without any real time to plan, it was easy enough to throw together old bits of our parents' or grandparents' clothes, mismatched, patched in some cases, the wrong sizes. Goofy hats. Big shoes. Mascara moustaches. Sticks with bandana sacks tied at the ends, filled with old socks. It kind of worked. We got a couple of polite-yet-snide *Aren't you a little old to be trick-or-treating?* Comments, usually from people whose shrubs were cut perfectly, walkways swept, who kept their good couches underneath plastic covers. That type.

Just a bunch of hobos, Craig answered, making it sound like he had a terrible head cold. We all sped off, cracking up each time. And we got into the spirit of it, though even then I felt a pang of nostalgia. We were *goofing* on Halloween, not getting *swept up* by it like we used to. It made the energy different. Funnier, sure. But less pure. Looking back, I guess that's how it goes when you grow up.

Not that I got the chance, since that was the last night of my life.

He said cynically.

. . .

Mrs. Eleanor Gracie's house was classically festive. Two jack-o'-lanterns on the stoop. A bouquet of colored Indian corn hanging on the door knocker. We'd all known her from elementary school, and even then she'd seemed old. Sitting in a circle on the floor while she'd taught us music, controlling the cacophony of a bunch of third graders with access to xylophones, maracas, and jingle bells. She greeted us, as ever, with a smile, knowing us at a glance, though not saying our names (which I guess had to do with her dementia, now that I think about it). Handing us the plate of cookies, she told us we could take two each. And we did, putting them into the little wax paper envelopes she handed us. We thanked her as a group and the smile on her face was the same generous, good-hearted one known by probably three generations of kids in town.

The poor woman.

We carried on until the chill got to us, probably being the last or close to last group out, our range extending a good deal farther than the younger kids'. We headed back to Craig's house, bustling inside, bringing the scent of the night air in with us. At least we'd had fun. And more importantly, we'd gotten Mark out of his funk, for a while, anyway. But as we were waiting around for his dad to come pick him up, I could see him start to sour again.

So to head off his bad mood, I started talking like the Cookie Monster. As far as the cookies from Mrs. Gracie went, we were generally agnostic. They weren't as prized as, say, a Three Musketeers bar or a bag of peanut M&Ms. But they were a step up from Dots or a little box of licorice Good 'N' Plenty, for sure. As such, I felt it fair game to raid my friends' bags for them, loudly repeating the stupid phrase *Nothing like coo-keys!*

I shoved them in my mouth, one after another after another. All eight of them. The funny-yet-not-funny part: that's what made it lethal. I heard that a few times over the years from Beth, telling the story to a friend or something. If I'd just had the two I'd been given, I'd have probably gone to the hospital and felt nasty, but I wouldn't have died. Like most of the kids who ate a cookie or two.

But who knew? All I knew was Mark was gathering up thunderheads again and I wanted to keep the mood light. So with crumbs all over the front of my father's torn Army jacket from 1952, I was pleased to see Mark give me a tight smile before he turned and walked to his dad's idling Chevy Nova, his shoulders hunching the closer he got to it.

Last time he ever saw me. At least I left him with a smile, am I right?

I could tell something was wrong by the time I got home after walking back from Craig's. Not wrong, wrong. Just wrong. Like maybe I'd had too much candy and cookies. Or laughed too much. My stomach hurt. I didn't think too much about it. Beth was getting ready for bed, my mom helping her wash the glitter off her face (she'd gone out with her friends dressed as a fairy). Dad was in the living room watching television.

Welcome to the last effortlessly happy night of your lives, sorry.

I went to my room. On the way, I probably said hi to my dad. Probably ignored my mom and Beth. Changed out of my thrown-together costume, probably wiped the crumbs from the jacket and shirt. I say probably, because you never remember the moments when things are fine, not really. But when things take a turn, well—those details burn in permanently.

Like the way my fingers started to tingle as I was dumping out my bag of candy. It was weird. One minute they were fine, the next they felt like they had little ants crawling all over them. I held them up and noticed them trembling. My chest tingled, too. And the skin on the back of my scalp. Creepy. I remember straightening, looking at the backs of my fingers, taking a deep breath or two like I'd gotten light-headed and only needed to calm myself. My skin was pale, normally. But the backs of my fingers were suddenly splotched with little red marks, and super pale between those.

The panic started around then. I don't know if I realized how serious a problem I was having, or if the poison just kicked my heart rate up to triple-speed. Not too much of a difference. Either way, something wasn't right.

And what did I do? Did I go tell my folks?

Nope.

I sat there, like an idiot, for another fifteen or twenty minutes. Those minutes might not have made a difference at all—I'd like to believe that, in a strange way—but who knows. Why didn't I do anything? I was embarrassed. A vague feeling I'd get in trouble. Half convinced I was imagining things. Looking back, my thinking wasn't clear, even by then. Blame it on the poison. Oh, I knew something bad was going on. I just couldn't quite put together how bad.

Little black dots fluttered in the edges of my vision, shadowy butterflies. The pain in my stomach turned into something much worse. Stabbing me. All right, that was hard to ignore. I tried to stand, but the pain kept me doubled over. Worse, when I groaned in pain, something came up into the back of my throat, hot. I gagged on it and coughed, sending a spray of bright blood across the covers on my bed. More came out after it. Take it from me: seeing a long line of blood stringing out from your mouth makes it hard to deny something terrible is happening.

"Mom?" I called out. My mouth filled with blood again. The taste of thick, sweet metal gagged me, some of it shooting out of my nostrils this time. Everything inside me felt wrong. My heart flopped around like a squirrel trapped in a fishing net, racing and seeming to miss beats. My guts wriggled, on fire.

I heard the first ambulance by then—or, rather, it first registered with me. You hear sirens every now and then, don't think much of them. I may have heard one earlier, but this other one cut through my thinking because I half wondered how my mom could've called for one so quickly.

At my door, I held on to the knob, leaning into the doorframe. The world tilted to the left. I opened the door just as my mom came out of the bathroom, wiping her hands on a towel. Funny, her first expression was of annoyance. I'm guessing she figured the blood was part of my costume, however little sense that made (Gene Simmons as a hobo?), and I was now dripping the fake blood onto the hallway carpet. But it didn't take much more than a look in my wide eyes before the towel dropped from her hands and she called for my dad.

Beth poked her head out from the bathroom, then ducked back in, frightened. I staggered for a few steps, then went down to my knees. My limbs were doing stuff on their own, no longer interested in listening to me. My insides felt like they were coming apart, firing off all the wrong signals at the wrong moments. More blood made it hard to breathe. Mom tried to hold me up, but my stomach muscles clenched so hard I couldn't straighten. She called again for my dad, this time with a note of unmistakable panic.

"What is it?" he called from the bottom of the stairs.

"Just get up here!"

When he reached the upstairs hallway, he muttered something about Jesus—but then he was there, fully taking it in. "Is it his tongue?" he said. "Did someone put a razor blade in something? Timothy?"

I couldn't get a word out by then. My throat closed down to a skinny straw. All I could hear was my pulse slamming in my ears, along with a whooshing roar. A moan from deep in my chest was all I could manage.

"What's wrong with him?" Beth screamed.

Dad got his arms up under mine and dragged me back into

my bedroom, laying me down on the bed. He and Mom crowded over me, Dad jamming his fingers into my mouth, searching around for a razor blade.

"I can't see." He grabbed the light from my bedside table and held it in my face, looking into my mouth. "I don't see anything. Call an ambulance!"

"What?" my mom said, clearly horrified at the panic in Dad's voice.

"An ambulance! Call! Now!"

"But what do I tell them?"

"He's hemorrhaging! His muscles are like knots!"

"Mom?" Beth wailed.

Mom sprinted into her bedroom down the hall. Her voice sprang up into an even higher range as she screamed into the phone for help. Meanwhile, my dad flipped me onto my stomach and, for some reason, started hitting me between the shoulder blades with the flat of his palm, as if I were choking. More blood rolled out. A lot of different sounds competed with the thuds: the white noise rising inside my ears, Mom's terrified pleading with the police department, Beth's panic, the wail of sirens outside.

I'll tell you the weird thing. Time slowed down to where I felt like I had all the time in the world to examine each second as it passed. And some part of my mind was perfectly clear, watching it all. That part made a calm observation: *this is what dying is like, and today is the day you're dying.* Just matter of fact. Nothing fussy, not slobbered over with fear, pain, panic, or the rest of what whirled around. Calm. A statement of fact. I don't know about your life flashing before your eyes—though it felt like there was plenty of time for it—but having that clarity and that distance was something I'd never experienced before. Or since, really.

Around then, I started going in and out. One second, my dad is pounding me on the back. The next, I'm looking up at the ceiling, staring at the light while he and my mom lean over me, their voices muffled as they're calling for me. Then, Mom's at the window, shouting, *Why aren't they coming here?* Red flashes shine on the wall across from the window. Along with them, there's a shimmering orange, like from a fire.

But for me, the ambulance is too late.

Yeah, I felt that line pass by me. That line of no return. My chest didn't work. When my limbs seized up, my chest locked up with them. That calm voice noted my breathing had stopped. In one last burst of panic, I rolled from the side of the bed, somehow staggering to my feet. The last reserves of energy in my muscles trying to override the catastrophic failure of my nervous system. Pure adrenaline. In desperation, I barreled to the door of my room, each step feeling impossible, like the worst kind of nightmare have-to-run-but-can't-run scenario. Something in my head sounded as though it sizzled. The last steps I ever took in my life brought me past my bedroom door—still plastered with stickers of The Fonz and Darth Vader, a little strip of Dymo-mite tape, embossed with the raised letters of my name, TIMOTHY LANE —and out into the hallway.

I didn't feel the floor when I hit it face-first. That was it for me.

My heart stopped about seven and a half minutes later.

See what I mean? Horrible. Even telling you about it puts me in a dark place. Living through it (though, really, I didn't actually live through it) was worse, I may confidently attest.

And if you skipped it, I don't blame you at all. No one wants to think too hard about death, their own or anyone else's. So why put you—not to mention *myself*—through the telling of the worst night of my life?

Because of the ambulances.

Seeing them in that footage from the news reminded me of something I'd long forgotten. As I'd been dying, I'd seen the red from their rotating lights shining on my bedroom wall. And the shimmering orange light. In all the chaos, I didn't think too much about it—but, remember, at the time I didn't realize I wasn't the only kid dying at that moment in the neighborhood. As I watched the orange and red light flickering on the wall of my bedroom, that weird, clear part of my mind noticed it, just for a moment.

Oh, there must be a fire. That's why all the sirens. That's what I thought.

But that footage from the news showed ambulances, like it should have. The firetrucks were all pulled over on the sides of the road. No hoses. No ladders. No fighting of fires.

Because there *were* no fires. Just dozens of kids poisoned, five of them dying.

Let me say that again.

There were no fires.

So what—you may ask—was that shimmering glow on the walls?

Don't know?

Don't feel bad. I'm not sure, yet. Not entirely.

But you know who I think *was* sure? Maybe not always, but within the last few weeks?

Karen.

36

———

I GO TO THE WINDOW, THE SAME ONE MY MOM HAD LOOKED OUT when she'd wailed about why the ambulances weren't coming. The yard's contours underneath the snow, bright in the sunshine, are familiar to me as ever. A glimpse of Kyle's house. I can't quite see Karen's or Andy's house directly. The street heads off toward downtown.

What did Karen realize? Or see?

I turn back to Alyssa, go to the iPad. Type.

Where are we buried?

"Buried?"

Yes. Can you find out? Not just me. All of us.

"Uh, maybe? Probably. You don't know?"

No.

It's hard not to feel like kind of an idiot at a question like that. There's a pretty understandable expectation that you know where your body is at all times. Natural that the expectation would extend to include death. But the truth is, I don't actually know. At the time, I only saw my family around the grave. Saw the coffin. The cemetery—but they all kind of look alike around here. I was also, no surprise, a little distracted by the whole tragedy part to think much about the location. Afterward, no one talked much about my grave. My mom never went to it. She had a thing about it. She just drank and looked through old photo albums. My old schoolwork. I even caught her, more than once, leafing through a stack of my old D&D character sheets. That's how she did it.

My dad was different. He'd go to the cemetery, usually taking Beth along with him. Leave little things at my grave. Sometimes normal stuff, like flowers. But a lot of the time it was weirder stuff, like he'd take one of my old Hot Wheels and put it at the foot of my headstone. Or a green plastic army man he scrounged up from the closet in my bedroom. It was touching that he did all that, but did he think I was pining away for toys? Whatever, that's Dad. He has his own way of dealing—or not dealing—with his emotions.

So, yes—I've seen my grave. When Dad and Beth visited it, they—surprise, surprise—thought of me clearly enough for me to see them, and thus also see my grave. But I have no idea where it actually is. They never told my mom, *Hey, we're heading over to Sleepy Knoll Cemetery to visit Timothy.* Really, they never even said *grave*. It was always *We're going to visit Timothy.* We weren't religious, so there wasn't an obvious go-to cemetery. And to be honest, I never thought too much about what they'd done with my body. Didn't really want to know, because embalming fluids and cosmetic glue and whatever other horrible things went on with it.

"It's probably in some of the newspapers from around then," Alyssa says. "Maybe online. Or, if not, I think the library might keep that kind of stuff."

My library card might be expired, I type.

"Ha ha. I can check." Alyssa smiles.

Tell them you're checking for a ghost. They won't think you're crazy at all.

"Oh, I'll just keep that to myself, thanks. But they're closed today. Christmas and all." She glances at the door and keeps her voice quiet. "Do you think if you find your body, you'll finally be able to move on?"

Not sure, but I'm out of other ideas. So maybe?

"And the demon will let you go?"

No, he's a dick.

"So how will you get away from him?"

One impossible problem at a time, thanks.

"There's got to be a way to do it."

I'd like to think so.

She looks up at the ceiling, biting her lower lip. "Can you distract him?"

Like how?

"Like with—I don't know. Can you knock things over? Make him think you're somewhere else?"

I doubt it. And even then, I still need to figure out how far away I can get. The whole thing seems impossible.

"But it's not."

You're more confident than me.

She paces. "The world's not crawling with ghosts, right? You're the first I've ever come across. So that tells you something."

That I'm an idiot.

"You're not an idiot. You're just fourteen. You figured out how to communicate with me, didn't you? That's not dumb."

I've been stuck in my house for thirty-eight years. That's not smart.

She looks up from the screen. "You're being too hard on yourself. I'm sure I wouldn't do any better."

Nice of you to say, but don't be too sure.

"Don't beat yourself up. It's a bad habit. You start to believe it."

I think I started out believing it.

"You're fine. It's just a problem. There's a solution. We'll find it."

We. What an amazing word. It hits me like a shot in the heart, a vital nutrient I'd been lacking for decades. *We.* That two-letter word has the power to neutralize the worst word of all: *alone*. And I know all about that one, trust me. *We*. Now that I think about it, there's probably no better word.

I love you, Alyssa.

No, I didn't. Calm down. I only *wanted* to.

What I *did* type was, *Thank you. Really.*

"Don't thank me until we figure out how to stop you from watching me in the shower."

I'm—wait. No, I'm not—

She smiles. "Kidding. Got you."

I like the shampooing part the best.

Her eyebrows go up.

Kidding.

"Of course. I have to get the comedian ghost."

"Alyssa," her mother calls from the bottom of the stairs. "Na-Na's on the phone. Come down and say hello, please."

"Just a sec!" Alyssa looks around the room, her eyes flitting past where I'm actually standing, giving me the briefest moment of feeling like she's seeing me. "All right. We're leaving for my other grandparents' for the afternoon, but when I get back, we can see what else we can find online. Do you want me to leave this open so you can search on your own?" She points to the iPad.

Yes, definitely. Great idea.

"See? Neither one of us is a dummy."

"Alyssa?" her mother calls again.

"Coming!" She gives one glance back as she heads to the stairs.

I'm practically vibrating. Basically the best conversation I've ever had with a girl. Laugh all you want, but it's true. Incredible. I go to the door and watch her hurry down the stairs, her ponytail bouncing.

Maybe I shouldn't leave, after all.

Kidding, again. Relax. I'm the comedian ghost, remember?

When I turn back around, Groan is standing by the desk. I freeze. He bats the iPad to the floor.

He points his finger at me. "I fucking warned you."

The sunshine coming in through the window casts the faintest of shadows around his legs. The detail sticks out to me. I've never seen him in the daytime. Ever.

I ponder that curious fact in the half second before Groan kills me with a historic ferocity. Like, my limbs rip off. Like, he shoves my torn off hand down my throat. Like, I've never, ever seen him that mad.

37

I come to in the closet. Takes a little while for me to get my bearings—but as I remember what happened, I shrug off the disorientation. What the hell was Groan doing showing up in the daytime? How could that even happen? Unsure what time it is, I poke my head out through the door. Night. Great. Groan's probably ready to serve up some more pain.

I got careless. Convinced he didn't remember. Well, he did. And I ignored what'd happened with the Ouija board, whatever the mechanism is that let him leverage my own senses. It bothers me that he's watching me this closely.

I lean back into the closet. Come on, Karen—what did you figure out? And where are you? As I ask myself the question, I decide Groan's probably wondering the same thing. Maybe that's why he's so pissed. I mean, think about it. You're a demon, happily torturing your band of misfit, broken ghosts. All is well. Then, out of the blue (I assume) one of your hostages disappears, getting out way past any point she should have. What the hell is that all about? And if you're a dumbass like Groan, questions don't go down too well. You live for making others feel stupid, but you get furious when you feel stupid, because deep down you really know you're not that bright (the bully instinct in a nutshell).

So if I'm Groan, I'm upset. Worse, because I'm not used to being upset, I'm furious. Willing to be extra vigilant. Extra violent.

But something about it doesn't make sense. Why drop by on Christmas Eve acting all normal? Like nothing in the world's any different than it's been for the past thirty-eight years?

I cross my arms and stare at the ceiling.

Because he didn't want to let me know. That's why. Christmas Eve was an act. But when he killed me in Alyssa's room, he couldn't control himself. He just reacted. He's furious. He's furious because Karen outplayed him. He's watching everything. I think back to being over at Andy's house, looking out the way Karen disappeared. Heading that way myself, only to get stopped by the tether. What was I missing?

Hold it.

It's right in front of my face. First of all, I was *all the way down the street at Andy's house*. Second, I was able to get all the way into Kyle's house, even in the daytime. None of that ever happened before. I mean, I never tried going that far at night, but I tried it during the daytime a thousand times over the years. Never a step past the brook. Ever.

Holy shit.

Groan is weakening.

The thought lights me up. I pace the closet. That feels like the missing piece. Now *that* would make Groan furious. Like *atomic* furious.

Another thought clicks into place: Is Groan weakening *because* Karen's missing?

That stops me in my tracks. I think through the timing. It could be. The night when I first got out past the edge of the yard into the street? A month or so back, right around the time the house sold. Couldn't have reached Andy's house then. Out of the question. But then reaching Kyle's house. Shit, that was just this week. And if Karen's been gone for about that long—how could those *not* be connected?

So let's say Groan's got four ghosts. Hostages. Whatever you want to call us. And one of us finds a way out, however that happens. And suddenly the others can get farther away from their homes.

How much farther?

Twenty-five percent farther?

Because Groan's lost twenty-five percent of his power to hold us in place?

Because Groan's lost twenty-five percent of his *source* of power?

Us. He's feeding off of *us*.

Boom. Another piece of the puzzle.

As for the *how* and the *why*, I don't care. But here's what I do know: Groan can't figure out I'm onto him. Sure, he's an idiot. But he's cunning. Betrayal. Lies. Paranoia. Sneakiness. He's full to the brim with all of it—so he's likely to spot anything like it in an instant. I have to start thinking in terms of doing what he *won't* expect. If there's any key to this, it's that.

Under normal circumstances, I'd stay all night in the closet. And under normal circumstances, Groan would probably stick around to make sure I did. But I have a feeling he thinks he's nailed me so good I won't press my luck. I also have a feeling he's maybe not here at all, but off somewhere hunting for Karen, desperate to get his full strength back.

Only one way to find out.

I step out from the closet. The house is dark. Silent. I drift over to the living room door and look inside. Christmas tree is still up. Bits of wrapping paper, a bag with cards in it, still on one of the end tables. Which means I've only been gone for half a day. Coming back from being killed isn't usually a quick thing. More proof that Groan's weakening?

The first floor of the house is clear. The more I look, the more certain I am of it. Doesn't feel like he's anywhere nearby. I drift upstairs. Everyone's asleep. I go into Alyssa's room, cautious. She's in her bed, buried underneath sheets and a comforter. I find her iPad on her desk. The glass on the front wears two new cracks from when Groan slammed it to the floor. Hopefully it still works?

At the window facing Kyle's house, I pause. The moon is out, lighting up the midnight snowscape, shadows deep blue. Has Groan laid into him, too? Probably worth checking. As I'm about to head out the wall, something catches my eye, something on the floor in the corner. A familiar tickle of dread brushes the back of my neck. The urge to race down to the closet flares, but I ignore it, instead crouching by the corner.

Where half of Groan's hand is curled up like dead earthworms in the summer sun.

Jesus. His pinky and ring fingers with their long, dirty nails, along with the outside edge of his palm. It's nasty. Did it happen when he slammed the iPad? But how? I've seen him do all kinds of crazy things and never take any damage at all.

Or . . . hardly any damage. I realize it's not the first time recently Groan has lost a part. Just the night before, with Lollipop. Half his ear came off then. I'd been a little too distracted to think much about it. I look at the part of his hand on the floor. I reach out and poke it. It's cold and stiff. Repulsive.

He's falling apart because he's feeding off of us, and one of us is gone.

But what feeds him? He doesn't suck our blood like he's a vampire. All he does is terrorize us.

Wait.

He terrifies us.

Is he feeding off our terror? *All* our terror. Karen, Kyle, Andy?

And what if—maybe—that supply started to dry up even before Karen escaped? I think back to Halloween—when I'd first talked back to him. Given him some lip. He definitely didn't like that. Did that turn off the spigot of what keeps him strong, even just a little? Maybe just enough to let us get a little farther from our houses? Maybe enough for someone clever to find a break in the boundaries?

Clever like Karen.

I start thinking about the timing of things again. What if my talking back to him loosened his grip? Even a little. Maybe Karen did the same thing. Is it possible the two of us started working the same angle without even knowing the other was there, let alone doing the same thing? We're the two oldest ghosts, after all.

I straighten. Look out the window in the direction of Karen's house.

Because the sunset. She'd seen fire.

She's a step ahead of me. What's the step?

Before I can get any further with my train of thought, I hear a noise from outside the door. Worried that it's Groan, I duck halfway through the floor, ready to dart to the closet. After a second, I recognize Jacinta's voice. She's talking in her rodent voice. "Come here, cutie. Don't do that."

Kid almost gave me a heart attack.

I come back fully into Alyssa's room. I want to get over to Kyle's, tell him my theory. He'll find the holes in it—it's his superpower. Annoying, but in this case probably useful.

"Oh, you're too silly," Jacinta whispers. "Be careful on the railing."

I pause before heading through the wall to Kyle's. On the floor next to me, Groan's torn off fingers flick, once, twice. I look to the door. I fly across the room, listening. Jacinta isn't quiet, even walking down the hallway in bare feet. She even breathes loudly. Careful, I slip my head through the wall, peeking. Jacinta is in her pajamas, hair tussled. A plastic mouse gripped in her hand. Just when I'm convinced she's making a trip the bathroom, I catch movement out of the corner of my eye. Another one of her dolls, the stuffed mouse, her main squeeze, is marching along the top of the railing on the stairs.

By itself.

Jacinta laughs, pure happiness.

"Ooooh, it's a playground slide," she whispers.

The mouse raises its stuffed arms, motioning for her to follow. I lunge through the door, trying to stop her, but by then she's at the top step, waving around that other toy. Leaning.

When Groan appears—just behind her—he turns his head to me, giving me a smile. Not a happy smile, either. With his good hand, he shoves Jacinta, sending her tumbling down the stairs. She screams.

"You don't listen, do you?" Groan says. He vanishes.

Footsteps, as the family wakens, rushing out of their bedrooms.

PART V

38

THEY'RE HOME FROM THE HOSPITAL BY LATE MORNING. GOOD THING, too, because I'm losing my shit. I mean, I know Jacinta isn't dead. But she was messed up. I've never heard screaming like that. And then I spend all night in the closet, convincing myself she's got a fatal head injury. Blaming myself. Blaming Groan. Sick about the whole thing.

When I hear the car pull up in front of the garage, I go to the window. Alejandro goes around to the back door and lifts Jacinta out. Poor kid's still in her pajamas, left arm in a big cast that goes all the way up over her elbow, bending her arm at a fixed angle. Some kind of brace and bandages over one of her ankles, too. Gripping her stuffed mouse in her good hand. Talking. They all come into the kitchen looking exhausted. All night at the hospital, no fun.

"Let's get you up to your room," Alejandro says.

"I want two water bottles," Jacinta says. "One for drinking. One for making into an IV for Widge. And some bendy straws. And some tape. Do we have any more tape, Daddy?"

"You should probably just rest, sweetie."

"But poor little Widge broke his little arm, too. See?" She

hurls her mouse down onto the kitchen floor and lets loose a high-pitched scream.

"How about we hold off on any more screaming, love?" Lilibeth picks Widge up from the floor and gives him back to Jacinta.

"But he needs to go to the hospital. His arm is broken."

"Tell you what," Alejandro says. "We'll get him patched up as soon as you're in your bed and settled. Okay?"

He carries her to the stairs, her nonstop words trailing them. Alyssa's at the fridge, drinking something labeled vitamin water.

"You should take a nap, honey," Lilibeth says.

"Nah, I'm all right."

"Ten hours at the hospital might argue otherwise."

Alyssa looks at her. She doesn't say anything. I wonder what she's thinking. It might be: How do you get rid of a demon?

Wish I had an answer on that one. Boy, do I.

Later, Schuyler comes over, parking a little compact car behind the Cruzes'. I've been trailing Alyssa all morning and early afternoon, waiting for her to reach out to me. Or to even take out her phone. Neither of which she does, to my growing annoyance. The single message she sent to Schuyler was so quick I couldn't even get in close enough to type anything before she had the phone back in her sweatshirt pocket.

As Schuyler walks inside, she dangles the car keys in front of Alyssa. "Free at last, free at last—thank the RMV I'm free at last."

"Hey, that's right," Alyssa says. "Nice."

Driver's licenses. Yet another thing I'd missed out on.

"How is she?" Schuyler asks.

"Even weirder on the drugs they gave her."

"I want some."

"Feel free to tumble down my stairs and break your arm, darling."

"Hard pass."

"Thought so."

They pass by Alyssa's parents with a couple of brief words and head upstairs to Jacinta's room. Jacinta's voice burbles out from the open door, a steady fountain. Now, whatever else I've thought about Schuyler, she knows how to make a kid feel good. She whips off her backpack and introduces Jacinta—propped up on a mountain of pillows, a table with juice boxes, straws, water, and snacks next to her—to an entire broken arm survival kit. A thin, flexible ruler for scratching under the cast. Three small bags of glitter and a tiny bottle of white glue. Half a dozen colored markers, rubber-banded together. A sheet of stickers of farm animals. And, ironically, a bag of googly eyes, two of which she proceeds to glue onto the cast inside a smiley face she draws. Jacinta loves every bit of it and the two of them rapid-fire so many words at each other that it's almost like listening to another language.

I watch it all from just outside the door, keeping out of Jacinta's sight, wondering if Groan is also watching. While they're fancying up her cast, I prowl the edge of the hallway, trying to sense His Nastiness. I look out the bathroom window, scanning the yard. Daytime apparently isn't the barrier it used to be. But—as before—I don't catch a hint of anything. Even in the spot where I'd found his torn fingers, nothing. The fingers, by the way, disappeared at some point during the night. First thing I checked after sunrise. He'd clearly taken them back. And for some reason, I picture him shoving them into his mouth and gulping them down.

"Big spider. It frightened me," Jacinta says.

My attention snaps back to her.

"Creepy," Schuyler says.

"And he has a huuuuuuge stinger and he crawled all the way up in the corner of the ceiling and I hid under my covers."

"I hate nightmares like that."

"It wasn't a nightmare. I was awake. I was awake from 11:19 on.

I checked on my iPad. But luckily Sealy and Manty Ray chased it away."

"They chased it away?"

"They flew up in the air and chased it away."

"Those are good friends to have."

"I don't think seals and stingrays really eat spiders."

"They don't have to—as long as they chase them away," Schuyler says. "I love your imagination."

"It's not my imagination. It happened at 11:26. That's when I decided to get some water for my midnight drink. That's when Widge marched into the hallway. Before I got pushed down the stairs."

Schuyler and Alyssa exchange a look.

"Were you sleepwalking?" Schuyler said.

Jacinta laughs. "I was wake-walking, because I was awake since 11:19. Widge needs to learn how to behave and stop doing such silly things at night."

Schuyler finishes up with a spiral of blue glitter on the elbow of Jacinta's cast, blowing the spare glitter off. "What do you think?"

"I think it's the most beautiful cast in the whole world."

"You are welcome. Now don't go breaking the other arm, though—that's the last of my glitter."

"You can buy more."

"Buy more? Are you planning on breaking your other arm? Your leg? That's nuts."

"The hospital was fun."

"But I bet it hurt."

"It felt like—BOOM! And it hurt so much."

"Then you won't break your other one, right?"

"No. Maybe they can give me a cast, anyway."

"Maybe they can. You just deal with this one for now. I'll leave the markers with you, in case you want to have your friends sign it. Or if you want to decorate it more."

Do I believe her about the spider? Lollipop?

I kind of do, which worries me even more. What the hell is Groan up to? Messing around with her toys. Messing around with her. Am I missing something? Has Groan been shadowing her? If I'd been more vigilant, would I have found him lurking around Jacinta's room? Watching her while she sleeps? Mumbling? Doing weird stuff—like with my dad?

Oh, no. No, no, no.

Is Groan trying to possess her?

The thought goes off in my head like a bell—a big-ass Hell's Bell. Does he see a way in with her that he doesn't with anyone else? She's not like everyone else, that's for sure. If she can see me —well, can she see Groan? Can he see into her? Is her condition something he can take advantage of, like he did with Eleanor Gracie?

And what do I do this time? They just moved in. Am I supposed to haunt them out of the house like I did with Dad? How's that going to work?

Alyssa and Schuyler head into Alyssa's room when Lilibeth brings some food for Jacinta. I keep my distance, staying just on the other side of the wall, leaning my head through enough to see and hear them. If Groan is watching me, hopefully that won't rile him up too much. But I also need Alyssa to figure out where I'm buried. Me and the others.

"Do you think it was the ghost?" Schuyler says. "Could he have pushed her down the stairs?"

"Schuyler."

"Well, if your house is haunted—"

"My house is not fucking haunted."

It's not? And why is she getting so defensive?

"Fine," Schuyler says, watching Alyssa closely. "Forget I said it."

"I will."

Alyssa picks up some random clothes from her chair and dresser. She's so oddly focused that she may as well have hung a sign that says *Bring up the ghost again and you may see yourself out.* Schuyler eyes the cracks on the front of Alyssa's iPad but manages to contain her questions. With effort.

In the other room, Jacinta sings, off-key.

Great.

39

———

"She thinks you're Scary-Eyes. Or whatever you call him. Mr. Groan," Kyle says.

We're in the back entry to his house. Not too far, just inside—not as far as I could get at night, but farther than I've reached during the daytime.

"That's crazy," I say. "She knows I'm not Groan."

"She thinks you've been fooling her."

"I've been totally honest with her."

"How does she know?"

I look through the windows on the back door, out across the snowy yards to my house. The corner of the roof just above my old room is barely visible. "Shit. You're right."

"You shouldn't swear."

"Sometimes you should, Kyle."

He crosses his arms and raises his eyebrows. I ignore him.

It's Groan's fault. Alyssa's started to trust me—and then this. Kyle's got it right: Why wouldn't she think it's me? That everything I've said to her is a lie? I'm furious at Groan. Doing the right thing is hard. Telling the truth, being honest. Messing everything up and having no shame about it? Easy. Building takes time. Smashing things doesn't. For all I've ever hated him, I've never hated him this much. "How are we going to find out where we're buried now? Or any of it? What about your family?"

"The Roths?"

"Yeah. What about their devices?"

"The kids are only one and three. They don't have any."

"But the parents must."

"They don't use them."

"What do you mean they don't use them?"

"They used to. Now they're on a diet. An electronics diet."

"You've got to be kidding me."

"Something the lady read about. They put their phones in this crystal dish on the table in the hall. With their car keys. Every time they come in the house. They don't grab them again until they leave."

"Perfect. All right. Fine. What about Andy's family?"

"They're away."

"Yeah, I know they're away. But they'll be back."

"They're old."

"How old?"

"Really old."

"Like, give me a number." I remember how he'd called Karen —twelve-year-old Karen—old.

"Older than my grandparents." He scrunches up his face. "Maybe one hundred?"

So guessing ages isn't Kyle's strong suit, apparently. Still, they could be old. My dad's age. Even older. That's not good. I think of Dad, with the old flip phone he kept around for fifteen years. No screen on it.

"Okay, that's not going to help," I say. "What about Karen? Did she ever say anything else about the flames?"

"A little." He chews the corner of his lip, squinting.

"Go on."

"After she discovered Mrs. Gracie hiding them."

"After—hold it. *Mrs. Gracie?*"

"Yes."

"The one who poisoned us?"

"She says it's really the demon. Not the real Mrs. Gracie."

"Seriously? *That's* how the demon looks to her?"

"Yes."

"Groan is such a"—I bite back on the swear word—"jerk. For looking like that." I mean, what he looks like to me is bad enough, and Scary Eyes sounds pretty nasty, too. I have no idea what *Flibber* is supposed to be, but Andy's terror is clear. But to be chased around and murdered by Mrs. Gracie, over and over again? Another burning hot coal added to my fury at Groan.

I turn back to Kyle. "Hold it. What do you mean *hiding them?*"

"Well. She's out there during the day."

"Mrs. Gracie?"

"Yes. And she does a thing. Out beyond the edge."

"Does what?"

"I'm not sure. But Karen was. She watched. For a long time. Years and years. I've seen it, too."

"Mrs. Gracie?"

"No. Scary Eyes. Sometimes I see him. Down over there." He points through the house. "Across the street."

"Doing what?"

"He walks, leaning over. Like he's talking to the ground. And he'll straighten. And lift his hand and cut himself on the wrist, then he'll lean over again. Back and forth."

"How often?"

"Pretty much every day."

"Every day?"

"Yes. Karen tried to interrupt her. It never worked. Forever, it felt like. But it worked, just recently. A couple of times. And that gave her the idea—because she saw the colors. Like sunset. Like flames. She's not sure. But she's going to come back and tell us."

Once again, Karen impresses me. I rack my memory, trying to recall even as much as a hint that Groan was outside in my yard, doing something, anything, during the daytime. Nope. Never saw it. "I've never seen it. Never. Not once."

"Well, Karen did. And so did I. And Andy."

"That doesn't make any—" I stop myself. Hold it. I think back to looking out my window earlier. The window that faces south. From which I can see Kyle's house and, if there weren't a couple other houses in the way, both Karen's and Andy's. Which also happens to be the direction Karen escaped.

Now I understand.

Groan never did anything in my yard because he didn't *have to*. What he did in the other kids' yards did the trick. It blocked whatever it is he doesn't want us to see, for all of us. Me included. My house. I play through the angles in my mind. Something starts to click into place.

"Do you remember what happened when you died?" I ask Kyle.

He flinches.

"Sorry," I say. "I've got to ask. I know it sucks to think about. But what happened? Once you actually died. How long did it take you to figure it out?"

"It was terrible."

"Of course it was terrible. But did you see anything? Or were you just—gone for a while?"

"Gone for a while."

"Like—the second you died?"

"I don't remember."

"It must've been. I don't think I knew anything for, I don't know. A couple of days? A week, maybe?"

"Why?" Kyle asks.

"What if Groan—Scary Eyes, Mrs. Gracie, Flibber—did something to us, that night, and for a few nights and days after?"

"I don't understand. Did what?"

"Distracted us. Or blinded us. Or something like—I don't know—drawing a bag over our heads."

"A bag?"

"So we couldn't see."

"Couldn't see *what*?"

"What don't we have, Kyle?"

"What?"

"What don't we have? That most people who die have. At first."

He shakes his head. "I don't know."

"Our *bodies*. We don't have them. Not now. And maybe when we needed them, our friend made sure we couldn't see them."

"Why would we need to see them?" Kyle says.

I step through the wall to the outside. Kyle follows. I look in the direction of Karen's house. The way she went, when she escaped.

"Because they're how we move on," I say. "This—ritual thing he does. Karen figured it out. Most of it. Probably all of it, knowing her. It's that way." I raise my arm, pointing toward the center of town.

"What is?"

"Where we're buried."

"Buried?"

"Yeah. Buried. And I'm willing to bet anything that somehow our bodies are signaling to us. By shining, or glowing. Like flames? Get it? The fires Karen mentioned. I even remember glimpses of them from the night we died, not that I knew what they were. But he's been blocking it. Hiding them from us. Ever since we died. Do you understand?"

Kyle frowns. A pair of crows in the top of a hemlock tree take flight, one of them croaking loudly.

"Do you remember when I said there's a time you should swear, Kyle?"

"Yes."

"What do you think?"

He doesn't hesitate. "Do it."

"The *fucking* demon who killed us has been *fucking* hiding our bodies from us ever since we died. Hiding the way out."

40

What's with these people? Normally, if you put even two of them together, one of them is looking at their phone. Sometimes both of them. But, no. Not today, when I most need them to. Alyssa reads a book. Downstairs, Alejandro is asleep on the couch, catching up on a night of missed sleep. Lilibeth is on her phone, but—and this is weird—she's using it as a *phone*. Telling her mother what happened with Jacinta. Then her sister. Then her other sister. Then her closest friend.

For a second, I imagine haunting them. For real. A couple of scenarios pop into my head. Poking my head through a pot on the stove, so when they lift the lid, *hello*. Hanging myself just underneath one of their coats, surprise. Of course, I could barely manage any of that with my own dad, so forget about it with the Cruz family. No bond. No connection.

Great. What's that leave me with? Fart smells? I roam the house, seeing if I can do anything at all. I try manifesting near Alyssa, digging deep, using everything I've got. And, nothing.

Of course, there's one person who can already see me. I drift into Jacinta's room. The kid's asleep, finally. The cast arm is propped on a stack of small pillows. Her mouth's open. Looking at her like that, so vulnerable, I squirm with guilt. I wasn't the one who pushed her down the stairs, but it's hard not to feel responsible. Her good hand is wedged underneath a plush baby rabbit. The kid couldn't be any sweeter—which infuriates me, thinking about what Groan wants to do to her. But how can I stop him?

Wait a minute.

Why has Groan been so bent in the first place? Why did his ear and fingers come off? Why have the tethers let me and Kyle get farther from our homes than ever before?

Because Karen escaped. It weakened him.

So what happens if the rest of us escape?

My guess is Groan is done for.

Okay. I take that sliver of hope and tuck it next to the other sliver of hope I have. So what if there's only one way I can make this work and probably ten thousand ways it can go wrong?

"Do you want to sign my cast?" Jacinta is awake and looks right at me. She smiles. "Isn't it pretty?"

I nod. She smiles.

"You can sign it if you want," she says.

I go over to her bed. I try to pick up a marker, but of course I can't. Instead, I mime like I've just picked one up and make like I'm signing my name with a big John Hancock flourish.

She laughs. "You signed it with a ghost pen."

I nod.

"And ghost ink. Yay."

I give her a thumbs-up. Then I look at her broken arm and bandaged ankle, cross my arms in front of my chest, and frown deeply. I mouth *I'm sorry*.

"It's okay. I know you didn't do it."

I scratch my head, as in *what do you mean?*

"You're funny," she says. "It's that stinky shadow creature who did it. He's mean."

Leaning back like I'm surprised, I mouth *Oh, no.*

"I know all about shadow creatures," she says. "Ethan rides my bus with me and he tells me all about them. He's fifteen and thinks he's too old to be friends with me. He's a thaumaturge. Which is a hard word to remember. It's kind of like a magician but Ethan gets mad when I say so. But it is. And he's told me about shadow creatures. They come into your room at night and watch you. And their eyes glow. I've Googled it. I could show you the pictures. But I'm not afraid, so I just tell them *Get out, shadow creature!* and they usually do. Even this shadow creature. He only pushed me because I didn't see him. And I realize now he was probably the one making my toys move, which is naughty. They're my toys. Not his. Don't you think?"

What? She keeps going.

"I'm not afraid and I'll stand up and hold up my hand and say *Stop!* Although not too loud, or my mom and my dad will wake up and I'm not supposed to be loud at night even if I'm not sleeping, which is a lot. Sometimes I go to bed at bedtime and then, boop, my eyes open up at 11:19 or at 1:22 or at 3:06 and then I'm awake for the rest of the night so I'll just watch brain games on my iPad under the covers. Do you like brain games?"

I nod, then hold up a finger like I want to make a point.

"Yes, ghost boy?" she says.

Miming creepy hands and a long chin, I stand at the foot of her bed.

She smiles and holds up her hand. "Stop!"

I tilt my head.

"It works. And if he sneaks up on me again, I'm going to be angry, even though I like the hospital. I like the IV and the nurse with the sparkly stickers on her shirt. I don't like the X-ray machine because it's hard to hold still and it's loud, even with quiet-phones on. Why would he push me? I try to be nice to everyone. Even shadow creatures. That's what my mom calls my superpower." She giggles.

She has some kind of superpower, all right. If I'd seen Groan sneaking around my room when I was nine, I'd have never come out from underneath my covers. I sure as hell wouldn't ever have slept in my room again. I also probably wouldn't have ever talked about it, either, but Jacinta doesn't seem to hold anything at all inside, which is actually kind of awesome. I give her another thumbs-up. Again, I mime like I'm Groan and go over to her toys, pretending like I'm picking them up and making them walk around.

She laughs. "Okay, you can play with my toys, shadow creature. See? Sharing is a nice thing and they're nice toys and as long as he doesn't wreck them and always puts them back, then he can do it. Maybe it will make him nice. But even if it doesn't, it makes me nice for doing it, which is what my mom says and Miss Adams says at my school. We take movement breaks together and I talk to her about shadow creatures. And she doesn't interrupt me like Ethan does, especially when he thinks I'm using words wrong, and once he told me to get a dictionary and he said it really mean. Would you ever tell me to get a dictionary in a mean way?"

I shake my head, *No way, of course not.*

"See? My mom said it's because Ethan is fifteen years old, but you look like you're fifteen years old, too. Are you fifteen years old?"

I shake my head.

"Are you fourteen years old?"

I nod.

"But you wouldn't tell me to get a dictionary? Who even does that?" She laughs again. This is a kid who broke her arm last night after being pushed down stairs by a demon. "I'm going to tell Ethan I don't need a dictionary and he shouldn't say things like that. I'm also going to ask him to sign my cast."

I'm trying to think of a way to get her to open her iPad so I can type. I don't even see the thing.

"Uh oh, I think you should go, ghost boy," she says. "The

shadow creature is coming and he doesn't like you. I disagree with him, by the way. You seem very nice. And you can visit me anytime you want to even though I'm not allowed to talk to invisible friends anymore around my mom or my dad or my sister. But I'll try to give you a wave from across the room. Like this." She lifts her good hand and waves at me.

Groan? In daytime again? I smile and wave at Jacinta and then dart off through the floor to the closet. Too much stuff to do, I can't risk Groan catching me and killing me again, even if I'm coming back quicker than ever. Standing there nestled between coats and jackets and the vacuum cleaner, I extend my senses, trying to see if I can feel him. Jacinta isn't wrong—I get the feeling of someone staring at me from behind, that crawling sensation of being watched that's one of Groan's specialties. The feeling is behind me, then above, like he's taking a circuit of the house, checking to make sure I'm not sitting around with the Cruz family, laughing as we all play a game on one of their iPads. I even catch the stench of him.

"Mind if I join you, buddy?" he whispers in my ear.

Before I can shoot off like a cannonball, he grabs me by the shoulder, sinking his claws deep into my flesh, holding me in place. I crane my neck around and there he is, leaning over me, taking up the bulk of the closet. *My* closet.

He looks around. "Smells like farts in here. And jizz."

I try to tear myself from his grip, but no go.

"No wonder you like it so much," he says. He fake shudders, making a face of deep disgust.

"Get out," I say.

"*. . . of my little whack-shack,*" he mimics. "Oh, if these walls could talk, am I right?" He shakes his head. "You've got a problem, buddy."

"Let me go, jerk."

He looks at me. "What'd you say?"

"Haven't you done enough shitty business today?"

"I'm just getting started. My only problem is that I'm running low on kids' arms to break."

"Yeah, you're so tough. Pushing a little girl down the stairs."

"Oh good lord, look at him." Groan sends his fingers into my shoulder. Blood runs down my side. "He's gotten tough all of a sudden. Little constructive criticism, buddy—it sounds more impressive when it's not squeaked out in a high, shaky voice like yours. What's-her-face upstairs could deliver the line with more balls. She's going to be a fun project, don't you think?"

Actually, I have been thinking about it. "Leave her alone."

"Maybe next time I'll break her neck. Or worse."

"Don't."

His grin widens. "I can't wait until I have her murder her whole family. But even their ghosts aren't going to stick around with you, in case you're getting your hopes up. Especially not that hot little piece of yum-yum. She can't stand you, if you haven't noticed. Didn't take much. You know why she's giving you the cold shoulder? I mean, other than the fact that most girls find you about as interesting as a piece of dog poo waved around on a stick. The real reason. The reason why she'll never let you near her tap-tap-tappy screen, let alone her soft and perkies." He smiles, wide enough for me to see the blackened teeth at the back of his mouth, falling apart in his gray gums. "You're welcome. I've saved you from yourself."

"What are you talking about?"

"Look, we both know you're a weak-kneed little perv when it comes right down to it. Right? Well, rather than her wasting her time figuring it out on her own, I did her a solid and spilled the beans. You're not the only one who can type, cowpoke. My spelling might not be great. For example, not sure how many *Es* are in *penis*. Or *Is* in *wiener*. Pretty sure I didn't spell *pee-hole* the right way. Or *poop-cutter*. Oh, and the thing about lapping up her panty-waste came out a little weird, but she figured it out by saying it out loud." He leans in even closer. "By the way, sorry to say that none of it made her damp and squirmy. Like any red-blooded female, she finds you repulsive. Turned pale. Puked. And what's funny is I'm not even making that up." His eyes shine as he laughs.

"But it gets even better, Dimrod. I've discovered method acting. Do you know what method acting is? It's when I pretend so hard that I'm you, that I'm basically you. I just have to think: What would a wormy little skid-mark machine do that's not at all embarrassing? And when I can't think of anything, because there *isn't* anything, I just go with the next idea. So, get this. Turns out I can leave a lick on the glass of the shower door when it's all steamy. Lots of licks. They show up perfectly. Most of them about crotch height. I can also get some other licks about the height and distribution of your dream girl's nibbles."

He sticks his gray tongue out and wiggles it. I lean back so it doesn't touch me. That prick. No wonder Alyssa won't talk about me with Schuyler: she thinks I'm a pervert. No wonder she's avoiding her iPad.

"You are welcome," he says.

I want to punch him in the throat. I don't. Instead, I glance down at his other hand—half of which is still missing. That's a good sign. He's got that creepy bowler pulled down over his ears, but my guess is that if I were to knock it off his head, his ear is still gone, too. He thrusts his damaged hand up into my face. Man, he doesn't miss anything.

"This?" he says. "You think this is funny? It's not, snot-breath. You made me so damned angry."

"I never said it was funny."

"Well, I said it's not. And don't go getting any ideas." He pokes the nail of his index finger into the corner of my eye, just hard enough to drive my head back. "This isn't weak, because I'm getting stronger. Stronger than ever, right?"

"Sure. Whatever you say."

"It's not *whatever I say*. It's what is. Just look around, buddy.

You think I'm weaker when I'm standing here with you in your little fortress of solitude? Does this look weak to you?"

He shoves me back so hard that I slip out of the closet. He reaches after me and pulls me back by my throat. "All right. I'll tell you. It's because I ate her." Groan pulls me right up to his face. He smacks his lips. "Warned her. But she's like you, Dimothy. Stupid. Dumb. Doesn't listen. So she runs away, thinking she's so much more clever than I am—always a mistake. Do you know she didn't even get halfway down the street before I got her? Lunged out from a patch of shrubbery, took her legs out from under her. The excitement of disobeying me wore off pretty quick, I can tell you. Because I pretty much lost my temper, sad to say. Well, sad for her. Okay for me, because I finally gave in and devoured her. Her toes. Her fingers. Her lips. Her ears. Her heart. Oh, look—my mouth is watering just thinking about it."

He mashes my face into his chest. Cold drool spills over the back of my neck.

"That's what happens when little assholes push me too far." His voice sounds wet and sloppy. "The bad thing is I don't get to play with them anymore. True. My own fault. But the good thing is I'm stronger than I've ever been."

He pushes me back and lifts me up, both of his clammy hands around my throat.

"Think how much fun we're going to have now that I can get in here every night and every day. Great, right?" Then he brings me in close to his face again. "You and your new buddies, am I right? Oh, they're going to love it, too. Especially little Andy. Do you know sometimes he gets so scared he craps his pants?" His tongue darts out in glee. "It's one of my favorites. Can't help himself. I kind of wish you could see it!"

Groan takes his damaged hand from my throat and slaps me across the face with it, his own face instantly empty of anything but fury. "But the next time I catch you huddling with those two other meat-beaters, either one of them, ever—I'm going to eat Andy, too. Do you fucking understand, Timothy?"

My cheek stings, half-numb. I can't squeeze a word out.

"Don't just stare at me with your buggy little eyes," Groan whispers. "Answer me."

"Yes."

"Yes what?"

"Yes—I understand."

"Because no one gets away from me. No one. Ever."

He puts his hand on my face and shoves me backward. I stagger out of the closet. He follows.

"Okay. Now you've pissed me off again," he snarls. "I don't like being this angry. I've never wanted to rip you apart this bad before."

I try to get away from him, but he's bearing down on me like a locomotive. I stumble through the walls into the living room. Alejandro is still asleep on the couch. Groan grabs at me but I manage to scoot just out of his reach. I feint left, then go right. He reads me, blocking my escape. When his claws dig into my arm, I tear loose, spinning through the wall until I'm standing outside the house, beneath the branches of the big sugar maple tree. Groan flies out after me. I try to bob and weave out of his reach, sprinting across the snowy yard in the bright sunlight. He's right behind me. Without the closet to hide in, I don't even know where to run. So I haul ass across to the corner of the garage. He's right on me. Instead of ducking back into the breezeway or the garage, I go down the little hillside to the brook.

"Get back here!" Groan shouts. "Take it like a man!"

I spill through the brook, feeling the cold water around my ankles, and then I'm up on the other side, speeding across the yard next to Kyle's. The tug of the tether doesn't kick in.

"You're such a chicken-shit," Groan calls out. "I'll just wait for you here. How about that? Because you're going to come back.

Because you know what's going to happen if I catch a glimpse of you talking with those other two nimrods."

He stands on the other side of the brook, his chest heaving, his skin extra pale in the direct sunlight, dark circles under his eyes, his mouth a crooked cavern lined with stalactites. His raggedy clothing is faded, part of the brim of his hat hangs loose. His eyes dance with malice. I try to think of where to hide.

"And while I'm waiting," he says, "I'm going to fix your little hidey-hole to make sure you're never going to want to be in there again." He runs one hand across the back of his neck. "I think it gave me a rash. You're disgusting."

He turns and stalks back to the house. Just before he reaches the garage, he calls back over his shoulder, "Don't think you're sparing yourself your ass-whooping, either. The longer you wait, the worse it's going to be. Believe it."

Groan slips through the wall of the garage.

I've got nowhere to hide.

41

———

Kyle's eyes go wide. "In your hiding spot?"

"Yeah. He walked in like it was nothing."

We're in the basement of Kyle's house. Yes, I'm ignoring Groan's warning.

"We're dead," Kyle says.

"We're already dead, Kyle."

"But how can he do that? He can't get into our hiding spots. That's why they're hiding spots."

This isn't going to be pretty. "He says it's because of Karen."

"Karen would never give anything away. Or tell him anything. Ever."

"She didn't tell him anything."

"I told you. She wouldn't."

"Kyle. He says he got her. Maybe he's lying—but you said yourself she's gone. For a while now. So I don't know."

"He—" His face crumbles, starting from his eyes. "No."

Poor kid. I get it. I mean, I did the past four decades pretty much on my own—but I'm older. Here's Kyle, starting out scared as shit. Then Karen comes along, pretty much takes him under her wing. Keeps him from feeling alone. She's smart. She figures out a system. She brings Kyle and Andy together, probably makes them feel like a little gang. Or a family. She gets the jump on what Groan's doing, all by herself. Puts the clues together. Has the courage to make the run, all by herself. Karen is everything for these guys. Even I feel the stab of grief, and I didn't know her.

"I don't believe you," Kyle says.

"I'm sorry. Groan's a bastard."

Kyle clenches his hands, turning from me, hiding the tears. He shakes his head.

"Look—we'll finish what Karen started," I offer. "Because she figured it out. She did."

"And look what it got her!" Kyle shouts.

"No. Don't say it like that. It's going to get the rest of us out of here. Everything she did mattered."

"Out of here? How? He got her. And we can't even hide from Scary Eyes anymore! How are we going to escape now?"

"Together. That's how."

"I don't believe you."

"Well, I don't believe Groan. Scary Eyes," I say. "All that talk about possessing Jacinta? Having her murder her family? It's a lie."

"You hope it's a lie. That's not the same."

"No. It's a lie. He hasn't got a chance with her. She's different —but she's not like Mrs. Gracie. Or my dad. He's got no way in. I listened to her. Most of what she says is logical if you follow it. She's just different." It makes even more sense now than when I first guessed it in the closet with Groan's leering face two inches from my own. I played along, but I saw it for what it was: bullshit. He's trying to keep my focus on that so I can't see what else he's doing. Subtle, for Groan. I'll give him that.

Kyle isn't buying it. "He got into your closet. He wasn't lying about that. Obviously."

I stare at the casement window across the basement. The

trees behind Karen's house are just visible. Smart girl. How much did she figure out?

Maybe not everything.

"Unless he was," I say.

"You said he was right there."

"He was. But I don't think *that's* what he was lying about."

"But he said it. And he was there."

I turn to him. "What if the lie isn't that he can suddenly get into our hiding spots because he's stronger? What if it's that he could *always* get into our hiding spots? The whole time."

"He couldn't."

"Why not?"

"Because he would have."

"Are you sure?"

"You're not making any sense."

"Hear me out," I say. "What if he can get in there anytime he wants, always could. Just like how he can show up in the daytime. What would we have done?"

"I don't know. That's horrible."

"Think about it. If we had nowhere to hide—what would we do then?"

"Get killed."

"Okay. Maybe we'd get killed. But then what? What if you'd never found a single place to hide? What would you have tried?"

"Anything."

"Exactly. Anything. Everything. Like—leaving."

"But we can't leave."

"Karen did."

"And he killed her."

"Maybe he did. Maybe he's lying." I look back toward my house. "Probably he is."

Kyle can't handle the sideways thinking. "But you said he said he did."

"*He* said he did. But like I said: He lies. That's the most important thing about him."

"Then where is she?"

"I don't know. But think about it. She figured it out. In time. Because she was smart, she paid attention, she watched what he did. And he's obviously been doing something to keep us from seeing where our bodies are. Something that keeps him busy pretty much every day, right?"

"So?"

"So I think if we'd had no place to hide all this time—we'd have been a lot more desperate to leave. And we would've tried harder. More often. Earlier. Do you see what I'm getting at?"

Kyle nibbles at the corner of his mouth like he's solving a tricky long division problem. "He let us think it. Even though it wasn't true?"

"Even though it wasn't true. Because if we always have a place to hide—a place right in our homes—then we're never going to leave. Right? We're too scared, especially when we have a place we feel safe. And it worked."

"But why didn't he just get us? Like Karen?"

"Because he wants us just like we are. Not gone. But *here*. Afraid. He's been feeding off us the whole time. Us. Our fear. Our whatever—I'm not sure how, but it makes sense. And now that Karen's gone, he's not stronger. He's weaker. I've seen it. He's falling apart. He's desperate—which is why he's playing this whole game. Lying about possessing Jacinta. Maybe lying about Karen. It's all to keep us from seeing what's right in front of our faces."

"That we can get away," Kyle says.

"Like Karen did."

"But if she got away—why didn't she come back? She promised she would."

"Maybe she's trying. Maybe she can't. I don't know—but I don't think Groan knows, either, and it's driving him insane. I bet he's looking for her every free second. He's probably doing it right now." I go to the wall. "Let's go over to Andy's."

"It's daytime."

"I bet we can."

"How?"

"Because if Groan's hunting for Karen, he's not minding the store. Or the tethers. And he's weaker, right?"

"I don't know about this."

"Only one way to find out."

We both slip through the wall, out into the yard. As we start toward the street, I keep an eye out for Groan. I'm sure he's going to take it out on us if he sees us together—but I'm willing to gamble he's too busy to notice. We get closer to the street and still no tether. We reach the street.

"Well, look at this," I say. "Still walking."

Kyle scans the trees, the houses, the rooftops like he's ready to book it back to his house. "He's watching. I know he is."

"I don't feel him. Do you?"

"No. But that doesn't mean he isn't."

We cross over the section of Field Drive next to Karen's house. "Listen, when we get to Andy's, don't mention the thing about the hiding places."

"Why not?"

"Because if something goes wrong—I don't want him to have no hope at all."

"He'd freak out. He's terrified of Flibber. Like, beyond terrified."

At the corner of Field and Chestnut, still no tug. "Has he ever described what the hell Flibber looks like?"

"Not really. He usually starts to cry," Kyle says. "But I think it's like something from *Sesame Street*. Only scary."

"Groan is such an asshole."

Kyle doesn't even blink at the swear word. I'm clearly becoming a bad influence. We hustle across Chestnut—after waiting for a couple of cars to pass, because of stupid habit—keeping our eyes out for Groan. Nothing. Before we pass through the snow-covered rhododendrons, I scan the neighborhood. A car backs out of Karen's driveway, exhaust steaming in the cold. Do they even realize their resident ghost is gone? Probably not. Another invisible story going on around them, layers and layers of life and death, from the tiny to the immense, unfolding unimagined, over, under, and around, always changing.

I slip through the wall, following Kyle.

When Andy sees me, he comes tearing across the living room and crashes into my leg, holding tight.

"Hey," I say. "Hello."

The kid doesn't let go.

Kyle looks at me. "He did this with Karen."

I reach down and hesitantly pat Andy on the head. "Good to see you, buddy. Maybe if you can give me back my leg?" He doesn't budge. Grips me tighter. I'm not really annoyed, but it's not exactly convenient. I walk with him still on my leg over to the kitchen. Andy doesn't giggle. Doesn't really say anything. He's just crushing my leg, his eyes screwed shut. "Does Karen have some trick for peeling him off?"

"She lets him hang on," Kyle says. "He'll let go eventually."

The house is neat. Still. Early afternoon sunlight falls in bright rectangles beneath the windows. Nothing looks new in the house, but it's all kept up. They even have an old-style phone hanging from the wall in the kitchen, green with actual buttons, a long curling cord connecting the mouth-ear piece with the part on the wall. Next to it, the hallway. I carry Andy down it and stop at the window at the end.

"We made it this far," I say to Kyle. "Right?"

"Right."

"Should we see how much farther we can get?"

"Is it safe?"

"I'm not sure *safe* is what we should be waiting for. What do you think?"

I look down at Andy. His hair flies off in several directions. "Hey, Andy. I'm going to need my leg back, okay? We're going to take a little walk, see how far we can get. Would you like that?"

He acts like he didn't hear me. Just squeezes tighter.

"Outside. The way Karen went. Come on—let's give it a shot," I say.

"No," Andy squeaks. More head shaking.

Kyle and I exchange a look.

"It's fine." Kyle comes over and squats next to Andy. "We might be able to get away."

Andy shakes his head.

"I don't mind checking it out on my own," I say. "But I can't really walk too well with Spider-Man on my leg. Maybe you could hang on to Kyle? How's that sound?"

"Flibber," Andy says.

"Say what?"

"Flibber."

Each time he says it, he crushes my leg.

"Flibber's busy right now," I say. "It's daytime, remember?"

Andy peels one hand from my leg and points his finger outside. "Flibber."

Kyle looks at me, eyes widening. I go to the window, dragging my heavy leg. I don't see any sign of Groan.

"Go check some of the other windows," I tell Kyle.

He slides through the beige wall into what I guess is a bedroom.

"Tim," he whispers after a few moments. The tone of his voice says it all. I curse under my breath and limp through the wall. A tall bed, wide, takes up half the room. Bureau. Walker. Knitted throw across the blankets, all of them lined up and smoothed. The scent of old people. Kyle crouches by the window facing east.

I pause. Put a hand on Andy's head. "Seriously, man. I need you to let go of my leg. Nothing's going to happen in here. I promise. But, come on." It takes a little more prodding on my part, but Andy lets go of my leg. He doesn't go far from it, though, basically bumping into me with each step I take. Fine. At least I'm not dragging all his weight.

Staying low, I come up to the other side of the window, across from Kyle. "Where?"

"Right next to the corner of that blue house."

"You're sure?"

"Take a look."

I peer out the window, trying to keep out of sight. The backyard extends past the deck for about twenty yards. At the far end is one of those outdoor stoves, a couple of wooden Adirondack chairs, all wearing blue tarps underneath a mantle of snow. Two houses stand on the other side, both of them on the street behind Chestnut, Fox Ridge Road. Both are small ranch-style houses. The one to my left is white with black shutters. The one to the right is a pale blue, faded and looking worse for the wear. Groan stands next to the corner. Still as a scarecrow, he's draped in the shadows of an overhang.

"Shit," I whisper. I sink down beneath the window and look at Kyle.

"We're dead," he says.

Andy tears off through the wall in the direction of the kitchen.

"He must have followed me," I say.

"We're dead."

"You like saying that a little too much, Kyle."

"But he's right there."

I inch my eye up to the window again. Yep. He's still there, watching. His face is pale in the shadow of the overhang. I get the sensation he's looking right at me, right in the eye.

"He hasn't moved," I say.

"He will."

Groan tilts his head, but remains in place. Is he going to rush us? Take us all on at once?

"Maybe he's waiting for night," Kyle says. "When he's strongest."

He was strong enough to kill me in the daytime yesterday. Still, he's been falling apart; maybe it took more out of him than he let on. And all three of us are together now. He might need to wait until night. I slide out of sight again. "Maybe. But I think he's mostly sending us a message."

"That we're out of luck."

"That's what he wants us to think. But we're not. We've got a leg up on him. He's the one who should be worried."

"He's not scared of us."

"Don't be so sure."

Honestly, I don't know if I believe it myself. But no point letting it show. Having two panicked kids to deal with isn't going to help.

"You know what?" I say. "I'll get him out of here. He's pissed at me, not you guys."

So maybe he'll spare you having your heads ripped off right after he stuffs your torn-off hands into your mouths, I helpfully don't add. Even if it's true.

"What are you talking about?" Kyle says. The idea of being alone doesn't go down well.

"I'll lead him back to my house. He can take it all out on me. Blow off his steam, whatever. I still need to find out where we're buried, even with everything he's done to make Alyssa think I'm gross. She can't stay off her devices forever. I'll be back soon enough, hopefully with the info." I stand. "You just lay low. For all he knows, you guys still think your hiding spots work. He'll probably keep that up—so all you need to do is get home when I distract him."

"Probably?"

"Probably. I mean, he is a demon."

"He'll know."

"Not necessarily. Karen learned a lot. But even when she got away, he never said anything to you about it. I don't think he likes us all knowing the same things."

"Karen was—never mind."

I arch an eyebrow. "Karen was what?"

Kyle puts his fingertips to his temples for a second, closes his eyes, then looks back at me. "Nothing."

"Smarter than me?" I take a not-so-wild guess.

He doesn't say anything.

"Well, I'm doing the best I can, Kyle," I say. "And maybe you're right. Maybe she's the smartest fricking ghost ever to haunt this little corner of Andover. But I'm all we've got right now, unless you've got some better ideas?"

He juts his lower lip out. Then shakes his head. "No."

"Fine. Now if you don't mind, I'll lead our favorite homicidal maniac away from you and kitchen sink Spider-Man over there, let him beat me to death and get it out of his system. We'll go from there. Okay?"

Maybe I'm a little harsh on him. Sure. Because maybe I'm a little sensitive about being called a dummy. Or about actually being a dummy.

Or both.

So when I'm ready to do it—and by *ready* I mean resigned to it—I tell Kyle to get ready to book it over to his house. I'm going to head in Groan's direction, make sure he's focused on me alone. I can see Kyle through the front entryway.

"I'll be back when I can," I say.

He nods.

I turn to the kitchen sink. "Bye, Andy. Stay in there for a while."

"Bye!" he calls out.

Hesitating just makes it worse, so I plunge out through the back wall. A row of long icicles hangs off the roof, glimmering in the sunlight. I wave to Groan—but he's not there.

"Where'd you go, dickface?" I whisper as I look around. He's not by the blue house, not in the backyard, not in the stretch of little trees bordering the yard. I spin around, but he's not on the roof, waiting to leap down on top of me. I don't see him anywhere. I hurry around to the street side of the house in time to catch a glimpse of Kyle hot-footing it through the walls of his house.

Is Scary Eyes in there waiting for him? Did I mess up again?

But, really—it's not me. It's Groan. *He's* the problem. How the hell can you deal on any level with a shameless, sneaky, lying, violent, evil being and not come up short? A surge of anger burbles into my throat. I step into the road, staying right in the middle even as a black pickup truck passes a half inch away from me.

I raise my arms. "Hey, you ridiculous pile of shit! Groan! Asshole!" I look around, this way and that. "I'm right here. You're so much stronger now? Come on—let's see it!"

A mail truck whooshes by me, the wake of winter air barely registering. I stride across the rest of the road, following the snow banks toward my house. The hemlock trees sway on the breeze, the snow on their branches weighing them down.

"Oh—I get it!" I shout. "You can't handle me, right? You have to go for the little kid—see if you can't get him to poop himself. What a tough guy you are, what a complete and total—"

I still don't see Groan, but I feel something. On my legs. My torso. My shoulders. I'm almost at the brook, where the weathered post fence sags above the culvert. The water flows fast around snow and black rocks. I take another step. And another.

But no more after that.

All the weight of gravity stops me from even moving any part of me more than a few inches forward. I sidle left. Then right. Nope.

The tether holds me back.

Away from my house.

42

I stand in the lengthening afternoon, seventy yards away from my house, unable to get any closer, and hang my head. Kyle's right. Hell, the *universe* is right. I can tell myself what a genius I am, but no one else is having it. Because I'm not.

Damn it.

Groan sealed me off. Somehow. When I wasn't paying attention. When I was congratulating myself a little too soon. All this time, he's been hard at it, knowing exactly what he needed to do to make sure I can't figure out where we're buried. To make sure Alyssa is permanently out of reach. And who knows what else he's done, desperate to make sure his three remaining hostages don't have the slightest chance at getting away. He knows how serious it is and he's not going to give an inch. Karen took him by surprise—I'm pretty sure of that. Knocked him sideways. But he's recovered and he knows how to seal up any plug left. There might have been some small window of time where we could've gotten out, but it's gone.

Groan outplayed me.

. . .

Kyle doesn't even want to come down out of his attic loft hiding spot. After half an hour of badgering, he finally gives in, climbing down and passing through the walls and floors of his house with me to the yard.

"He's definitely watching," he says.

"Probably. Who cares." I start off toward Andy's house.

Kyle looks around, still half-panicked, and hustles after me.

"He'll see we're together," he says.

"He saw it already."

"He'll be even more pissed."

"Yep."

I don't slow. Kyle struggles to keep up with me.

"What do we do now?" he says.

"See who he cuts off next."

"See—what? He's going to—we should go back to my house."

"And leave Andy on his own?"

"You think he's going to do that?"

"Yes. Which is why we need to stick together."

Andy doesn't mind the company. I even let him stay locked around my leg. There's nothing in his house even resembling a computer, or modern phone, or iPad. I spot a tall book of maps of Eastern Massachusetts on one of the shelves, but my fingers slip right through it. So do Kyle's and Andy's.

A big bay window in the living room faces the street, lets in the late afternoon winter sun. Little porcelain figurines line the windowsill: a postman, a shepherd and lone sheep, a snowman, a bear with a sheet over him and a jack-o'-lantern in his hand. A trick-or-treating bear, how adorable. I shake my head.

"Do they ever use fancy phones, Andy?" I ask.

"No. They don't even watch cartoons. They're old."

"They do anything else?"

"They make grilled cheese sandwiches for lunch." It comes out like *sam-midges*.

"I could use a grilled cheese right about now."

"The people in my house make pancakes all the time," Kyle says. "That's the worst for me. I love pancakes. With syrup. And butter."

"Pop-Tarts," Andy says. "Chocolate."

"No," I say. "Strawberry."

The memory lingers, all of us, I'm pretty sure, recalling that amazing smell coming up from the toasters of our youth.

"Why do I miss breakfast most of all?" Kyle says.

"Because breakfast is the best," I say.

"Apple Jacks," Andy says.

"Fruity Pebbles," Kyle says.

"Boo Berry," I add.

"Oh," Kyle says, drawing the syllable out, a look of wonder on his face.

"I once ate a whole box of it in a single sitting," I say. "Turned my poop blue."

"No it didn't," Kyle says.

Andy looks back and forth between us, smiling.

"Blue. Not kidding at all," I say. "Man, I could eat five boxes of it now."

"And poo-poo blue," Andy says, delighted at the prospect.

"So much blue poo-poo," I say.

The kid cracks up.

"Vanilly Crunch," Kyle says.

"Peanut Butter Crunch," I say.

"Cap'n Crunch!" Andy yells.

"Quisp."

"Alpha-Bits."

"Freakies."

Kyle and I hurl them back and forth at each other, both of us smiling. Andy's pleased as punch by the whole thing. Because we conjured it, if even for just a few moments: the landscape of a lost childhood we all remember. The cartoons. The commercials. The cereal (and the prizes in the boxes!). The ridiculous names, the bright colors in the milk.

God, for a moment, I can't talk.

Look at this little club of ours.

Ninety-two minutes.

We still have some daylight left. I'm keeping an eye on the angle of the sun. Sneaking peeks outside the windows, looking to see if Groan's trying to give us the business again with his creepy-scarecrow routine. I don't see him. Not yet. He's coming, though.

Kyle lies on his back in the middle of one of those old, woven, oval rugs, brown, orange, and yellow, recalling the Aurora Model dinosaur scenes he'd built. A shadow passes by the kitchen window, which I can just get a glimpse of from where I'm standing.

"Kyle," I say.

". . . and I always felt bad for the woolly mammoth, because he was trapped in the tar pit . . ."

"Kyle."

He stops talking and looks at me.

I look at Andy. "Do you know when these people are supposed to be back?"

Seems a little bit complex for the kid, so I'm not hoping for much.

"Springtime," he says.

"*Spring*time?"

"They go away for all winter."

"Seriously?"

Andy nods.

"You mean you spend all winter by yourself?" I say.

He nods, like it's no big deal. Man, I was bouncing off the walls when there was no one in my house. This kid puts up with something similar every year. I guess you can get used to anything.

"Well, you might want to get into your hiding spot," I say, calm as can be.

Kyle sits up like he's on a spring.

"Flibber?" Andy doesn't even wait for my answer before he's off through the walls and safely (but not really) in his cabinet beneath the sink. Can't blame him.

Kyle looks after him, that little line between his eyebrows.

"Don't tell him," I say quietly.

"But it doesn't work."

"You want him hanging on to *your* leg for the next six hours? Then go ahead and tell him."

I'm up, heading down the hallway in the direction I'd seen the shadow pass. If Groan's coming for us, I want to figure out the best way to keep him away from Andy for as long as I can. One of the back bedrooms is made up as a guest room, with checker-patterned drapes straight out of 1972, two wall shelves with old sports trophies (1975 Slugger of the Year, 1977 1000 Meter Swim First Place), and a sewing machine off to the side of the window. Approaching the window, I search for Groan, ready for him to bust through the wall like a hideous Kool-Aid Man. But when I look out the window for my least favorite demon, I freeze.

Alyssa stands in the snow behind the deck, looking at the back of Andy's house, wearing a black jacket and jeans, her hair blowing, her face burnished by the cold. She glances around at the neighboring houses and the street, not doing a good job of looking innocent. Sticking close to the back of the house, she goes up to the kitchen window and presses her face to the glass, shading the glare with her free hand, like she's saluting. She moves away from the window.

I slide through the wall. Just as I do, she lifts her phone, getting ready to take a picture. I slip between her arms and tap the screen, snapping off four pictures in a row. She yelps and holds the phone at arm's length, looks at the camera, then lifts her gaze to the back of the house. I take a bunch more pictures (it's the only button I can hit). Instead of flinging the phone down, she brings it back to her face.

"Okay." She makes the camera setting go away. Before I can reach for the little yellow notepad, she taps on it and it fills the screen.

It's me thank God you're here, I type. Standing so close to her, I keep crossing her boundary, sending wave after wave of ripples along my shoulders and back. Can't be helped. Before she can respond, I keep typing. *Not the demon. Me, Tim. He's locked me away from the house somehow. He's been pretending to be me. Ignore everything he said.*

"It's really you?" she says. "How do I know?"

Because I'd never be gross.

"Easy to say."

No, really. Doesn't it seem weird that it suddenly changed?

I can see her thinking about it.

"Prove it."

After a moment, I type the words to the chorus of her favorite song—that one I hated so much. Even typing the words sticks the horrible melody in my head, but, hey, desperate times, desperate measures.

"I love that song," she says.

I don't. Remember?

"Oh, that's right."

And you tried to get me to prove I'm a ghost by making me guess how many fingers you were holding up. Which makes no sense.

"It made sense at the time." She stares at the phone, her mouth scrunched to the side. "Your spelling is better."

Than Groan's? No doubt. Even he copped to it.

Yes. I'm not a stupid demon, that's why.

"He's disgusting."

He's worse than that. He's the one who pushed your sister down the stairs.

"We have to move," she says.

I've got a better plan. How'd you know I was here?

"I didn't. I'm just doing some research."

The houses where the other kids died.

"Exactly."

Smart. There's three of us left. The other two are inside the house right now. Andy and Kyle.

She looks up at the house, unsure. I don't expect to see Andy, and I don't see Kyle, even though he's probably watching from somewhere. Alyssa certainly wouldn't be able to see them, even if they were outside.

Did you find out where we're buried???

She pulls her head back, surprised. "Like twenty-five minutes ago."

Where?

"Place called Summer Grove. All four of you were buried there."

Where is it? Summer Grove.

"On the other side of downtown, maybe a mile past it or something."

Can you show me? On the map thing?

"Yeah, sure."

As she pulls up a map and moves it around with her finger, I look at where the sun is: across the street, just about touching the treetops.

Eighty-two minutes, give or take.

"Here." Alyssa makes the map bigger, pointing to a patch of green shapes like an uneven pair of lungs, crossed back and forth with gray lanes. Summer Grove Cemetery, it reads. I try to make sense of where it is, then realize it's not too far from the pond we used to swim in, a little place with a dock and a float and a town rec building. The road leading to the pond curves down past the cemetery, which rises beyond a winding stone wall, stretching up along a shaded hillside. If Karen disappeared trying to reach it, she went off in exactly the right direction.

Alyssa makes the map disappear and brings back the notepad.

I know where it is, I type.

"But can you even get there?"

Maybe. I'm not sure.

"I thought you couldn't."

I thought I couldn't ever get this far. Now I can't get back to the house. So who knows.

"What am I supposed to do about the demon?"

If we can get to the cemetery, I think he's done for. We're keeping him strong. If we're gone, he's gone.

"Are you sure?"

No. But I'm willing to try.

"You definitely don't sound like the demon."

Nicest compliment I've ever gotten.

But if we're going to make a break for it, Groan can't know. He seems like he's been busy, so that might be possible—which, wait a minute. Has he been too busy? I look behind me, in the direction of the cemetery, the way Karen went.

Can you wait here for a minute? I type.

"I—uh, sure." Her fingers grip the phone clumsily and her teeth chatter. I hadn't realized how cold it is.

I'll be quick.

I dart off along the side of the house. Through the trees separating the yard from the next one along Chestnut. I pass between tree shadows from across the street. I speed up. It's hard to know exactly where I stopped the night I tried to go the way Karen had gone, since it was dark, but I have a feel for the general area. I reach it. And pass it. Right through it. I keep going. By the time I'm halfway across the next yard, I'm sure of it. Nothing tugs at me. There's no tether.

But Groan probably figures we don't know that. He probably thinks we won't even try to make any kind of move at all until nightfall.

In seventy-five minutes.

Alyssa gets the plan, once I explain it to her. She's amazing. Hits me with a few questions, comes up with a couple ideas I never would've thought of, and she's all in. If I'd known her when I was alive—well, I would have been too shy to ever say anything to her. But if I hadn't been such an idiot, she's exactly the kind of friend I'd have wanted to have. Friend. Girlfriend. Either.

"How will I know you've made it?" she asks.

If my plan works—a big if—and my theory is right—maybe even a bigger if—then Groan himself won't have anything left of his power once we escape. *Good question. I'll be gone. So will the demon. I guess that's the sign.*

She nods. "Good luck, Tim."

Thank you thank you thank you. After a second, I add, *You're amazing.*

With a smile, she says, "So are you." She turns and heads to opposite edge of the house. She waits until there aren't any cars passing by, slips out to the edge of the driveway, and hurries to the sidewalk next to the snowbanks, trailing puffs of white condensation in the freezing air. I watch her for a minute, then look around the rest of the yard. I pass back into Andy's house. Kyle's been watching from the kitchen window.

"What was all that?" he says. "Who's she?"

"Alyssa." I lean down next to the sink. "Andy, come on out. It's all clear."

After a second, Andy crawls out through the wooden door.

"Guys, we're leaving," I say.

They both stare at me.

"Karen was right." I cock a thumb over my shoulder. "The cemetery is that way. She figured it out. And I think she made it."

"Groan said she didn't," Kyle says.

"Groan lies."

"But you couldn't follow her."

"Not then. I think now we can. If we hurry." I move down the hallway. "Karen figured out what Groan's been doing. He's been hiding the signal from our bodies with the barriers he puts in place during the day. That stuff he does. And here's the thing—Groan figured out you guys were talking."

"No he didn't. We had a system," Kyle says.

"A brilliant system. Worked for a long time. But he caught on. And I think he trapped her away from her house, like he's doing to me right now."

"She didn't say anything about that."

"She didn't want to worry you."

He has nothing to say to that. She was smart.

"The point is," I continue, "she worked out, or guessed, or however she did it, that for Groan to rearrange the boundaries—which we thought of as tethers—in one spot means weakening them in another. And that it's hard work for him to change them in the first place."

"You don't know that for sure," Kyle helpfully points out.

"Can you think of another reason Groan didn't come and kick our butts earlier? He was right outside. Watching us."

"He wanted to scare us."

"Sure. He always wants that. But why not more? Why not really drive home the message by pounding the crap out of us? Killing us. I think it's because he can't. Not yet. Because he blew it all on shifting things around to keep me away from Alyssa. He's weak already from Karen being gone. This took a lot out of him. He's probably gathering back his energy to come take care of us tonight. So we have a little time right now."

"To what?"

"To get the hell out of here before he knows we're gone."

"Are you serious?"

"Kyle, I'm a guy who ate a whole box of Boo Berry in one sitting. I'm nothing but serious. Come on."

We reach the edge of the house and pass through it. The sun shines through the trees. A little more than an hour before sunset.

"What if he sees us leaving?" Kyle says.

"I don't want to see Flibber," Andy whines.

"Alyssa's going to distract him," I say.

"How?"

"Groan half figured out how to use her phone. But he doesn't know everything. So Alyssa's going home right now—where she'll have a conversation with me."

"With you? How?"

"It won't be me. It'll be her friend Schuyler—pretending to be me. Groan won't know the difference. He's a moron."

"But he'll know you're not there."

"She's also going to have her sister pretend to see me. Groan's so paranoid he won't know what to make of it. It'll make him insane. He'll be all over it. Looking for me. Trying to figure out how I'm doing it. What's going on. He'll sweep through every inch of the house, the yard, the street, and probably all the way over here. Which is why we don't want to be here when he figures it out. Which means we're leaving. Now."

Andy holds on to Kyle's leg, looks up at me. Looks at Kyle.

"Come on, Kyle," I say. "What do you think? Have I missed anything?"

He frowns, that little line between his eyebrows appearing. "Do you know where the cemetery is?"

"Yes."

"Do you know where our graves are inside it?"

"No. But I think we'll know."

"How?"

"Because Karen said so. She caught a glimpse, remember? The sunset. The fire. I think she had more of it figured out than she let on. So if you don't trust me—do you trust her?"

"I trust Karen," Andy says.

Kyle looks at him. Then at me. Then off down the road where Karen disappeared. He looks back at me. "Let's go."

43

MOVING DOWN THE ROAD IS ONE OF THE STRANGEST THINGS I'VE
ever done. After being confined to the same hundred yards or so
for decades, each step forward feels like the world reinventing
itself. Cars pass by, some bright, others wearing shrouds of salt.
Birds flit overhead, crows and sparrows on the wing against the
December blue. Snow drapes the power lines.

"I remember that house." Kyle points to a white house with
red trim. The trees in front nearly hide it from the road. They'd
been nothing more than saplings when our school bus had
passed on the way to school.

It's disorienting. Some of the houses are the same. Others are
gone, replaced by bigger, fancier houses. Even the street signs
look different, with darker colors and bigger letters. The painted
lines on the street are brighter. The sidewalk isn't concrete, but
asphalt. The streetlights are taller and thinner. Everywhere, the
present blots out the past. Always. Forever. The river only flows
one direction and it takes everything with it.

Andy keeps bumping into me. "I want to go home," he says.

"That's where we're going," I say.

"My house."

"We're going somewhere even better. Somewhere you don't have to worry about Flibber."

"I don't like Flibber."

"Me, neither."

"Will Flibber follow us?"

"Nope."

"I hope not."

I look to the west, across the street. High clouds catch the gold of late afternoon. Forty-seven minutes. I don't see any flames yet. "But let's hurry, just to be safe."

Andy starts crying. "I don't want Flibber to follow us."

"He's not following us," Kyle says, an edge to his voice.

I look back the way we came. No sign of Groan. He took his eye from the ball. Looking for Karen. Rearranging the tethers. If luck holds, he's still back at the house wondering how Alyssa is talking with me, Jacinta seeing me. I don't want Andy to panic—and take off running back to his kitchen cabinet.

"What was your favorite toy, Andy?" I ask.

"A bunny named Bunny."

"Perfect name. Tell me about him."

Kyle sees what I'm doing. He joins me in interrogating Andy about his stuffed rabbit.

Forty-one minutes.

The center of town kills our strange conversation. The town library stands across a big intersection, a two-story brick building with a weathered brass cupola extending up from the middle of the roof, the sky blazing with sunset behind it. Traffic moves through a complicated series of lights, bright colors, arrows, a weird robot voice announcing *The crosswalk sign is on.* All around, people in cars and on the sidewalks, heading home from work, maybe going out for supper, just another weekday. The convenience store where I'd gleefully stock up on bubblegum cigars and copies of *Creem* magazine is a wine store. The pharmacy where my mom brought me to pick up prescriptions or calamine lotion after I'd waded through poison ivy now has bikini-clad mannequins in the front window. Hardware store, gone, a coffee shop in its place. Grocery store, gone, a CVS in its place. I see three or four signs for banks, but nothing that looks like a bank.

"Is Flibber coming?" Andy asks again.

Man, I'd be happy to never hear that question again. "No."

Kyle's looking jumpy, like it's all overwhelming him, too.

I point down the street that runs past the library. "It's this way. Come on."

Andy doesn't move. He holds up his hands. "Hold hands to cross the big street."

Kyle and I look at each other, then take the kid's hands. With the sun setting, we move across Main Street, dodging the cars so Andy doesn't get any more freaked out. Holding hands. Like three kids, maybe brothers, out trick-or-treating.

I'm confused about where we need to turn to reach the cemetery. At the bottom of the hill, two different turns open up to the left. I kick myself for not looking more carefully at the map when Alyssa showed it to me. And for not paying attention on summer afternoons when my mom drove me and Craig and Hugh to the pond. I would just stare out into the hot July air through the open windows of the station wagon, wearing swim trunks, towel draped over my shoulders, diving mask and kickboard by my bare feet. I never paid enough attention.

So I take a chance, skip the first left, and hike around the curve of the second one.

Nine minutes.

"It's getting dark," Andy says.

"Not yet, buddy." I point to the western sky, still slapped with broad strokes of ember red, fiery orange, a few feathers of wispy clouds gone purple. "See? We've got plenty of daylight."

Of course, by now the cars all have their headlights on, sweeping over us as they pass, deepening the illusion of Halloween. I'm thankful for the snowbanks and drifts, otherwise the cars would probably be close enough to stop Andy in his tracks.

"But I see the moon," Andy says. "And the moon is nighttime."

He's right. At the top of the street, the moon, nearly full, crests the horizon, shining through the trees. It glows copper, the biggest jack-o'-lantern of all.

"Then let's do the hustle." I speed up even more.

"Where's Karen?" Andy hasn't let go of my hand and I'm practically dragging him next to me.

"This is the way she went."

"Will we see her?"

"Only one way to find out. Let's keep going."

We reach an intersection partway up the hill. I take us to the right. The streetlights come on along the gently curving road. Houses sit back from the road, separated by low fields of snow carved by the wind. Big houses, some of them illuminated with little spotlights, others wearing incredible collections of holiday lights.

"Is that Flibber?" Andy pulls to a halt. He stares wide-eyed at a figure in front of one of the houses.

I yank his arm. "Come on. No. That's a snowman. See? Just a snowman."

He's dragging his feet. Man, it's amazing how heavy a scrawny ghost can suddenly be.

"Andy, come on—we're almost there. Do the hustle, remember?"

Something lopes onto the road up ahead, in a patch between the streetlights. We all flinch. A ghostly white mark at chest height darts across the road. A deer. A few more quick steps and it leaps the snowbank and disappears into the trees.

Andy's wrapped on my leg, gripping it like it's a ship's mast and he's at sea in the middle of the biggest storm ever.

"Just a deer," I say.

"What if he's running away from Flibber?"

"He's not. He's just hurrying home for dinner. He's fine."

"Deer don't really have homes," Kyle adds.

"Thanks, Kyle. Noted."

"Well, they don't."

"I want to go home!" Andy wails.

"Tim," Kyle says.

I pry Andy's arms from my leg. "Listen, buddy. We have to keep moving." I'm on the verge of adding *because Flibber may well be after us by now*, but I stop myself, figuring it'll only make things worse. "Come on. Let go. We all need both our legs to do this, okay?"

"Tim," Kyle says again.

"Don't need any more deer trivia at the moment, thanks."

"No. Look."

I glance up. About a quarter mile on, the road bends to the right, down to the pond. A smaller lane angles up to the left. Summer Grove Cemetery. And where it should be dark it shines with a light more alive than sunset. Oranges. Golds. Shimmering yellows. Hints of green. Of indigo. Rising from behind the gates.

Because the sunset.

Imagine drowning—and then suddenly feeling your foot touch bottom, safe. Now multiply that by a thousand. Imagine seeing the world with terrible eyesight—and then having someone put the right pair of glasses on your nose. More real than real. Crisp, bright. A signal. The ultimate signal.

Because the sunset.

This is what Karen saw when she peered past Groan's handiwork.

This is what we should've seen when we died, showing us which way to go.

I turn to Kyle. The colors reflect on his face, glimmering in his eyes. I look at Andy. He's captivated, little tears quivering in his eyelashes.

"Come on, guys." For a second, my words catch in my throat. Thirty-eight years. "We're going home."

44

We run. The moon paces us through the trees to our left. Ahead of us, unearthly light shimmers like the most beautiful northern lights anyone's ever seen. We cross through the light of the final streetlights before the gates of the cemetery. On the granite pillar to the right of the iron gates, a handprint shines like it was pressed out of liquid sunlight.

"Hold on a sec, guys." I walk over to it. Hold my hand out above it. My hand is bigger—but not by too much. It's probably bigger than Kyle's hand.

"What is that?" Kyle says.

"Karen." A weight falls off me. "She made it. She really made it—and she's telling you. *This* is telling you."

"But why didn't she come back for us?"

"Because she couldn't. Groan trapped her. Once he figured out she got away, he made sure she couldn't come back." I put my hand over the glowing print. Little sparks tickle my palm and the pads of my fingers. "But she left this sign for you. To tell you this is the right place. That she was here."

Kyle lowers his head, puts a hand over his brow. His chest hitches. Andy frowns at the sight of Kyle's tears and wraps his arms around his waist. Good guys, both of them. I wish I'd known them the whole time.

Reaching over, I pat them each on the shoulder. "This way. Let's finish this."

The gate is open and wide enough for cars. We hurry into the cemetery. Narrow lanes cross between stretches of headstones and tall trees. Ornamental shrubs wear cloaks of snow. Some of the smaller headstones are almost completely buried, nothing more than little pillows of snow. The hillsides rise and fall, lined with graves.

The sunset fires dance ahead of us, mesmerizing. As we draw closer, they sharpen, never still, revealing more detail, more intricacy. Like watching a fire, really staring at it—but with a depth I've never even imagined. No wonder most people don't have any trouble moving on. Smaug's treasure beneath the Lonely Mountain has nothing on what we're seeing. To our right, an oak about two feet across wears another of Karen's handprints, shining like a beacon.

"What now?" Kyle says.

"Follow it," I say. We hurry along, slipping between headstones and their delicate shadows cast across the snow by the moon.

Oh, Karen. You're a genius. The smartest frigging member of the Chestnut Street Ghost Society.

"She marked the trail for you guys," I say.

"What trail?" Kyle says.

"The trail to your graves. I'll bet anything."

By the time we reach the tree, I know I'm right. I spot the other marks, glowing bright, leading from one tree to another, off in two directions. And about two hundred yards out, I see one shining down low, on a tombstone.

"She stuck around," I say. "Found your graves. For when you got here."

"And the lights shine there, too," Andy says.

We're not all seeing the same lights. We each see our own. I see them down by a trio of birch trees, while the handprint on what must be Andy's grave isn't anywhere near them. Karen didn't take any chances—the guys are both younger than her, after all. She thought of everything.

"This one over here." I lead them by the series of handprints to the closest gravestone bearing Karen's signal. Her print shines like sunset reflecting on the surface of a lake. Below it, the engraved letters on the polished marble read:

Andrew Leonard Van Etten
Beloved Angel, Sleep in Peace
August 27, 1977 – October 31, 1981

Man, that's hard to read. I'm actually glad Andy can't. "Andy, it's yours."

He looks up at me. His face shines with the glow of a light I can't see. He looks back at the headstone. "I see into it."

The back of my neck suddenly crawls.

A familiar voice, dripping with malice, says, "Well, isn't this a pretty picture?"

We all snap our heads to the left. Groan leans against a marble obelisk not three yards away. Andy screams. Before he can dart off, I grab him by the collar of his Spider-Man costume. "Go! Go into it!"

He looks at me, eyes wide. I put myself between him and Groan, guiding Andy toward his gravestone. For a moment, the snow lights up, licks of golden illumination shining through from the ground below. And then Andy's gone, leaving nothing but an outline of bright yellow embers, a puff of glowing dandelion parasols, floating off and winking out.

"Oh, you little shit!" Groan charges us, his face a perfect fury, his eyes shining with rage.

"Yeah, a little late." I block Kyle, shoving him behind me as I duck out of Groan's way.

"I'm going to kill you both—and kill the fucking families you live with!"

As Groan flies past me, I step forward and twist my leg around his. I punch him in the back of the head as he stumbles. He falls into the snow.

Man, that feels good.

He whips up, clawing at me. I'm out of his reach by then. Kyle swings in behind Groan and kicks him in the back of his head. Jesus. I never would've expected it, but I guess I'm not the only one with some pent-up aggression. Before Kyle can go in for a second kick, I leap over and drag him out of Groan's reach. We break into a sprint as Groan scrambles to his feet. The trail of Karen's handprints leads off to a group of graves with little American flags poking out of the snow.

"Go. I'll lead him away," I whisper.

"What about your grave?"

"Don't worry about me. Just go!"

"I heard that, you little fuckers!" Groan roars. But unlike before, he isn't just winking out and appearing in front of us, zapping around like some horrible jack-in-the-box—because he's just lost a third of his remaining strength, which means he's only half as strong as he was a couple of weeks ago. And that's on top of whatever exertions he made trying to keep me away from my house.

I spin around. "You couldn't keep up with us. We outsmarted you, every step of the way, jerk. We won!"

If he were smart, he'd go after Kyle. But he's not smart. He's Groan. Bully-smart, and no smarter. He comes at me, his weird long legs spindling across the snow. His hat comes off. The side of his head where his missing ear had been is peeling skin in huge scraps, revealing a glimpse of bone beneath. Instead of trying to duck out of the way, I spring straight at him, hitting him midstride. My head crashes into his and we both go down in a tangle of limbs. He claws at me, but I'm just as quick, jamming my fingers into his eye socket, kneeing him in the nuts. The stench of decay rises from his clammy skin. He sinks his claws into my arm, dragging my hand from his eye. Fluid spurts across his gray cheek. A string of curses and grunts spills from his mouth. I clip him in the jaw with my other elbow. He tries to shove me away, which gives me the opportunity to roll to the right. I somersault and spring to my feet, ignoring the blood rushing down my arm.

Before he can get to his feet, I lay into the side of his head with my foot, once, twice, hard as I can. His head snaps to the side and he slides to the snow, at least momentarily stunned. I sprint to follow Kyle, ready to keep Groan away until he's safe. Down across one of the lanes and past a little hedge of trimmed shrubs, I catch up with Kyle, who was dumb enough to stop to watch.

"That was awesome," he says.

"Thanks—but go, hurry!"

The last of Karen's handprints shines at a granite headstone with a bronze plaque, tarnished from nearly forty years of New England weather. Embossed letters read:

Kyle Hart O'Brien

June 10, 1971 – October 31, 1981

When you look at the sky at night, you—only you—will have stars that can laugh.

We skid to a stop. Behind us, Groan shrieks in incoherent rage.

"Go, don't wait! Go!" I say.

Kyle looks at Groan, then looks at me. He leans over to me and wraps his arms around me, pulling me into a tight hug. I think it's actually a hug for Karen. She deserves it more than me —but I take it. For one second. Then I push back.

"Go," I say. "I'll see you on the other side."

He glances at Groan, then back at me, pale light wavering across his face and tears streaming down his cheeks. With a turn, he steps forward—and vanishes in an eruption of light from the ground. Sparks, like delicate fireflies, fill the space he'd stood, fading as they drift down to the snow.

Groan hits me from behind. I crash into Kyle's headstone.

"You're all mine, Dimothy," he hisses. Twining his fingers in my hair, he pulls my head back and bashes my forehead into the gravestone. Barely holding on, I gather my strength and hurl my own weight backward to slam down on top of him. Using my elbow as a pile driver, I smash him in the face a few times, then shove myself to my feet. Groan rolls onto his side and gets on all fours. He hangs his head, glaring at me. His jaw hangs loose from one side, his left cheek is split wide from his mouth to his earlobe.

"You'll pay for this." The words are garbled. He closes his eyes and mutters, lifting up one arm. He bites into his own flesh, sending black blood to steam in the snow.

I back away from him. Lights shimmer over a stretch of the graveyard down near the stone wall that divides the cemetery from the street. As I watch, the light vanishes, as though a curtain falls in front of it. I try to locate the right spot, but can't. When I turn back to Groan, he's on his feet, right behind me, a terrible grin turning up the good side of his face.

"Now it's just the two of us," he says, the words flappy and lisping. "You always were my favorite."

He slams his hand into my throat, his fingers tearing through my flesh. He pulls me in close. With his other hand, he reaches into his pants pocket and pulls out a hideous, fleshy spider, shoving it into my face. Lollipop. With a jerk, I slap it off. Just then, a wash of headlights sweeps over the scene. A car passes through the cemetery gates, throwing long dark shadows from the headstones across the hillsides. Groan turns. I take the opportunity to pound him in the face with my right hand. I yank myself free of his clawed fingers and stagger away.

The car moves slowly along the lane, turning toward the section of the cemetery where I'd seen the light of my grave before Groan worked his foul magic.

Groan turns back to me. Half his face is stove-in where I'd hit him—because he's seventy-five percent weaker than he's ever been. So, just because I can, I kick him so hard in the crotch that his legs lift up and slide back, dumping him on his ugly face. He grunts but pushes himself up onto his forearms.

"You'll still never find it. You're still mine," he spits through his broken face.

I recognize the car—it's really a tiny van—as it heads down along the outside lane. Leaving Groan where he is, I take off down the hillside, holding my hand to my throat to stem the bleeding. Even as I do, I feel myself growing weak like the many times he's killed me. Groan calls after me, a bellow of anger.

The van stops at the first curve near the wall. When the driver's door opens, the inside light comes on. Alyssa steps out. In the passenger seat, Jacinta is dressed in a bathrobe and wool hat. She's holding what looks like a plunger—the one she sometimes carries around when she's pretending to be a wizard. Alyssa turns on a flashlight, her hair blowing in the wind. She sweeps the beams over the nearest row of headstones. After taking half a dozen steps, she stops, training the light on a particular headstone.

"I found it!" she calls back to her sister.

Jacinta squints out the open driver's door. "Yay, ghost boy!" she cries. She's seen me.

I lift a hand as I run down the hillside. She raises the plunger in return.

"He sees you!" she says to Alyssa.

Alyssa straightens, looking around. She points the flashlight at the same headstone and calls out, "It's right here!"

Groan trails me, crawling through the snow. He's not fast enough to catch me. I guess I nearly split him in half with that kick of mine. I don't feel the slightest bit of pity for him, thinking of how many times he did as much, or worse, to me.

When I reach Alyssa, Jacinta cries out, "The ghost boy's there! With you!"

Alyssa glances around in the darkness of the winter night, her breath steaming across the beam of the flashlight. She trains the light on a pale marble headstone. "There. There it is, Tim."

I flash a thumbs-up to Jacinta, who bounces in her seat with joy. I turn to the headstone. Flickers of golden light edge the stone and the ground beneath it, glowing like the huffing flames along the bottom of a log in the fireplace.

Written on the front:

Timothy Carey Lane
September 23, 1967
October 31, 1981
Son

This is where I'm buried. This is where my parents stood and wept. Where my friends gathered. A final memory of me they all carried for the rest of their childhoods. Probably to this day. In the light, I also see my mother's tombstone. She's buried right next to me. Of course. Not how it was supposed to work, but how it turned out. No wonder my dad didn't want to move.

"Don't do it," Groan croaks. He crawls through the snow, shrunken and desperate. "I'm sorry. Don't send me back. I'll do anything. We can be friends. Timothy. We can be friends. Start fresh? I mean it this time. Please. I'm begging you. Don't make me go back!" His voice chokes with anguish. The first genuine emotion I've ever heard from his lying mouth, I'm sure. He's falling apart, a shadow tearing into shreds.

"Eat me," I say to him.

The beam of light on my headstone shakes from the cold. I turn to Jacinta, put a hand to my heart and bow my head at her, then blow her a kiss. She smiles, bouncing again in her seat, broken arm in a sling, plunger in her other hand. With a look at Alyssa, I say, "Thank you. For more than you'll ever know."

I put my hand to my heart again, and lean forward. She can't see me or hear me.

Doesn't matter. What it means to my heart—what it's *all* meant to my heart—is all that counts.

I turn to my grave. I see it now, the light coming through. And I know what it means.

45

———

BEFORE I TAKE THE STEP, I GLANCE BACK IN THE DIRECTION OF MY house. I'll never see it again. But that's the way it goes. You never know when it's the last time, most of the time. Trust me on that. Although as I look around, taking in the beauty of a winter's night, one final glimpse of the moon, one last look at this world, it strikes me that maybe, in a weird way, I'm luckier than most. Because I had thirty-eight years to say goodbye. That's a gift, when you think about it.

I'll keep the rest of this short. Like life.

So what happens when I step through?

Can't tell you. I can only tell you what it's *like*.

It's like October dusk and the smell of autumn leaves. It's like the scent of dinner filling the house. The sound of the TV in the other room. It's like coming back from trick-or-treating, the night alive, the future wide open and waiting.

Is that it, exactly? Literally?

No, it isn't. But it gives you the idea.

And that's all I'm going to tell you—I've told you everything else.

~

Keep up to date on my upcoming books, novellas, and exclusives by joining my private Readers Club.

As a welcome, I'll send you a free ebook of Sorcery of the Stony Heart *(the prequel novella to* The Books of Conjury *series), along with* A Spark of Will: The Trans-Atlantic Diary of August Swaine, *an exclusive novelette you can't get anywhere else.*

It's easy, just sign up here: **kevandale.com**

SPECIAL EXCERPT FROM REVOLUTIONARY DEAD

April 23, 1775

West Bradhill, Massachusetts

It was a terrible thing they were doing. Thomas Chase didn't understand why they'd brought him along, or what they planned on doing with his dead cousin, Nathan, out by the old lake—only that it was terrible. He supposed his uncle, Joseph, was mad with grief, but that didn't explain why Father didn't stop him. They left Thomas and his questions to watch the horses. He shivered, glad not to see the body any longer. A deep chill held the midnight woods. His breath hung in the air in rolling clouds, and steam rose off the horses' backs. He barely knew those woods, being so far out from the village, out in the lonely stretches that folks avoided. He didn't like them, either—too dark and still, with old trees close together.

A cold half hour passed before a hand fell on his shoulder. Thomas recoiled, but his father steadied him, the older man's face grim. He motioned and Thomas followed, pushing through branches and thickets until the trees opened on the lake.

Thomas looked around but didn't see the body.

At the lake's edge, moss-patched granite overhung the water. Moonlight shimmered on the water's surface a dozen feet below. His uncle grabbed his shoulder. Thomas flinched and looked up into his uncle's wide eyes and twitching mouth. Joseph shook him by the front of his cloak and pointed to the water. Thomas tried to pull away.

"Told you he wouldn't do it," Joseph said. His sour breath washed over Thomas.

"He'll understand," Samuel said. "He can't see your lips, that's all."

"This's why I didn't want him here in the first place, he's useless. Just have him do it," Joseph said. He shoved Thomas toward his father.

"You can't do this," Samuel said. "Leaving him out here won't make it go away—you of all people know that."

"Meaning what?"

When his father had nothing to say, his uncle leveled a pale finger at him.

"You don't stop now," he said.

Samuel stared at him for a long minute and stepped over and put a comforting hand on Thomas's face, turning his head toward the water again.

"Right there," he said.

His father pointed to a spot above the water. At first, it looked like another gray outcrop of rocks and moss. Then Thomas saw the body. Bent saplings and broken plants marked where it had slid down the face of the rocks toward the water. It hadn't made it all the way—a thick root held it in place.

His cousin Nathan.

Looking at the body made Thomas want to run back into the woods—he couldn't swim and didn't like heights, and the thought of having to touch Nathan twisted his stomach. Still, he hated everyone thinking of him as useless. He stepped forward and picked his way down. He slid in spots, feet shifting for traction, hands grabbing what they could to steady himself. Saplings and mossy fissures in the rock allowed him to work his way to the steep drop. His hands grabbed at the granite, his eyes drawn to the dark water below him. At one steep spot, he missed a foothold and nearly slid past the body and into the water. A few more steps and he stopped next to the body. Nathan's eyes stared at the moon, dry and empty. His head lay at a funny angle to his shoulders. A matted patch of hair and bone on the side of his head marked where he'd smashed against the edge of the wagon—Thomas didn't look at the wound.

He inched closer. A rock came loose and tumbled into the lake with a *ploonk*, rippling the surface. Steadying himself, he reached over and yanked on his cousin's jersey, hoping to free the arm over the root. The material ripped. Thomas grabbed the arm instead and shuddered at the feel of the flesh—like cold clay. Thomas pulled, scared and wanting to get the horrid task done with, wanting to get away from the dark lake.

The root let go from underneath the arm. The bag of stones tied to Nathan's ankles pulled his body to the water. Thomas lost his footing and slipped next to the corpse. Terrified of plunging into the black water with Nathan, he cried out. At the edge, his pants caught on a stone as his legs hung out over the water. He looked down just in time to glimpse his cousin slipping into the water. For a moment more, Thomas could see the hands, pale fish swimming into the depths. Once the trickle of dirt and stones ceased, the surface of the water smoothed and the moon shown on it. A few bubbles rose from below and soon ceased.

The stars to the east faded into a deep indigo sky as the two men and the boy came out of the woods and onto the road. Frost thatched the ground. Thomas rode the smallest horse, leading the riderless horse by the reins. His hands ached from the chill night. He wanted his own bed where he might forget the long night. Joseph turned around and spoke to them.

"I'll not lose him, I won't. This bloody curse won't take everything from us," his uncle said. "That's what this is. Do you understand?"

Thomas looked to his father, but Samuel kept his eyes forward.

Joseph turned to him. "And it's not anything like before. Not a single bit. This was an accident."

Thomas didn't know what he meant—only that he couldn't let go of the feeling of dread the lake had put into him.

"He's my boy," Joseph went on. "A good boy, not fit for leaving. Not yet."

The horses passed through a grove of birch. Dawn lightened the sky to the east.

"My good boy," Joseph said. He pleaded with them. Tears slid down his face. Thomas thought he should say something. Instead he looked away.

Will Thomas Chase learn the truth of the curse his uncle mentions— and can he survive the evil about to be released by it?

Revolutionary Dead *is available now.*

Revolutionary
DEAD
KEVAN DALE

ALSO BY KEVAN DALE

The Governor's Witch

The Magic of Unkindness

The Grave Raven

The Halls of Midnight

Sorcery of the Stony Heart

The Books of Conjury: The Complete Trilogy

Revolutionary Dead

The Devil's Key

Shades of the Grave: A Horror Collection

Find out more at www.kevandale.com